The PRINCE and the GOBLIN

Book One of the Goblin Trilogy

Written and Illustrated by

Rory Madge and Bryan Huff

Month9Books

THE PRINCE AND THE GOBLIN by Rory Madge and Bryan Huff
All rights reserved. Published in the United States of America by Month9Books, LLC.
No part of this book may be used or reproduced in any manner whatsoever without written permission of the publisher, except in the case of brief quotations embodied in critical articles and reviews.

Trade Paperback ISBN: 978-1-951710-37-8
ePub ISBN: 978-1-951710-45-3
Mobipocket ISBN: 978-1-951710-46-0

Published by Month9Books, Raleigh, NC 27609
Cover and interior art by Rory Madge and Bryan Huff

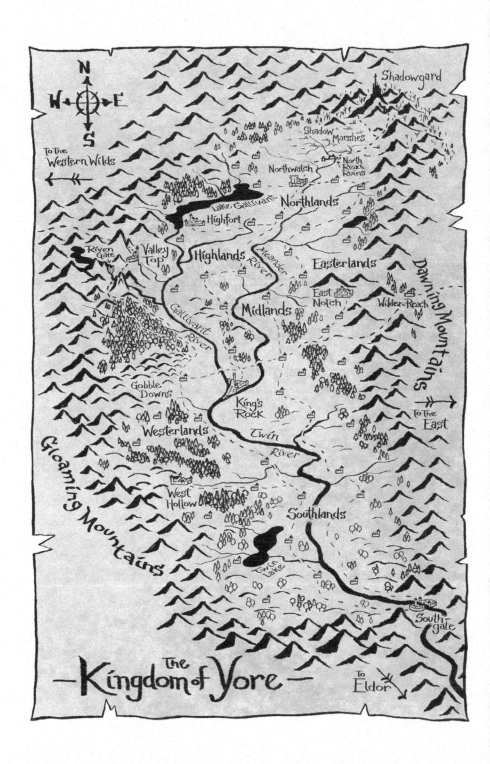

THE PRINCE and the GOBLIN

PROLOGUE

A Road Less Traveled

"GOBLINS!" shouted the guards along the village walls. "*GOBLINS!*" Under cover of darkness and heavy rain, the creatures had launched a surprise attack.

The warning cry echoed across town, as two cloaked figures—one short, one tall—hurried through the stormy streets. A goblin raid was least of their worries, though. They were fugitives on the run.

The clatter of hoofbeats on cobblestones chased them on. And suddenly, seven horsemen appeared behind them in the darkness, carrying bright torches and kicking up a spray.

The lead horse was a massive gray charger, ridden by a tall figure cloaked in black. The rest of the horses were white, ridden by soldiers in glinting golden armor and crimson cloaks.

The fugitives ran as fast as they could but had nowhere to go. Half-timber row houses lined both sides of the street, hemming them in. The horsemen bore down upon them.

Then they met the goblins! A dozen of the wild green creatures rushed up the street in the opposite direction, carrying loot sacks and swinging crooked weapons over their crooked heads.

The short fugitive pulled his companion into a sunken doorway at the street side, and the goblins collided with the horsemen right in front of them. CRASH! Horses reared. Swords rattled. Goblins howled and ran. And the fugitives slipped away.

Moments later, a loose board in one of the village's timber walls was pried back with an axe. The fugitives slipped out through the crack.

"Never thought there'd come a day when I was glad to see *goblins*," said the short fugitive, stowing his axe. His voice was old and gruff, but not without a certain pep. "Why'd you have to go showing off for that tavern girl?"

"Relax," replied the tall fugitive. His voice betrayed his youth; he could not have been more than fourteen. "We've escaped."

"Not yet, we haven't!" said the little man, hurrying on.

They scrambled through the storm-swept fields outside of town. But before long, the heavy hoofbeats chased them again. The diversion hadn't lasted, and the horsemen were back on their trail.

With the storm growing worse all the time, the hoofbeats were soon the only thing in the world the fugitives could still make out.

"We're lost!" cried the boy, unable to locate even his companion.

"No!" cried the little man. "There's a road!"

The boy found the little man standing at the beginning of the so-called road. Overgrown and churned to mud by the storm, it was barely a path. It quickly disappeared into a thicket of low trees that grew in a gully between two hills.

"This is our escape," cheered the little man. "A shortcut. A road less traveled!"

"More like, *not traveled at all,*" said the boy.

"Better still, if it means their horses can't take it."

He had a point. Every second, the hoofbeats grew louder and louder.

"After you then," said the boy.

Within minutes, the horsemen arrived. Their torches lit up the scene. It turned out the fugitives' little road actually branched off of a much larger one, which the horsemen had come by.

"Where'd they go, Captain?" asked one of the horsemen.

The rider in black—the Captain—said nothing, but dismounted and stalked about with torch in hand. Its light fell first on the beginning of the little road, complete with fresh footprints in the mud. Then it caught on something else, something the fugitives had missed—an old signpost lost in the thicket of trees.

The Captain raised the torch to reveal three signs. Two pointed along the main road, marking *The Way Round* and *The Village of Brew*. The third pointed down the little path, marking ...

"*The Gobble Downs!*" gasped another horseman. "Few ever make it out of those hills alive!"

"They're braver than I thought," remarked a third.

"They are fools," said the Captain. She threw back her hood and turned to her companions.

Her hair was tied back in a bun accentuating high cheekbones and rich brown skin. Her keen eyes gleamed in the torchlight.

"But they *have* escaped. Even if we could follow on horseback, with all the branching paths in those hills, they would already be lost to us. With any luck, they will continue to be as good at getting out of trouble, as they are at getting into it. And we shall meet them on the other side."

The next instant, she was swinging back into her saddle and setting her charger to gallop up the main road north, taking *The Way Round*. Her men followed immediately. And, one by one, they vanished into the storm.

CHAPTER ONE

Hob

In the long ago, far away Kingdom of Yore, under the hills known as the Gobble Downs, there lived a horde of goblins. No doubt you've heard of goblins before. They often appear in stories of long ago and far away, and when they do, they are always the *same*. They are stinky, green thugs and sneaks, who serve evil lords, covet shiny objects, and have absolutely no manners at all.

Well, by and large, the goblins of Yore were no better. In fact, they might've even been *worse!* And the Kingdom was infested with them. They'd been warring with the humans of Yore for longer than anyone could remember, with no end in sight.

Yet, even in times long ago and places far away, things were rarely as simple as they seemed, and this is a story about a goblin who was *different*.

His name was Hob, short for Hobblestraug, and he was a young goblin who lived with that horde beneath the Gobble Downs. He was small in size, standing only about three feet tall, even though some goblins were as big as bears. He had large, curious eyes, pointy, bat-like ears, and a little, upturned nose. And he always wore a floppy leather cap on his head and a rough hide tunic on his body.

One night, Hob was looking for something to read. He loved human books, but had only one tiny shelf of them. It was carved into the rock wall over the dug-out bunk at the back of his underground nook.

In the Gobble Downs, you had to either fight for a nook to live in, or find one nobody else wanted. And Hob's was *the one* nobody else wanted. It was a dark, dank hole with barely enough room to sleep or stand.

A torch on the wall illuminated a collection of old boots and dusty bottles cluttering the tight space—Hob's failed attempts at making the nook feel homier.

There was also a badly faded old tapestry that hung in front of the bookshelf, depicting what might once have been a goat. Hob hung it there to hide his books. You see, while reading wasn't exactly forbidden in the Gobble Downs, it certainly wasn't the *goblin way*, which made books hard to come by. And Hob had come by *his* books in a manner that he knew could get him into trouble. So he did his best to keep them a secret.

Nevertheless, he stood on his bunk, with the tapestry pulled back, considering his secret library. He'd read every book he owned many times, but that only seemed to make choosing one harder. And he had to get moving. Even without his books to worry about, there was no telling what kind of terrifying ordeal he might get dragged into, if he got caught loafing around in the Gobble Downs.

Hob pulled out a book called *Sir Swashbuckle's Last Stand*—before changing his mind and swapping it for *The Big Book of Derring-Do*. Glancing at the sword embossed on the cover, he smiled. He loved human adventure stories most of all—at least when the humans weren't fighting *evil* goblins—and this was his go-to favorite.

He slipped the book into his shoulder satchel, and swung the faded goat tapestry back into place. Then he hopped down from the bunk, lifted the torch from the wall, and ducked out through the sheepskin curtain that covered his nook's round entrance.

Emerging in the black, oozy tunnel outside, Hob snuck his way up it as quickly and quietly as he could, making for the surface and his *secret reading spot*.

A tangled web of similar tunnels sprawled between the nooks and caverns of the Gobble Downs. But, due to a lifetime of curiosity and frequent attempts to go unnoticed, Hob knew them better than anyone. He stuck to only the most rarely used tunnels, where the air was musty and cold, but the going was easy.

At one point, he was forced to stop where the little side-tunnel he'd been following intersected a wide torch-lit passage. Smells of smoke and goblin musk hung in the air there, and a terrible racket echoed up the corridor. All were coming from the Great Cave, the horde's central gathering place. It wasn't far off, and the area was often busy with comings and goings.

Hob made a break for it. He dashed across the wide passage to where his little tunnel picked up on the other side. Then, thinking the danger mostly behind him, he hurtled up the tunnel and around the next bend.

SLAM! A giant wooden shield seemed to fill the whole passage, and Hob crashed right into it. He fell hard on his back, causing his torch to fly out of his hand and his head to spin like a wobbly top.

"Wanna fight?" barked an angry voice. "I'll smash yer face!" Then it paused. "Oh, it's *you.*"

Hob's head stopped spinning at once. And it wasn't the threat of having his face smashed in that did it. It was the sound of that "*you.*" Blinking hard to clear his vision, Hob looked up from the tunnel floor.

Towering over him, holding the wooden shield, was Brute: a huge, burly goblin, with arms like a gorilla, a face like a bulldog, and the full-body odor of an unwashed sock.

Brute was the favorite son of the goblin chieftain, and the biggest, meanest young goblin in the whole horde. It was just Hob's luck that Brute had always had it out for him. Brute especially loved to rough Hob up and stuff him into cracks in the rocks, which were so tight that they often took hours to wiggle back out of.

Hob really didn't want to get "stuffed" just then. He couldn't afford any trouble while carrying one of his books with him. So, clutching his satchel, he scrambled awkwardly to his feet, and backed up against the wall of the tunnel.

"Well, looky here, boys," said Brute. "If it ain't *wittle Hobblestwaug*."

Peeking out from behind Brute was a rabble of goblins big and small, all armed to the teeth. Seeing their dented helmets and crooked blades, Hob understood why they were there. Although it went mostly unused, that particular tunnel doubled as a back passage to the horde's armory—the cave where the goblins kept their weapons and bits of armor when they weren't using them, or just *playing* with them.

"Hi, guys," said Hob, trying to sound casual, but really sounding like he was about to throw up.

"Hi, Hob!" came an earnest voice from the back of the pack.

There, waving at him, was Hob's brother, Grunt, a large, husky goblin, with a friendly face that bore a slight resemblance to Hob's own.

Now, technically, all young goblins in the horde shared the same mother, the Queen Goblin, which made them all brothers of a sort. But it sure didn't feel that way.

Hob and Grunt really did see each other as brothers, though. They'd been born in the same litter, reared in the same nursery, and that meant something to them. If Hob had a family, Grunt was it.

Grunt's enthusiastic greeting was not matched by the rest of the pack. They glared at him until he shrank back, looking sheepish.

Brute took no notice. "*Watch* where yer goin', Hobby!" he growled, advancing on Hob and shaking a fist. "Unless ya want a beatin'!"

"Sorry, Brute!" said Hob, trying to save himself. "I didn't *mean* to run into you. I was just in a hurry, and there was this corner here, and your shield was kinda large and hard to miss."

"Yer *head's* kinda large and hard to miss!" said Brute, giving Hob's head a shove, so the back of it banged against the wall.

With the exception of Grunt, the goblins all laughed.

"Yeah, watch where yer goin', *big head!*" chirped a tiny, weasel-like goblin named Snivel, suddenly emerging at Brute's side. He was Brute's chief lackey and hanger-on, and the only goblin who may have hated Hob as much as Brute did.

"Where ya hurryin' *to,* anyway?" asked Brute, peering around the tunnel with a scrunched-up face that suggested he was trying to think.

"Yeah, where?" echoed Snivel.

Hob was silent, trying to come up with an answer. The truth certainly wouldn't do.

Brute fixed him with a suspicious look. "You was sneakin' off again, wasn't ya?"

"Me? No, of course not ..." Hob lied.

"Then whadda ya doin' here, Hobby?" Brute pressed.

"Yeah, what?" echoed Snivel.

Finally, it came to Hob—the right answer. "The same as you!" he said.

This was *always* the right answer with goblins. Though, it could backfire, if, like Hob, you didn't know what you were signing up for.

"Yer comin' on the *ambush?*" said Brute. "But ya wasn't even picked this time."

"Yeah, Hobby never goes on ambushes unless ya make him!" said Snivel, mashing his fist into his palm.

It had backfired. Now, Hob needed an explanation for his explanation.

"Grunt invited me!" he said.

Everyone glared at Grunt again.

"I did?" Grunt asked.

"Uh-huh. *Just before*," said Hob.

"Oh … right," said Grunt, clearly not remembering. "And ya said, '*yes?* Even I was startin' to think ya didn't like ambushes."

"Hah! Good old Grunt," Hob chortled. "I love ambushes. The theft! The unsuspecting victims! Let's go *ruin* someone's day!"

From the looks he got, Hob thought he might have been laying it on a bit thick, so he added, "Grunt told me to meet him in the armory, but I ran a bit late."

"Well, keep up!" Brute snapped. "You've slowed us down enough already. The scouts spotted two humans up there, and I'm not lettin' either of 'em get away!" He turned to the rest of the goblins. "Let him through. He's Grunt's problem, not mine."

Not daring to go against Brute's orders, the others made way for Hob to shuffle to the back of the pack. As Hob fell in beside Grunt, Grunt looked over at him beaming. Then the rabble resumed its march down the tunnel.

—

CHAPTER TWO

Ambushes and Interlopers

Hob *didn't* like ambushes. But he'd never had the heart to tell Grunt the truth about that. The goblins of Yore got almost everything they had from either raiding human villages or ambushing any humans unfortunate enough to wander into goblin lands. And although Hob felt this was no way to live, it was the *goblin way*. So he just had to go along with it.

He was certainly *going along* this time. The pack marched on and on toward the site of the impending ambush, through tunnel after twisty tunnel, around gardens of moss and mushrooms, up dizzying ladders, and over rickety rope bridges that crossed deep chasms and underground streams.

The tunnels grew fewer and farther between as they reached the edge of the horde's domain, but they never stopped entirely. Hob knew of a few that carried on right out of the Gobble Downs. A vast network of these nearly endless tunnels connected all the goblin hordes in the great valley of Yore, so the goblins could travel between them without ever venturing above ground. This was important because all goblins shared a natural aversion to sunlight. It made them weak and dizzy, forcing them underground during the day. And, at one time, it had even been used by human magicians to keep them underground at *night*.

"Here we are," Brute announced, at last. "Find a hidey-hole, and wait for my signal."

The ambush party rattled to a stop in a cavern just below the earth's surface. Five short tunnels branched up from there, all leading to *hidey-holes*, tight chambers topped with trapdoors made to blend in with their surroundings above ground.

Hob followed Grunt up the nearest tunnel. They climbed slippery stone steps to the top, trailed by three of Grunt's friends: Ick, who was tall and lanky with a chimp-like grin; Uck, who was short and stocky with a bullfrog's jaw; and Skulldug, who was small and shifty with a wolfish snout.

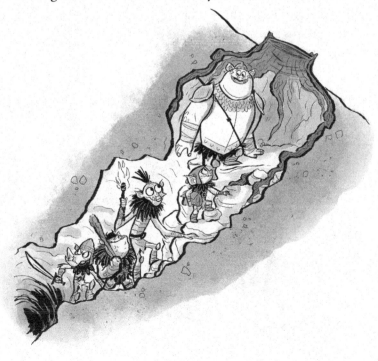

The hidey-hole Grunt led them to was concealed by an old stump with a top that lifted up on a hinge. A steady trickle of water seeped in around the seam.

Once the group had squeezed in below the trapdoor, Grunt lifted it up a crack so they could peek outside. The night was dark and stormy. But the goblins' keen eyes could see in low light, so only the rain hampered their vision.

They found themselves perched on one of several hillsides surrounding a small hollow. The steep hills were strewn with rocks, bushes, and dead trees, a few of which were sure to be concealing the other four hidey-holes.

Minutes passed in cramped silence. Then two travelers, cloaked and hooded, wandered into the hollow. The goblins had created many trick paths in those hills, and the travelers were following one. It was a dead end—a trap—but they couldn't see it, lost in the darkness and the storm.

Hob looked down at them, picking out as much detail as he could. He was always eager to see humans in real life. Though, he liked it much better when they *weren't* about to be ambushed.

One of the travelers was a tall boy, the other a short, little man. They had come to the spot where the path ended, and the boy seemed to be searching for a way forward. The man just stood there with his arms crossed, looking frustrated.

It occurred to Hob that the man might have been a dwarf! Hob had read about dwarves before, and this fellow fit the description perfectly. He was no more than five feet tall, built like a pot-bellied brick, and even had a bushy white beard sticking out from under his dark-brown hood.

Hob could hear both travelers arguing over the wind.

"Why did I ever let you talk me into this?" asked the boy. "You said this was a shortcut."

"It looked like a shortcut," replied the dwarf.

"It looked dangerous!"

"That's what shortcuts look like. They look dangerous!"

Hob turned to Grunt and the others. "Awfully loud for interlopers, aren't they?" he whispered, trying to make friendly conversation.

"Loud for whats?" asked Grunt.

"Interlopers," said Hob. "People who're somewhere they're not supposed to be."

"Why didn't ya say that then?" asked Ick.

"It feels different," said Hob. "And it takes longer."

"Longer than this?" said Ick.

"Yeah, ya talk funny," said Skulldug.

Uck, who never talked much at all, simply nodded.

"Ya *do* talk kinda funny, Hob," said Grunt, with a shrug.

"I guess so," Hob sighed. "Still, I wonder what they're doing here …"

He returned his attention to the interlopers.

"You know whose fault this really is?" the dwarf was saying. "That dotty old wizard's, that's whose. If he'd met us when he was supposed to, we wouldn't be in this mess. He always does this."

They know a wizard! Hob marveled. He was becoming more curious about them by the second.

"I wish he were here too," muttered the boy. "But we're on this quest now, with or without him."

They're going on a quest! Hob marveled again. He was suddenly transfixed. He'd never seen *real* adventurers before! Unfortunately, his opportunity didn't last long.

"Attack!" cried Brute, from the far side of the hollow.

And with that, Grunt and the others exploded from the trapdoor with such force that Hob—who was smaller and positioned in front—got ejected ahead of them. This sent him careening down the hill, leading the charge, until he slipped on a patch of loose stones and went tumbling head over heels the rest of the way.

Seconds later, as the other goblins came charging out of the darkness from every angle to surround the travelers, Hob landed face-first at the bottom of the hollow.

By the time he lifted his head out of the mud, the ambush was underway all around him. The boy rushed past, chased by a swarm of goblins. The dwarf rushed past, chased by another swarm of goblins. And a bunch of stray goblins just rushed about all over the place.

STOMP! STOMP! STOMP! Hob tossed and turned to avoid getting trampled by their feet. Then, his hand fell on something unexpected. *A book.*

Worried it was *The Big Book of Derring-Do,* Hob instinctively clutched his satchel. He felt his book still inside. The one on the ground was new! Although its cover was wet and mud-spattered, it might have been the finest book he'd ever seen.

Without pausing to wonder where it had come from, Hob checked to make sure no one was watching, and stuffed the new book into his satchel. The next instant, a foot slammed down right where it had been. Sensing a second one about to slam down on his head, Hob threw himself aside. *THUMP!* It was a narrow miss—one which put him in the path of another charging goblin. *THUMP-THUMP!* Two feet caught Hob in the chest and sent him rolling across the ground.

Everything was a blur. Then he was free. He'd rolled right out of the fray, onto an empty patch of grass at the bottom of a hill.

Hob pulled himself a short way up the slope to catch his breath. A few bruises were all he had to show for his struggle—and a new book! He squeezed his satchel to make sure it was safe inside with the first.

Then he returned his attention to the ambush. If only through sheer numbers, the goblins had already captured the boy and dwarf. The pair didn't appear afraid, as Hob would have been in their place. They were defiant, kicking and squirming even as the goblins fought to tie them up.

For a split second, Hob felt an unexpected urge to help them—to try to escape with them on their adventure! But it passed as quickly as it came. The next thing Hob knew, the captives had been bound and gagged for their trip underground.

"Take 'em to the dungeon. And take their loot to the pile!" shouted Brute. "Then get yourselves to the Great Cave for a feast!"

CHAPTER THREE

Adventure Calls

The Great Cave resembled a strange underground stadium. It was a vast space, with a high domed ceiling and a floor split into levels, rising up around a central, bottom ring. Giant, pointy stalactites hung from the ceiling, and matching stalagmites shot up from the floor. And, opposite the towering main entranceway, a tall balcony had been worked into the rocks—the platform of the goblin Chieftain.

The platform was empty, but the rest of the cave was bustling. On every level, goblins sat gathered around roaring bonfires, eating and drinking from wooden bowls and jugs. The fires filled the place with smoke and warm light, and cast dancing shadows upon the walls.

Hob and Grunt sat on rocks by one of the fires in the bottom ring. The goblins from the ambush were all there, eagerly telling stories of their victory, sometimes in turns, sometimes loudly over top of one another, and always to the delight of their listeners.

Brute was telling his own, much embellished, tale to a large crowd. It was a version in which he did most of the ambushing himself, while the others just stood by and watched.

"Yer awesome, Brute!" exclaimed one of his admirers.

"The best!" added another.

"*I know,*" said Brute.

Hob wasn't listening to any of them, however. He was thinking. That night's ambush had been as frightening and senseless as any, but Hob felt lucky he'd been forced to go along. He'd come back not only with his life, but with a new book to read, and, better yet, a new story of his own to tell. It was *almost* as if he'd gone on one of the adventures from his books, braving a terrible battle, and returning with a hard-won treasure. Not to mention, he'd seen the boy and dwarf—*real life adventurers!* It was like something out of one of his dreams.

Finally, a loud voice brought him back to reality.

"A burp!" shouted a jolly, fat goblin, hammering his jug with a spoon. "A burp to the ambushers!"

A "burp" was the goblin version of a "toast," and all the goblins in the cave took long drinks from their jugs, and joined in.

> *"O, gobble yer grub, an' guzzle yer beer,*
> *'Cause it's like music to the ear,*
> *When we fill with gas, an' let it pass,*
> *Loud and proud for all to hear!*
> *BRRRUUUUURRRRRP!"*

18

Hob drank too. Like everyone else's, his jug was full of gobble-beer, a frothy green liquid that smelled and tasted like tree roots. He swallowed hard, and let out the best burp he could muster, though it wasn't much. "*Brruup!*"

"You've hardly touched yer food," Grunt said, when the burping was done.

Hob looked down at the bowl in his hand. It was full of gray-green paste that looked like cat puke and smelled much worse. He stared at it with a wrinkled-up nose, trying to figure out how to get rid of it without offending Grunt.

"What's the matter with it?" asked Grunt.

"I'm never sure it's *sanitary*," Hob explained.

"No, it's '*gru-el*,'" Grunt corrected him.

"I know it's gruel ..." said Hob. Gruel was the goblins' staple dish. The recipe was simple: anything you could find, plus dirt, thrown into a pot, and boiled until thick and gloopy. "It's just ... I meant ... I dunno ..." He paused and let out a frustrated sigh. "Don't you ever wish there was more to life than this?"

"Like more *gruel?*" asked Grunt, turning over his bowl to lick out the last of its contents.

"Not exactly," said Hob. "I'm not even hungry for what I've got."

"I'm a'ways hung'y," said Grunt, still licking out his bowl.

"Have mine, then," said Hob, holding out his bowl for his brother.

Grunt took it, and continued feasting. He found something long and slimy and sucked it up like a noodle. "Mmm! I th'nk I g'd a worm in this 'un!" he said, cheeks full. "Or'a rat's tail!" *Crunch.* "Nope. Defin'ly a worm."

Hob pressed on. "I meant, more like, getting *out of here*. Going on an *adventure*. Like

those humans we ambushed. Don't you wonder where they were going? What it might be like to go with them?"

Grunt spat out his latest mouthful of gruel. "No," he whispered. "And don't let anyone hear ya talk like that. Those man-captives ain't goin' nowhere. And even if they was, ya could never go *with them.* They're humans. They're our enemies." He paused. "This is where we belong, Hob."

"I know," Hob muttered. "Just, sometimes I wonder is all …"

Before long, Hob was hurrying back up through the tunnels of the Gobble Downs. He'd excused himself from the feast by telling Grunt he was tired. But he had no intention of going to bed. Hob might not have been any closer to going on an adventure himself—but at least he had a new one to read about.

Soon, he reached the destination he'd set out for hours earlier—*his secret spot.* At the end of a far-flung tunnel, he came to a small underground waterfall, where fresh, cool water spilled out of a crack in the bedrock to fill a shallow pool.

Many goblins had been to that place before, but only Hob knew its secret. Hidden behind the waterfall was an opening to a long-forgotten passage to the surface.

He stopped at the pool to take a drink and wash his hands and face. The Gobble Downs was an exceptionally dirty place, and Hob always felt the need to wash. Then, with a quick glance around to make sure nobody else was there, he edged over to the waterfall and slipped in behind it.

He found himself at the bottom of a tight shaft, big enough for only one medium-sized goblin to pass at a time—or maybe one man. But Hob was much less than medium-sized, and he climbed easily up the steep steps and rock falls, never once bumping his head on the low ceiling.

Soon, the air began to stir, and the foul odors of the goblin caves gave way to the fresh scent of spring. Hoisting himself out of a hole at the top of the tunnel, Hob emerged at the back of an open-faced cave.

The cave sat beneath a rocky outcropping on the northernmost hillside of the Gobble Downs, overlooking the lands beyond. As he often did, Hob moved to the edge of the cave to take in the view. The rain had passed, and the sky was turning purple over the fields, forests, and distant mountains. For a moment, he imagined being in those places, far away.

Then he returned to the back of the cave, and sat down. In the shadow of the rock, it would remain dark until well after dawn, and he would be able to read for a while without the sunlight bothering him.

Hob opened his satchel, drew out his new book, and wiped the mud and water from its cover. Thankfully, not much damage had been done. It mustn't have been out in the storm for very long. And otherwise, it seemed in excellent condition. If anything, it was more beautiful than he'd first thought. It was thick and heavy, bound with rich leather, and embossed with gold. Its title read: *The Ballad of Waeward the Wanderer.*

Hob opened it to the first page. Though it was damp, the book made the soft cracking sound that books make when they've gone too long unopened. It brought a smile to his face.

At once, he began to read.

Chapter One:
Wherein Waeward Meets Princess Parabelle

A legend tells
of brave Waeward,
Who wandered
far and wide,
On a quest to save
his dying love,
So she might one day
be his bride.

Such trials did
brave Waeward face,
In search o'
his Lady's cure,
But for all his deeds
and wanderings,
He ne'er returned to her.

Who was this Lady
whom he loved?
Why did he disappear?
The story's long
and quite drawn out,
So it's written down
in here ...

The tale turned out to be a history, passed down to its author by Waeward's squire and traveling companion. As Hob read the first few chapters, a marvelous story unfolded. Hundreds of years earlier, Waeward traveled from a distant land to South Gate, one of the small early kingdoms that had once divided the valley of Yore. There, Waeward met the beautiful Princess Parabelle, and they fell deeply in love. He won a grand tournament for the right to ask her hand in marriage. But on the eve of their wedding, Parabelle fell sick and passed into a deep, feverish sleep from which it appeared she might never wake, forcing Waeward to set out on a quest to find a cure.

Hob paused, and stared wistfully into the distance. He knew he was supposed to hate humans, but he just couldn't! They went on heroic quests, built great kingdoms, and made wonderful things. He often felt like if he belonged anywhere, it was with them.

That may have been why he loved their adventure stories so much. They didn't just give him a temporary escape from the Gobble Downs; they gave him hope. On an adventure, anything was possible! Hob often fantasized about traveling with a daring band of humans, doing great deeds, and being accepted as not *just* a goblin, but as one of the *heroes,* worthy of an honorary place in the human world. Though, in reality, this had never seemed like the remotest possibility, until that night.

And it still wasn't, he reminded himself. Grunt was right. The travelers were captives now. And goblins were villains, not heroes. They didn't have adventures. Hob was imagining things that could never be. Would never be. No great adventure would ever come calling a goblin like him.

"*CAW! CAW! CAW!*"

The morning quiet was broken.

Hob spotted a small black speck in the northern sky. A crow. He closed his book, and crept to the edge of his cave. The bird was huge, with bristling feathers and powerful wings—a mountain crow from the north. Seconds later, it swooped into the hills of the Gobble Downs and out of sight.

"News on the wing!" Hob told himself.

The goblins of Yore had been training crows to act as messengers for an age, a trick they'd picked up from the evil old sorcerer who'd once been their master. And, as much as Hob wanted to keep reading, if there was news, he had to hear it. He returned *The Ballad of Waeward the Wanderer* to his satchel, hurried over to his secret tunnel, and lowered himself back inside.

Soon, Hob found himself back in the Great Cave. The goblin Chieftain had called the whole horde there to hear the crow's message, and the cave was even more packed than before.

Trying to avoid the boisterous crowd in the middle, Hob climbed a large stalagmite along the outer wall. He found a good ridge on the stalagmite to perch on, with a clear view of the Chief's platform, and he waited there for the show to begin.

After a few minutes, a spindly old goblin emerged from an entrance at the back of the platform. It was the horde's shaman, Toothless Cooty. He shambled to the front. "Open your eyes, and unclog your ears," he warbled, at the top of his shriveled lungs, "for Grand Chief Gobblestomp the Gargantuan!"

The Chief strode out onto the platform next, with the great black crow perched on his shoulder. This was clearly a proud moment for the Chief, as, for once, he actually had something "chiefly" to do. Though, he did look rather ridiculous doing it, like a giant pig-nosed toad, wearing a skull head-dress, and pretending to be a bird-stand.

"Okay, you lot," Chief Gobblestomp bellowed, bumping Toothless Cooty out of the way to take center stage. "Listen to what this here crow fella has to say. If ya hate humans half as much as I do, then yer gonna love it!"

Excited hoots and hollers rose from the crowd.

The crow gave the Chief's shoulder a hard peck.

"*Ouch!*" groaned the Chief. "Go on, then. I won't spoil the surprise."

The crow promptly shook out its feathers, and climbed right on top of the Chief's head. The Chief seemed a bit put out by this, but allowed it, nonetheless.

"*CAW!*" croaked the crow. "I bring news from the north. The Sorcerer of old has returned to his fortress of Shadowguard. And he calls on you to help him make war on the humans. *SQUAWK!* And so he shall speak."

The crow then spread its wings, and froze there like some sort of living statue. Its eyes began to glow green. And, without moving its beak, it began to emit a strange voice. Bodiless and booming, the voice echoed not inside the cave, but inside Hob's own mind! By the frightened looks of the goblins in the crowd, it echoed in their minds too. The voice of the Sorcerer.

"*THE TIME HAS COME, MY GOBLIN MINIONS, TO REMEMBER YOUR BONDS. YOUR MASTER HAS RETURNED TO THE VALLEY! YOU SERVED ME ONCE, AND SHALL SERVE ME AGAIN. FEEL MY POWER AND KNOW IT TO BE TRUE!*"

Every goblin in the cave began to shudder. Hob had to cling to his stalagmite to stop himself from being shaken off. Unearthly power surged through him, causing his muscles to quake and his skin to fill with fire. He felt like he might explode. He felt like he could crush the stalagmite in two between his arms. Then the feeling faded, and the voice returned.

"*THE TIME HAS COME FOR OUR REVENGE. THE HUMANS HAVE KEPT YOU UNDER-GROUND FOR TOO LONG. RISE UP, MY MINIONS! JOIN ME IN MAKING WAR ON THE HUMANS, AND THIS TIME THE VALLEY SHALL BE OURS FOR GOOD! SEND ME YOUR BEST WARRIORS. WE ATTACK WHEN THE FIRST LEAVES OF AUTUMN FALL.*"

And with that, the voice was gone. The crow relaxed, closed its wings, and gave its feathers another shake. It blinked, and its eyes returned to normal.

"*CAW!*" it added. "Each horde must send a troop of its best warriors to join the Sorcerer's Army in Shadowguard. All march on the third moon. *SQUAWK!*" Then it shuffled back down onto Chief Gobblestomp's shoulder.

"Well, there you have it!" said the Chief. "But, er ... I've got it from our shaman here, that there are traditions we gotta follow. And we've only got three moons to work with."

To goblins, who lived their lives at night, "moons" simply meant "days." So, three moons was not a lot of time.

"Tell 'em, Cooty," added the Chief.

The old shaman shuffled back to the front of the platform, reclaiming as much space as he could from the Chief. "Thirty an' five years ago," he began, in his most quavering, mystical voice, "the humans' magic sun-fire, so bright and terrible that it kept us underground even at night, disappeared. And I knew then, it must be a sign."

The old goblin paused for dramatic effect, staring around the cave meaningfully. After a few moments, however, it became obvious he'd forgotten he was the one speaking. Instead, he began scratching at something in his ear.

"A sign *that* ..." Chief Gobblestomp prompted him.

"Oh, yes! A sign that this day would come!" Toothless Cooty went on. "That the Sorcerer of old would return, and it would be time for us to serve him in his fight against the humans, once more."

He paused again. His finger climbed to his ear.

"And *so* ..." the Chief interjected.

"And so, the time has come to hold our traditional try-out for war," Toothless Cooty exclaimed. "A contest to decide who among you will join the Sorcerer's army. Yes! The time has come for *The Clobbering!*"

A hush filled the cave.

"Right!" said Chief Gobblestomp, bumping Toothless Cooty back out of the way. "So, we're gonna hold the Clobbering on the second moon from tonight. And everyone's gotta be there. We gotta make sure we send the Sorcerer all our best clobberer ... *ers*. That gives ya one moon to get ready! Good luck!"

Then, to Hob's horror, the goblins in the Great Cave all began to cheer.

"To war! To war!"

"The Sorcerer's back!"

"To war!"

CHAPTER FOUR

The Clobbering

The next night, the caves and tunnels of the Gobble Downs were abuzz. They were filled with the hustle and bustle of every able-bodied goblin going about his preparations for the Clobbering—every able-bodied goblin *except for* Hob.

He just couldn't bring himself to join in. *What a disaster,* he kept thinking. He'd read about the Sorcerer before, and he knew it was not good news the old wizard had returned. The last time the goblins had fought for him it had turned out *horribly.* What if Grunt ended up on the front lines? What if Hob didn't even survive the Clobbering? It was all too much to take.

And so, Hob just went about his regular business and tried to ignore the excitement growing around him.

His regular business was that of *Treasure Keeper.* It was Hob's job to sort, count, and care for the horde's ever-growing treasure pile—a task the Chief had personally assigned him, on account of Hob's knack for "knowin' numbers and 'memberin' stuff."

And Hob was working on some important sorting—important to him, at least. Sitting beside the towering treasure pile in its gloomy, vaulted cave, he picked through the backpacks that had been taken from the two ambushed travelers. Despite the goings-on, Hob had been unable to get the pair off his mind. He'd been eager to learn what they'd been carrying.

Two fine swords and scabbards, an axe, seven gold coins, some light camping supplies, and a couple rations of hardtack biscuits were all he found. But to him, each piece represented a clue about their lost adventure.

The entire treasure pile had been amassed this way, through centuries of looting from humans. Hob felt bad about that. But the pile did have its uses. It was from the pile that he'd "borrowed" all his books—except one, which he'd inherited from the wise old goblin who'd taught him how to read in the first place.

Pausing for a moment, Hob stared hungrily at the travelers' hardtack biscuits. They would just go to waste in the pile. He picked one up and tasted it. It was boring and difficult to chew, but at least it wasn't *gruel.* Deciding to save the rest for later, Hob stuffed the biscuits through the front ties of his tunic into a large breast pocket inside—a pocket he used for carrying items that didn't require his satchel.

"Hobblestraug!" Chief Gobblestomp barked, as he marched into the cave.

Hob froze, afraid the Chief might have seen him pocketing the hardtack.

"Excellent work!" the Chief continued. "The pile's lookin' nice and big!"

Hob relaxed. "Oh, thanks, sir," he said, standing at attention. "I'm just finishing up with the latest ambush."

"Good show," said the Chief, as he walked around the pile, examining it closely.

"Is there anything I can help you with?" Hob asked.

"There is!" said the Chief. "I need somethin' *shiny* to wear while I'm judgin' the Clobberin'."

"No problem," said Hob, happy to help. He remembered every item he'd sorted by heart, and he hurried to pick out a few of the shinier pieces for the Chief to accessorize with. "Do any of these catch your eye?"

"This one's nice an' shiny!" said Chief Gobblestomp, picking up a silver tiara and fiddling with it awkwardly.

"It goes on your head," said Hob. "But you should know—"

"I already *know* everythin' I should know!" said the Chief, adding the tiara to the front of his headdress.

"—that it's meant for a *princess*," Hob finished, entirely to himself.

The Chief wasn't listening. He was studying his reflection in a dusty old mirror half-buried in the pile. He seemed pleased with his new look. It screamed, "*toad-in-a-tiara.*"

As the Chief turned to admire his profile, Hob took the opportunity to get a word in with him.

"Um, sir, there's actually something I've been wanting to talk to you about …"

"Huh? What? What's that?" asked the Chief, not taking his eyes off himself.

"Well, it's about the Clobbering," Hob began. He took a deep breath, and blurted out the rest before he lost his nerve. "I know you said we all have to participate. But I was thinking, maybe, I might *not*. I mean, it's not like I could ever make the troop anyway. It makes no sense."

"Hmm," said Gobblestomp, turning to him. "No can do. Everyone's gotta try out. That's the rule."

Hob had expected as much. Still, he had to keep trying. "And you're *sure* there are no exceptions? Because I've been thinking—"

"See, now, there's yer problem," said the Chief. "All this *thinkin'.* You know what *you need*, Hobblestraug? A few good hits to the head! Why don't ya run along an' practice? The pile can wait till after the Clobberin'. There's a good fella. Out, out, out!"

With a powerful arm, the Chief shunted Hob out of the Treasure Cave. Then he stood in the entrance, making sure Hob ran off to practice.

Hob did run off—but not to practice. He made straight for his nook, intending to pick up *The Ballad of Waeward the Wanderer* before sneaking off to his secret spot to keep reading.

"Hob! Wait!"

A voice stopped Hob halfway down the passage to his nook. He looked back to see Grunt hurrying after him.

"You said we was gonna practice together!" said Grunt, catching up.

"Sorry, Grunt. I forgot …"

"That's okay! Plenty of time left!" Grunt gestured for Hob to follow him.

Hob hesitated. "Gee, I don't know. I've got important, um … stuff to do."

"What's more important than practicing for the Clobbering?" asked Grunt. "If you don't, you'll get …"

"*Clobbered?*" Hob volunteered.

"Yup."

"Don't worry," said Hob. "I've got everything under control. I've got a, um, *strategy.*"

But he didn't. The Clobbering was not the sort of contest that lent itself to strategy—owing to the complete lack of rules. All you had to do was grab a stick, step into the ring, and clobber away, until you either got knocked out or you made the troop.

"You can practice *that* then," Grunt replied. "C'mon. The Clobbering's tomorrow moon. You gotta!"

Unfortunately, when Hob looked up into Grunt's big, expectant eyes he simply couldn't bring himself to say "no."

A few minutes later, Grunt was leading Hob into the Great Cave for a practice session. They paused inside the entranceway. Looking down, Hob could see a wide chalk circle drawn around the edge of the cave's bottom level. The next moon, it would be the *Clobber-Ring*. But, for now, it was the *practice ring*. It was full of goblins rehearsing various fighting maneuvers—all of which looked quite painful.

Noticing Hob taking everything in, Grunt placed a hand on Hob's shoulder. "How lucky is this?" he said. "You was just sayin' how ya wanna get outta here and go on adventures and stuff. Well, bein' in the Sorcerer's army would be a real adventure, wouldn't it, Hob?"

"I guess so," said Hob, "in a *goblin-y* sort of way."

"Exactly!" said Grunt, missing the point entirely.

They descended to the practice ring. All around the outside, goblins sorted through barrels full of sticks.

"Oh! I know," said Grunt. "Let's pick ya out a clobber-stick."

"Mine's hickory!" volunteered an enthusiastic goblin, hitting himself over the head with a stick to test it.

"Hickory looks good, doesn't it?" Grunt observed.

"I guess so," said Hob.

A clobber-stick was the official weapon of the Clobbering, and if Hob was going to have to participate, he figured he might as well have one to defend himself with. He and Grunt began picking through the barrels, looking for a stick short enough for Hob—in hickory, if possible.

Once they found one, Hob gave it a test swing. It made a satisfying *swish*, which seemed to please Grunt.

"That's a good one!" he said. "C'mon, you can try it out!"

Grunt took Hob by the hand and led—or, rather, dragged—him into the practice ring. Hob's heart sank as they were joined by Ick, Uck, Skulldug, and several other rowdy goblins. The last thing Hob wanted was company!

"Um, Grunt, I thought it was gonna be *just us*," he whispered.

"Lucky, huh?" Grunt replied. "It'll be more fun with a group."

And it would be—for *the group*.

Hob and the others practiced head-butts, slew-foots, stick-tackles, and pile-ups. And Hob got the worst of every one. Soon, he was battered, bruised, and buried under a heap of bodies.

It wasn't going unnoticed, either. As Hob crawled out from beneath the pile, he saw a bunch of spectators gathered nearby.

"Pathetic," said one.

"What's wrong with him?" said another.

"I hear he's a *vegetarian* ..." whispered a third.

A few gasped aloud.

"He's gonna get pounded at the Clobbering."

"He's mincemeat!"

"Ground gizzard!"

"Chopped chum!"

"He's MINE!" said Brute, muscling his way through the crowd, accompanied by Snivel and a gang of other lackeys. "And I'm so glad I found him!"

Brute and company gathered around the spot where Hob lay in the ring, and sneered down at him malevolently.

"*So glad?*" asked Grunt, poking his head into their huddle. "I thought you didn't like Hob?"

Brute glared at him. "I'm glad I found him, so I can tell him what he's in for," he explained, turning back to Hob with a wicked grin.

"He's *gonna kill you,*" Snivel whispered giddily, giving away the "surprise."

"Shuddup!" snapped Brute.

"Aye, aye," said Snivel, not really shutting up.

"So here goes, Hobby," Brute went on. "As soon as the Clobberin' starts, I'm comin' straight for ya. I'm gonna get to ya first. And I'm gonna pound ya, till that big ol' head of yers is knocked good an' empty. And then, *if* ya survive, maybe you'll know not to be such a *weirdo*. Got it?"

"Got it, Brute!" said Snivel.

"I was talkin' to *him*," snapped Brute.

Snivel stuck out his tongue at Hob, as if Brute scolding him was somehow Hob's fault. Hob scowled back.

"Don't count Hob out," Grunt interjected. "He's got a *st-stragedy*. Don't ya, Hob?"

"Er, well ..." Hob mumbled.

"Don' matter," Brute interrupted. "Ain't no stragedy that'll stop *this!*" He punched the air violently with both fists, causing Hob to flinch.

Except for Grunt, the nearby goblins all laughed.

That was it. Hob had had enough. He couldn't hold back his frustration any longer. "You think this is funny?" he shouted at them, jumping to his feet. "That a try-out for *war* is some sort of game? Does going to fight for some crazy old magician with a vengeance complex really sound like a *good idea* to you?"

The goblins' laughter gave way to stunned silence. Their faces turned menacing. They looked ready to *clobber* Hob right then. Especially Brute.

For a second, Hob held his breath, instantly regretting what he'd just said. Then he un-said it. "B-b-because, to me, it sounds like a *great idea!*"

Suddenly, the goblins were all laughing again.

"He's right!"

"It is a great idea!"

"An awesome idea!"

"He's *still* gonna get pounded though."

"Oh, totally."

Brute alone seemed unimpressed. It made no difference to him what Hob thought. "See ya tomorrow, Hobby," he growled.

Then he and his followers strode off, shooting Hob threatening glances as they went.

Once they were gone, Hob fled the practice ring. He had no way of saving himself—no strategies, no plans. But one thing was for sure; more practice wasn't going to help.

"Hob, wait! Where're ya going?" shouted Grunt, catching up to him in the tunnel outside the Great Cave's main entrance.

Hob stopped and turned back to him. "Away from here," he muttered.

"But what about all that stuff ya just said?" asked Grunt, looking confused. "If ya kept that up, the other guys'd probably lay off ya. They might even help me get ya through the Clobbering." He paused. "Please, Hob, just this once, don't go sneakin' off. I've got a bad feeling ..."

Hob didn't answer. There was no way to make Grunt understand. "See you tomorrow, Grunt," he said. Then he turned and stalked away.

Hob wanted to forget Grunt's pleas—forget everything. He returned to his nook, plucked *The Ballad of Waeward the Wanderer* from his shelf, tore the blanket from his bunk, and stuffed both into his satchel. Then he hurried off to his secret spot.

The night was almost over when Hob pulled himself above ground. Wasting no time, he sat down gingerly on his blanket, smarting from his bumps and bruises, and cracked open his book. He couldn't wait to escape into *The Ballad of Waeward the Wanderer*—his last and only refuge from the nightmare that was the Clobbering. If he was going to get his brains pounded out the next moon, he figured he might as well finish the book while he still could.

He picked up right where he'd left off, and quickly lost himself in the tale.

Brave Waeward searched the Valley of Yore, but could find no way to wake Princess Parabelle from her cursed sleep. Then a mysterious traveler told him of a legendary Fountain of Youth, which was located in an ancient Lost City hidden somewhere deep in the mountains north of the valley. It was said water from the fountain could cure any illness with a single drop. The traveler gave Waeward cryptic directions, and sent him on his way. Waeward outfitted himself in a city called Valley Top, perched on a mountainside at the western edge of the valley, and set out from there into the wild lands beyond.

By the time Hob looked up from his book, dawn had come, and the sun was nearly up. Even in the recesses of the cave, it was getting too bright for him to see. But he had to know if Waeward ever found the Lost City. He crawled beneath his blanket so he could keep reading.

Feeling hungry and tired, Hob remembered the hardtack biscuits in the pocket inside his tunic. He reached in, and pulled out a handful of crumbs. The biscuits were a bit squashed from clobbering practice. But they were still edible. Hob nibbled away on handfuls of the crumbs, as he continued to read.

Waeward wandered the wilds for many months, following the traveler's cryptic directions as closely as he could, so that he might locate the Lost City, where it lay hidden in the mountains. This took him on a winding route, stretching as far west as the sea, before leading him back to the lands north of the valley. And he had many thrilling adventures along the way.

Finally, Waeward reached the Lost City. He searched the ruins for the Fountain of Youth. But before he could find it, something found him. *A dragon!* To Waeward's horror, the city and its treasures were being guarded by a terrible fire-breathing serpent.

Hob rubbed his tired eyes. He'd now read late into the morning. His hardtack crumbs were all gone. And he couldn't help but struggle to stay awake. Still, he had to know how the story ended!

Waeward gathered his courage. He was about to face his greatest challenge yet. He had to find the Fountain of Youth to save Princess Parabelle, even if it meant slaying the dragon. Soon, one way or another, his wanderings would be over. Slowly, cautiously, he crept through the city streets, sword drawn, muscles tensed. And then … And then …

Hob awoke with a start. Where was he? What was happening? He'd fallen asleep in the middle of reading!

He peeked out from under his blanket.

"Oh no!" he cried.

It was dark out—*too* dark. He threw off his blanket, and ran to the edge of the cave.

"Oh *no!*"

The moon and stars shone down on him. It was the middle of the night. Hob was late for the Clobbering!

How had it happened? Where had a whole day gone? Hob hurtled down the tunnels in a state of distraction, willing his feet to carry him as fast as they could toward the Great Cave. Maybe it wasn't too late? Maybe the others hadn't noticed he was missing? Maybe, maybe, maybe ...

SLAM!

Hob ran into someone, and stumbled backward. There was Grunt, staring down at him, looking distraught.

"Grunt!" Hob cried. "Thank goodness it's you!"

"Where've ya been?" asked Grunt. "Yer in *big trouble* ..."

"So, I'm too late, then? I missed the Clobbering?"

"Not *exactly* ..."

"What do you mean?"

"Well, when ya didn't show, Brute got pretty mad, and demanded the whole thing be called off till he could find ya. He's takin' a search party to yer nook, right now."

Hob's stomach sank so violently that he thought it might fall out. "My *books!*" he cried. He tore off, leaving Grunt behind.

Hob sprinted straight for his nook. But by the time he got there, Brute, Snivel, and a bunch of other angry goblins were already gathered outside.

A few of the smaller ones were going in and out, ransacking the place. Almost everything Hob owned now lay in a pile on the tunnel floor, which Brute was sifting through for clues. Atop the pile, stacked on the faded goat tapestry, were Hob's books!

Hob gasped audibly, and the whole search party turned to see him. He whirled around, and shot back up the tunnel.

Brute gave chase.

SLAM!

Hob ran into Grunt again. Grunt must have been following him down from the upper levels.

"Lemme go, Grunt!" Hob cried.

But before Grunt could get out of the way, Brute seized Hob from behind, and lifted him right off his feet. Holding Hob up by the scruff of his furry collar, Brute turned him around so they were face to face.

"Tried to skip out on The Clobbering, eh, pipsqueak?" Brute said, grinning nastily as he savored this new excuse to torture Hob. "Bet ya wish ya'd taken yer licks, now, huh? 'Cause we found some pretty interestin' stuff in yer nook there … I wonder if ya got any more *on ya!*"

Brute then flipped Hob over, held him by one foot, and shook him up and down. Hob closed his eyes and gritted his teeth. Blood rushed to his head. He thought he might faint. Finally, *The Ballad of Waeward the Wanderer* tumbled out of his satchel, and landed with a *thud* on the tunnel floor.

CHAPTER FIVE

Deep Down and Out

Water oozed out of the rocks above Hob's head, coating them in a layer of slime before trickling to the floor with a steady *drip, drip, drip*. The sound drummed at Hob's ears as he sat in a hard, lonely corner of his hard, lonely cell. If pressed, he would have said that a couple hours had passed since he'd been thrown into the dungeon. But counting *drips* wasn't a reliable way to tell time, so he couldn't be sure.

Located on the deepest, most miserable level of the Gobble Downs, the dungeon was little more than a dead-end hallway lined with cells—simple holes in the rock, barricaded by doors of rusty iron bars—and lit by a single sputtering torch bolted to the wall beside a single snoozing guard.

The grim place had only one redeeming feature. Hob's cell happened to be directly across from that of the captives. This allowed Hob to satisfy his curiosity about the mysterious boy and the dwarf. Even in the meager light, he had a better view of them than at any time during the ambush.

Hob sat in his corner watching them. The boy was young—maybe fourteen years old—and had a charming face, with green eyes half-hidden under a mop of shaggy golden hair. The dwarf was much older, and had a bushy white beard, rosy cheeks, and dark, mischievous eyes. Both wore simple traveling clothes, filthy from days on the road.

They spent most of their time huddled together, whispering. And, every once in a while, the boy would peer around, and add to some sort of drawing he was scratching on the floor with a stone chip. It was clear to Hob they were planning to escape.

Then it dawned on him. They were *planning to escape!* And he was *there to help them!* In the most unexpected fashion, fate had given Hob the chance he'd always wanted. The chance he'd never thought possible. If he could prove his worth to the boy and dwarf right then, they might just take him with them!

What Hob had in mind would be risky, but there was nothing left for him in the Gobble Downs anyway. Even if he managed to survive his imprisonment and the Clobbering, the Sorcerer's war was still coming. And Hob wanted no part in that. He had to try.

He scrambled up to his cell door and knelt there, clinging to the bars. "*Psst! Psst!*" he whispered across the hall to the captives.

They glanced back at him, looking annoyed.

Hob didn't let that stop him. "I can help you," he whispered.

"What?" hissed the dwarf.

"You're planning an escape, right?" Hob went on. "You're going on an *adventure,* right? I've always wanted to go on an adventure. Take me with you, and I can show you a way out of here!"

The boy and dwarf exchanged incredulous glances. Then they glared back at Hob.

"We're not escapin'!" snapped the dwarf. "Who said we were escapin'?"

"Don't worry!" Hob pleaded with him, trying to calm him down before he woke the snoozing guard. "I'm on your side."

"On our *side?*" the dwarf blustered. "We're tryin' to save the valley from the *likes of you!*"

"Shh!" hissed the boy. "You're saying too much."

"No, that's perfect!" Hob cut in. "I wanna save the valley from the likes of me *too!*"

The boy chuckled in spite of himself.

Meanwhile, the dwarf only got more upset. "Take the hint, goblin. I meant, '*no!*'"

"Aw, ease up," said the boy, flashing Hob a charming half-smile. "The goblin's got a dream."

"Well, he can *dream on,*" said the dwarf. "He's *not* comin' with us!"

The boy elbowed the dwarf in the shoulder.

"And we're not escapin'!" the dwarf added, for good measure. "So, go away! *Shoo!*"

"But, but—"

Hob was just about to keep pleading his case, when—*BANG!*—the door at the end of the hall burst open, waking the snoozing guard beside it, and nearly putting out the single sputtering torch. Chief Gobblestomp squeezed into the dungeon.

Hob's one big chance had evaporated. Crushed, he sank back into his cell, and stood there waiting for the Chief.

The Chief stopped outside seconds later, holding a rusty key. "Let's get this over with, Hobblestraug," he said, unlocking the cell door, and drawing it open, causing it to *whine* ominously. "I was really lookin' forward to the Clobbering, and it's been put off till after yer trial."

"My *trial?*" Hob squeaked, sensing things were about to turn from bad to worse.

The Chief nodded. "Yer to stand trial before the Queen."

"Here we are," said Chief Gobblestomp. He halted in a narrow tunnel out-side the Queen's residence—*the Deep Cave*—which was also on the lowest, most miserable level of the Gobble Downs. He filled the whole passage with his bulk, blocking the cave's entrance from view.

Hob stopped behind him, feeling doomed already.

"Oh, and just to warn ya," the Chief added, "there are a few others in there too."

"Huh? How many?" asked Hob.

"Well, all of 'em, really," said the Chief. And with that, he ducked in through the entrance, and stepped aside to reveal the Deep Cave.

The cave opened up beyond the tunnel mouth, a bowl-shaped cavern of black rock filled with goblin spectators. They covered the upper ledges of the steep, craggy walls, holding fiery torches, and staring down with wild, gleaming eyes.

More frightening than the sight of the crowd, however, was the sight of the figure seated directly across from the entrance. The Queen Goblin on her throne!

The Queen was the mother of every young goblin in the horde, but none of them ever thought of her that way—perhaps because of how terrifying and un-motherly she was. She was nearly twice as tall as Chief Gobblestomp, more than twice as wide, and easily three times as ugly, with a toad-like face and a giant mouth packed with short, pointed teeth.

Her throne was carved out of the cave wall atop a wide stepped platform, and was flanked by two back exits, one to either side. Perched on the back of the throne was the Sorcerer's crow, only adding to the nightmarish quality of the scene.

"Yer Mightiness," Chief Gobblestomp called out from beside the en-tranceway. "I bring you Hobblestraug, the accused." He paused. "*C'mon now*," he whispered to Hob, peering back into the tunnel.

Heart pounding, Hob stepped forward past Chief Gobblestomp and into the Deep Cave.

Jeers and insults rained down on Hob from the crowd above. He knew Brute would be up there somewhere, enjoying the show. Grunt would be there too, ashamed and worried. But Hob didn't look for either of them. He kept his eyes fixed ahead and his feet shuffling forward. When he got as close to the Queen as he dared—which wasn't very close—he stood to face her judgment.

"Hobblestraug!" the Queen bellowed, her deep, gurgley voice echoing through the cave and turning Hob's insides to jelly. "Do you know why you stand before me?"

"*SQUAWK! Why?*" croaked the Sorcerer's crow, from atop the throne.

Hob tried to stop shaking long enough to answer. "Umm … Because I missed the Clobbering?"

"No," gurgled the Queen.

"Because I missed the Clobbering to read a book?"

"No!" gurgled the Queen. "Though you are a truly miserable excuse for a goblin …"

"*SQUAWK! Miserable!*" croaked the crow.

"… you're guilty of something *far* worse!"

"I *am?*" Hob gulped.

"*YES!*" bellowed the Queen.

The crowd cheered wildly at the verdict. But the Queen raised a stubby hand to silence them. She wasn't done.

"The books discovered in your nook," she continued, speaking as sweetly as a giant monster with a deep, gurgley voice could speak. "*Where* did you get them?"

Hob was sure from the pointy-toothed grin twisting across her face that she already knew.

"The treasure pile," he admitted. It hardly seemed worth lying. She was going to punish him no matter what.

"I *know*," gurgled the Queen. "The treasure pile's the only place to find books in the Gobble Downs. And as Treasure Keeper, you had plenty of chances to *steal* from it."

The cave filled with the sound of a hundred goblins all gasping at once.

"I always thought of it more like *borrowing*," Hob mumbled, mostly to himself.

"*Enough!*" shouted the Queen. "Do you know who that pile belongs to?"

"To the horde?" Hob ventured.

"To *ME!*" bellowed the Queen. "No one steals from *my* pile and gets away with it! GUILTY! Off with his head!"

"*SQUAWK! Off with his head!*" croaked the crow.

The crowd cheered again. And this time the Queen let them.

"*CARL!*" she bellowed.

On her command, a figure entered through the back passage to the right of the throne. It was a gigantic, three-headed, three-*hooded,* executioner troll! Goblins kept trolls around to do the jobs even they found unpleasant, and judging by the enormous axe it carried, Hob knew what this one's next job was going to be.

As the troll lumbered forward, its three heads bickered amongst themselves.

"She's talking to *me,*" said the left head.

"She's talking to *me,*" said the right head.

"She's talking to *all of us,*" said the middle head.

"But, *I'm* Carl," said the left head.

"No, *I'm* Carl," said the right head.

"We're *all* Carl," said the middle head. "We've been over this."

"But that's just confusing," said the left head.

"Yeah," said the right head. "Are we *one* Carl with *three* heads, or *three* Carls with *one* body? Because, if we're *one* Carl, then she's clearly talking to *all* of us. But if we're *three* Carls, then she could be talking to *any* of us."

"Shut up! Shut up!" roared the Queen. "I'm talking to *all* of you. *All* of you, chop off that little goblin's head!"

"Yes, Your Mightiness!" the troll's three heads replied. "Right away!"

Hob tried to run. But the next thing he knew, he'd been seized by the troll, dragged forward, and made to lie with his neck on the steps of the throne platform.

"Off with his head!" the Queen shouted again, just for the fun of it.

Out of the corner of his eye, Hob watched as the troll raised its axe, the blade glinting in the torchlight. Everything was happening so fast! Hob couldn't think! He didn't know what to do!

Then a jumble of voices and heavy footsteps rang out in the cave, and the troll froze.

"In here!"

"Whoops!"

"Now we've got 'em!"

The troll lowered its axe as its heads looked toward the cave's front entrance. Hob looked too.

Just inside the entrance, the boy and the dwarf stood frozen in their tracks. Each carried a stolen goblin saber in one hand, while the boy carried the sputtering dungeon torch in his other. They turned to flee, but ten armed guards—led by the sleepy fellow from the dungeon—followed them into the cave, blocking their exit.

I knew they were escaping! Hob thought, in spite of himself. Though, he had to admit, it didn't look like they were going to get very far.

"Any other options?" shouted the dwarf, swinging his saber to keep the ten armed guards at bay.

The boy scanned the cave. His gaze swept quickly over the crowd above, all the goblins paralyzed with shock and confusion. Then it landed on Hob, the troll, and the Queen on her throne.

In that instant, Hob could have sworn the boy made eye contact with him—recognized him even! But the boy's expression quickly changed to one of pure relief.

"There!" he exclaimed, pointing past Hob toward the back exit to the left of the throne. "Run!"

The boy and dwarf took off across the cave, making straight for the back exit. And the guards tore after them, joined by Chief Gobblestomp, who'd been standing by the front entrance the whole time.

The guards immediately threatened to overtake the fleeing captives, particularly the short-legged old dwarf. But, while the dwarf kept hustling for the passage to the left of the throne, the boy suddenly veered toward the throne itself—and Carl the Troll!—which surprised the guards, jamming them up for a second as they decided whom to follow. The six leaders and Chief Gobblestomp went after the boy, while the four slowest carried on after the dwarf.

"What are you *doing?*" the dwarf shouted.

The boy had no time to answer. He charged in at the troll—just wide of the spot where Hob lay—brandishing his sword and letting out a wild war cry. Provoked, the troll swung its axe at him in a violent, horizontal arc. The boy ducked the axe, and rolled right through the troll's legs, jabbing the creature's oily loincloth with his torch.

"*YEOW!*" the troll screeched, dropping its axe and grabbing its smoking backside.

CRASH! The pack of goblin guards promptly slammed into the troll, having failed to anticipate the boy's evasive maneuver.

Hob scrambled out of the way, as the whole lot of them fell over in a heap, big Chief Gobblestomp on top.

Peeking around the pile, Hob saw the boy pop up out of his roll. The boy glanced back, flashed Hob a daring smile, and hurried on. Had he planned the *whole thing?*

Hob didn't have time to think about it. The goblin spectators on the ledges above had now recovered from their initial shock, and they began streaming down the walls of the cave, pushing and shoving as they rushed to chase the captives.

Having arrived at the back exit, the dwarf dueled with the four goblin guards who'd pursued him there. He was clearing the way in hopes that the boy would reach him before the oncoming swarm. Two of the four guards already lay unconscious on the floor. *Shwing!* The dwarf disarmed the other two with a flourish of his stolen saber, and—*clonk!*—he jumped up and banged their helmets together, sending them to join their friends. He looked for the boy.

"Just thought I'd ditch the crowd!" the boy exclaimed, as he shot past the dwarf and out the exit.

"*Show off*," grumbled the dwarf, bolting after him.

That was when Hob realized he too had been given a chance to escape. With the crowd distracted by the captives, and the troll tangled up in a pile of guards, there was no one to stop him. So, as everyone else streamed for the back exits to chase the captives, Hob took off in the opposite direction, running straight out the cave's wide-open front entrance.

He ran so fast that he'd already started up the passage outside when he heard the Queen bellow from her throne.

"Look, fools! The *thief* is escaping too!"

"Escaping with the man-captives?" someone cried.

"No, you idiot!" bellowed the Queen. "He went *that way!*"

"*Idiot!*" croaked the crow.

Hob went on running as fast as he could. Though it was a bit narrow, the main passage outside the Deep Cave was straight and empty, and it climbed steadily upward. Hob wanted to take it as far as possible before the other goblins caught up. He had to get to the surface, get out of the Gobble Downs altogether, if he wanted to live.

Still, before long, loud footsteps and angry voices filled the tunnel behind him. With his short legs, Hob had no hope of outrunning the larger goblins in a straight line. He had to find another way out. Eventually, the mouth of a small side-tunnel opened in the wall ahead, and he slipped inside it.

Hob hurried on through the winding little tunnel, trying to recall the best back-routes from there to the surface. He should have been paying more attention to where he was going though, as a sputtering torch soon lit up the tunnel ahead of him, and he came face to face with the escaping captives.

Before Hob could even react, the dwarf tackled him, pinned him with his back to the ground, and pressed a stolen goblin saber to his throat.

"Stop!" Hob croaked. "Don't you recognize me?"

"All I see is GREEN!" growled the dwarf, putting pressure on his saber so its chipped blade bit at Hob's skin.

"Wait," said the boy, peeking down at Hob over the dwarf's shoulder. "It's *you*."

"Yes!" Hob croaked. "You saved me from that troll! Don't let *him* kill me!"

"He didn't *save you*," the dwarf growled, increasing the pressure on his blade. "He was just losin' those guards."

"I know what I saw," Hob croaked.

The dwarf glanced back at the boy suspiciously.

"W-well, I couldn't just watch him get beheaded," said the boy. "It seemed like a win-win."

"*Ugh,*" groaned the dwarf. "You really *are* goin' through a *phase*." He stared back down at Hob in disbelief. "I mean, *this* is a cry for help! What're we supposed to do with him now?"

"Take me with you!" Hob pleaded, suddenly. He had another chance to try to prove himself, and he wasn't going to let it slip away. "I'm escaping too. And, like I was trying to tell you before, I know a way out. A *secret* way. I can show you. But you *have to* take me with you!"

The dwarf paused, squinting at Hob. "No deal. Point us in the right direction, and *maybe* I'll let you live. But I can take it from there myself. My sense of direction is uncanny."

"So you *know* you're headed back toward the cave full of goblins?" asked Hob.

The boy shot the dwarf a worried look.

"Uh, sometimes you have to go backward to go forward," muttered the dwarf.

"Not with me you won't," Hob went on. "You need me. These tunnels go on like this for miles in every direction."

"But how do we know we can trust you?" asked the boy.

"Because I'm not like other goblins," said Hob. "You saw. They're trying to kill me! It's this whole thing where I messed up the Clobbering because I was reading, and my books were borrowed from the treasure pile, and—"

"Okay! Okay! *Shhh!*" hissed the dwarf, clapping a hand over Hob's mouth. "We don't need your life's story." He looked back at the boy, exasperated.

"If it means we don't have to spend who-knows-how-long fighting our way out of here, then I'm all for it," said the boy.

"Fine. Be that way," grumbled the dwarf. "But no more talkin', goblin. Just get us out of here, quick and quiet like." He stood up, letting Hob—and Hob's mouth—go free.

"Thanks!" Hob wheezed, hopping up, and extending a hand for someone to shake. "I'm Hob."

An awkward pause followed.

"Er … I'm *Ed*," the boy replied, shaking Hob's hand hesitantly. "And this is Monty."

Monty crossed his arms and scowled.

"It's a pleasure to meet you both," said Hob.

"Remember how I said, '*no talkin'*?'" asked Monty.

"Oh, right. Well, follow me."

It was a long trek from the bottom of the Gobble Downs to Hob's secret spot, but he made sure to set a good pace, guiding the captives through the endless maze of twisting tunnels. Ed and Monty kept up well, with their stolen sabers drawn and Ed's dim torch lighting their way.

Still, because the trio had to stick to only empty back passages, their route was far from the most direct. And when they neared the heart of the Gobble Downs, where all the tunnels tended to converge, they found the other goblins had arrived there before them.

Suddenly, the curving passage ahead filled with bright torchlight, the sound of footsteps, and armed shadows that stretched around the bend. A goblin search party!

"Go back! Go back!" Hob whispered, beginning a frantic retreat.

They had to get out of that tunnel fast. Followed by Ed and Monty, Hob took a small passage rightward at the next fork. It led directly into a larger one.

At the intersection, they met Carl the Troll!

In a moment of shock, the troll's three heads stared at Hob and the fleeing captives. Hob couldn't order another retreat, not with a swarm of goblins already filling the tunnels behind them.

"Run!" he yelled.

He bolted to the right again, up the new tunnel. Ed and Monty followed as the troll charged after them.

"C'mon!" Hob cried, rushing past the next intersection and around a wide bend. "C'mon!"

Monty huffed and puffed but couldn't keep up with Hob. And Ed hung back to make sure his old friend didn't get left behind. As such, Hob was well ahead of them both when he skidded around the bend and encountered yet another goblin search party, this one led by Brute, Snivel, *and* Grunt!

Hob froze a dozen paces off.

"*Hob?*" Grunt exclaimed.

Their eyes locked. It was obvious Grunt knew Hob was leaving. Hob said nothing; there was no time. He just turned and sprinted back around the bend—*out of sight*. He couldn't let Grunt know he was escaping with the captives. It would be too shameful, even for Hob.

"Get him!" Brute roared.

"But what about finding the man-captives?" asked Snivel.

"Forget them! Bring me HOBBLESTRAUG!"

Hob shot straight by Ed and Monty, who were still following his previous path around the bend.

"This way!" Hob cried.

The captives reversed step and followed him back to the intersection they'd just passed. They found Carl the Troll already blocking it.

Without slowing, Hob ducked through the troll's legs and up the passage to the right. Ed and Monty followed, dodging the startled troll, and racing after Hob. With a roar, the troll turned and gave chase.

The passage soon opened into a bottomless cavern with a twenty-foot-wide chasm in place of a floor. A rickety rope bridge stretched from the end of the passage to a timber platform on the far side, where three new tunnels opened up.

Hob shot out of the passage and across the bridge, stopping on the platform to wait for the others.

Monty started across next.

Ed leapt out after him. "Hold on!" he cried, ditching his torch, grabbing on to the bridge, and cutting the ropes with a swing of his saber.

SNAP! The bridge fell away with Ed and Monty on board, leaving the troll stranded at the end of the passage, surprise etched on all three of its faces.

Ed and Monty swung with the bridge across the chasm, hitting the far wall with a *thud*, and dangling below the platform.

Carl the Troll glared across at Hob. Then it started backing up the passage. It was going to try to jump!

Tucking their sabers into their belts, Ed and Monty climbed the planks of the rope bridge as if they were the rungs of a giant ladder, scrambling toward the platform.

"Hurry!" Hob shouted down at them. "Hurry!"

"What do you *think* we're doin'?" Monty shouted back at him.

A short way up the passage on the far side of the chasm, Carl the Troll halted its retreat and began to charge. Its footsteps echoed like thunder out of the tunnel.

Monty and Ed heaved themselves onto the platform.

"This one! This one!" Hob cried, waving them into the smallest of the three tunnels there.

He waited as the pair crawled inside. The troll reached the far side of the chasm and launched itself. Hob ducked into the little tunnel after the others.

SMASH! The troll cleared the chasm, but not one of its three heads had accounted for their target's small size. They hit the tunnel opening hard and got jammed inside, with the rest of their body too big to fit. They were stuck, unable to do anything but watch, and *bicker,* as Hob and company got away.

"We'll get you!"

"He means, *I'll* get you!"

"Not *this* again!"

A short time later, Hob brought Ed and Monty to the little underground waterfall. It spilled cool and clear into its pool, just like always.

"This is it," Hob said. "My secret way out."

"A waterfall?" said Monty, taking a stubborn tone. "I'm not swimmin'."

"It's *behind* the waterfall," said Hob. "That's what keeps it secret."

"How do you know about it, then?" Ed wondered.

"Don't ask questions," hissed Monty. "He talks too much already."

"I found it while taking a bath," said Hob, "which is another reason it's secret. I'm the only one here who bathes." He knelt by the pool and rinsed his hands in the water.

"You can't bathe *now!*" Monty snapped.

"I'm just washing up," said Hob. "In case you hadn't noticed, this place is filthy."

The dwarf shook his head. "What's *wrong* with this goblin?"

"Not his commitment to hygiene, that's for sure," said Ed, chuckling. He joined Hob at the pool to wash up.

Monty stayed put, with his hands on his hips—as dirty as ever.

"Okay," said Hob, standing, and shaking dry. "All set?"

"All set," said Ed.

"Then here we go." Hob sidled up to the waterfall, and stared into the darkness where the curtain of water diverged from the rocks. Before then, it had just been the gateway to his secret spot. Now, it was the gateway to his new life. He slipped behind the curtain and was gone.

CHAPTER SIX

Left Behind

Hob moved to the front of his secret cave, and stood at the very edge of the Gobble Downs. A soft wind blew, carrying a thin rain. Both were cool on his sweaty face. He closed his eyes and let out a sigh. He was alive. He had escaped.

Hearing a scuffling noise behind him, he turned to see Ed pulling himself out of the tunnel at the back of the cave. The boy had managed the steep, tight climb with astonishing ease.

They were joined *much later* by Monty, who had managed the climb with no ease at all. He flopped out of the tunnel, panting and wheezing, with cheeks so red and puffy they made him look like a bearded tomato.

"Dagnabbit ..." the old dwarf puffed. "Last time I trust a goblin ... Secret tunnel my rump ... Tryin' to kill me ... Little blighter!"

Ed decided—wisely, Hob thought—to give Monty some space. The boy joined Hob at the front of the cave, where he looked down from the hillside and across the darkened plain beyond. The breeze tousled his golden hair and tugged at his cloak and tunic.

"Where are we?" he asked.

"My secret spot," said Hob.

"I mean, geographically?"

"Oh. The northern edge of the Gobble Downs."

"So, we're all the way through, then?"

"Yep," Hob confirmed. "I told you I had a way out!"

"And you weren't lying," said Ed, sounding a bit surprised. "I don't know how to thank you."

"It was nothing," Hob mumbled.

"So, if we go north from here, we'll hit the mountains?"

"It's actually *northwest* to the mountains, across that field and through the woods." Hob pointed off into darkness.

Ed turned back to Monty. "Did you hear that?"

Monty just groaned.

"C'mon!" said Ed. "We can't stay here forever. What if they search above ground?"

"Fine," Monty grumbled, rolling onto his belly, and hoisting himself up. He joined the others at the front of the cave, still panting. "That's *it*, lad," he announced. "I'm quittin' the pipe. Turns out, breathin's more important than you'd think."

"I've heard *that* before," said Ed, rolling his eyes.

And with that, they set forth from the cave. Monty in the lead, followed by Ed, followed by Hob.

They didn't get far. After only a few steps, Monty and Ed stopped and rounded on Hob.

"And what do you think *you're* doing?" Monty asked him.

"Coming with you?" said Hob, earnestly.

Ed opened his mouth to say something, but didn't get the chance.

"Oh, no you're *not!*" barked the dwarf. "There's no way I'm lettin' a *goblin* join this expedition!"

"But I helped you escape," said Hob. "I thought we had a deal!"

"Well, the deal ends *here*," said Monty.

"But I can't go back," Hob pleaded. He looked to Ed. "And I told you, I've always wanted to go on an adventure."

"*Well* ..." the boy sighed.

"No," said Monty. "I'll kill him before I let him tag along any farther."

He drew his saber, and thrust it at Hob. "He's still the *enemy.*"

Ed studied Hob. He didn't seem convinced that Hob was the enemy, but he deferred to Monty's judgment anyway. "Sorry," he said, "but you would kinda cramp our style. You should probably find somewhere else to go."

Ed turned away, and he and Monty set off down the hillside, leaving Hob behind.

"But I don't *have* anywhere else to go ..." Hob mumbled to himself.

Suddenly, the air didn't feel so refreshing anymore. The cold wind whipped at Hob's face. The clammy drizzle weighed him down. And for a long time, he just stood there, feeling miserable and abandoned. He had escaped the Gobble Downs, but he was still trapped. Goblins didn't have adventures on their own.

CHAPTER SEVEN

Following Along

Then, deserted on that hillside, Hob came to a sudden realization. Goblins didn't have adventures, because none ever tried! Well, Hob would try! There was finally nothing stopping him. And if his adventure just happened to start out in the same direction as Ed and Monty's? Well, there was nothing stopping *that,* either!

The next thing Hob knew, he was charging down the hillside, as fast as his short legs would carry him. He had the wind at his back and a lightness in his heart. For the first time in his life, he felt *free.* The feeling propelled him out over the plain between the hills and the forest. It was a long run, wet and windswept, through grass up to his knees, but Hob hardly noticed.

He didn't slow down until about halfway across, when he caught sight of Ed and Monty up ahead. Then, since Hob could see quite well in the dark and they could not, he hung back in the shadows, and began to "*adventure along*" behind them.

The trio reached the edge of the forest just before sunrise. This was fortunate for Hob, as darkness was his only advantage out on the plain, while the trees would give him cover even during the day. Their leafy boughs swayed up ahead, silhouetted in the predawn light. The rain had stopped, the birds had started to sing, and Monty was demanding a nap.

"I've had it with all this walking," the old dwarf complained, coming to a standstill at the tree line.

Ed, who was in the lead, was forced to turn back.

Hob scrambled for a place to hide, and found a boulder sticking up out of the grass a short distance from the forest. He dashed in behind the rock, peeking over the top at his unwitting companions.

"You promised me a nap when we got to the woods," Monty grumbled.

"You're *rrriiight* …" Ed yawned. "I guess we could use a rest." He looked up at the sky. A swath of purple was spreading from the east. "We should be safe for now. They won't cross the plain in daylight. But let's get under cover, okay?"

He looked to Monty for confirmation, but Monty was already gone.

"*Zzzzz … Zzzzz … Zzzzz …*"

Loud snoring came from the forest, and Ed turned to see the old dwarf falling asleep in the trees.

Ed chuckled, and joined him.

Thinking it unsafe to follow until Ed was also asleep, Hob rested his head on the mossy boulder, and listened for the boy to stop stirring. Unfortunately, Hob was more tired than he realized, and, before his wait was over, he fell asleep himself.

A few hours later, Hob awoke, slumped against the boulder. When he opened his eyes, sunlight flooded in. The late-spring morning had dawned cool, clear, and bright. And, while that might sound lovely to a human, it was troublesome for a goblin like Hob.

He tried to stand, but the light made his head swim and his knees wobble. Blinking rapidly, he staggered around, attempting to find his balance, and then promptly fell over.

Hob lay facedown in the long, wet grass, allowing himself a moment to recover. Then he groped for the boulder, and used it to hoist himself back onto his feet. He chanced opening his eyes a crack, and nearly collapsed again. But, this time, he held fast to the rock, and stayed upright.

Squinting hard and using a hand to shade his eyes, he peered around. The world was an over-bright blur, but the dark green of the forest was unmistakable. With any luck, the shade of the trees would allow him to see. Hob made a break for it, lurching out from behind the boulder, and running dizzily across a short stretch of grass.

He broke through the underbrush, and collapsed against the first trunk he came to, closing his bleary eyes. After a few quiet breaths, he opened them again, first one, then the other. To his relief, he could now keep them open. Although the forest was still too bright for his taste, he could see, and his dizziness was fading.

As Hob stood recuperating in the shade, he admired the world around him. To someone raised underground, it was a wonderland. He found himself at the edge of a small clearing, ringed by thick oaks and pines. They sheltered him, their limbs reaching overhead to form a canopy of dappled green. In the center of the clearing, a single beam of sunlight broke through, bright—but not *entirely* blinding—and beautiful. It spilled, golden, upon the forest floor. One of the forest goblins' little footpaths ran through the beam, leading deeper into the woods.

Never had Hob felt so surrounded by life. Unseen creatures scurried noisily through the underbrush. A pair of red squirrels played chase up a tree. And the birds' cheerful songs, which had begun in the early morning hours, were now in full, harmonious refrain.

Then, suddenly, all of it stopped. A few finches even scattered from a nearby bush. Something was coming. Hob ducked in behind his tree, just as Ed and Monty burst through the bush and into the clearing. Hob peeked out at them. They were following the goblin footpath.

"I'm just saying, you woke up awfully early for someone who was so tired and grouchy last night," Ed yawned. "Couldn't we have slept a *bit* longer?"

"When I'm up, I'm up!" said Monty. "*Teenagers*," he added under his breath, "always sleepin' their lives away."

"We only got three hours," Ed complained.

Monty stopped in the beam of sunlight, and stretched his back. It cracked audibly.

"This isn't one of your usual city capers, lad," he said. "There's no sleepin' in. If we're not careful, we could die horrible deaths, dragged by our nose hairs over beds of rusty nails … or worse!"

Ed looked stricken. "And here I was, worried about getting lost in the woods and having to live off berries and stuff."

"Berries?" Monty gasped. "That *would* be worse. If I don't get some meat in me soon, I'll waste away."

The dwarf rubbed his belly, and it responded with an unhappy grumble. In terms of wasting away, though, it looked like he had a *long way to go*.

"But seriously, lad," Monty went on, glancing around the clearing. "We can't lose any daylight. Even now, there could be a goblin hidin' behind every tree!"

Hob yanked his head in to avoid Monty's gaze. Unfortunately, the quick motion only caught the old dwarf's eye.

"Shh!" Monty whispered, as he moved in for a closer look.

Hob stood frozen behind the tree, holding his breath. He could hear Monty's footsteps approaching. *Crunch, crunch, crunch.* There was nowhere for Hob to hide. The nearest trees were too far, and the underbrush too low.

Then he got lucky. Sensing Monty coming, one of the finches took flight from the branches above. It flew right past Monty's head in a flutter of wings.

"Hah!" Monty laughed. "Only a wee bird." Shaking his head, he turned to leave.

Hob let out a silent sigh of relief. And when Monty and Ed followed the goblin footpath into the forest, Hob crept after them.

The wind *rustled* in the treetops as the little procession picked its way through the woods, Ed and Monty breaking trail and Hob sneaking along behind.

Drawing on a lifetime of sneaking experience, Hob always stayed back just the right distance from his guides, darting from tree to tree to keep out of sight and treading lightly to avoid crunching on leaf or twig.

They walked all day long. And all day long, the trees around them grew older and more gnarled, and the forest around them grew thicker and thicker, letting in less and less light.

Finally, when the sun began to set, and the shadows turned an inky black, Ed and Monty stopped again for the night.

"Harder!" Monty barked. "And faster too!"

He and Ed had camped out by the bank of a small stream. Ed struggled to start a fire by rubbing two sticks together, while Monty supervised. Hob watched from his latest hiding place in the trees.

The sun had now completely set, and darkness loomed around them. Yet, as Ed and Monty fretted over night's arrival, Hob couldn't help but welcome it. Even the shadiest parts of the forest had let in enough sunlight to bother him over time, and he'd grown tired of squinting.

"If you don't like my work, why don't *you* do it?" Ed complained, grinding his uncooperative sticks in frustration.

"Because, *you've* gotta learn," said Monty.

"Gotta learn to rub sticks together?" Ed scoffed. "I'll just buy a new tinderbox when we get back to civilization."

"And what'll you do *until* then?" asked Monty.

"I'll make you do it for me." Ed pushed the two slightly warmed sticks into the hands of the irritated dwarf, and reclined on the bank of the stream, hands folded behind his head.

"Typical," Monty grumbled. "Old Monty's got to do everythin'!"

Still, he went to work making the fire. After much grunting, groaning, and ranting about "stubborn youths," he stepped back to reveal his masterpiece.

"It's all in the wrists!" he boasted.

The wood was wet, and gave off more smoke than flame. But the fire was lit. And *lit* was as good as *roaring*, if you were as desperate for warmth as they were. It was turning out to be a frosty spring evening, and Ed and Monty were soon huddled over their tiny fire.

Hob wished he were so lucky. He could only sit curled up at the edge of the trees, far from the fire, silently shivering.

He'd been sitting like that for so long that his limbs began to go numb, when a voice gave him a jolt. He stood, searching for its source. Then he realized there wasn't one! The voice wasn't coming from the forest, but from inside Hob's own mind. It was the Sorcerer's voice, quieter and more distant than it had been in the Great Cave, but still strangely clear.

"GOBLINS OF THE OLD FOREST," it said, *"TONIGHT MARKS THE BEGINNING OF YOUR MARCH. TROOPS FROM NEARBY HORDES GATHER AT HIGH-HOLE IN THE MOUN-TAINS. JOIN THEM, AND TRAVEL TOGETHER TO SHADOWGUARD!"*

The Sorcerer was speaking to the forest goblins! Hob knew their tunnels and burrows ran beneath the forest floor. And if he was overhearing a message meant for them, he mustn't have been far from the crow channeling it—likely perched before a large audience in the goblins' main burrow.

"VENTURE ABOVE GROUND ONLY WHERE THERE ARE NO TUNNELS BELOW. REST ONLY WHEN YOU CAN NO LONGER WALK. AND LET NOTHING STAND IN YOUR WAY!" the Sorcerer finished.

Hob scuttled deeper into the trees, taking cover behind root and bush. Had Ed and Monty heard the voice too? Or was it only goblins who could hear the Sorcerer?

Hob peered back into the clearing. His companions weren't searching for some strange, disembodied voice, but remained huddled over their little fire. Ed picked up a stick, and began prodding the embers absentmindedly.

The pair stayed that way for quite some time, sitting in silence.

Then the dwarf remembered something, and began fishing around inside his overcoat. He pulled out a small object. "Looky what I managed to save from those rotten goblins, hidden in my secret pocket!"

Monty held up a small wooden smoking pipe. It had a curved stem and a dome-shaped metal cap that snapped into place over its chamber to secure its contents for travel.

"You *said* you were quitting," Ed groaned. "That thing's poison, you know. It's turning your lungs to soot."

"I am. I am," said Monty. "But I can't quit without takin' a last puff first, to make it official."

With a flick of his thumb, he opened the pipe's cap on its hinge, and used a small twig to light the chamber inside with flame from the campfire. He leaned back, and took one last puff, and then another, and then *another*, sending each little toxic wisp up into the sky.

Ed shook his head.

"Did I ever tell you, lad," Monty went on, puffing obliviously, "about the time your old man and I got trapped inside the lair of a hairy-backed giantess, and fought our way out using nothin' but—"

"—one of her giant toenail clippings as a sword?" Ed recited. "Yeah."

"Hah!" Monty laughed. "Didn't think you knew that one!"

"I know all your tall tales," Ed told him, with a grin. It seemed he couldn't stay mad at the old dwarf for long. "Everyone does. You two were *famous*."

"I suppose we were, weren't we?" said Monty, chuckling to himself. "Those were the days, lad, fightin' off early goblins raids, huntin' for treasures to help your old man in his quest, and slayin' a beast or two along the way." He went to take another satisfied draw on his pipe, but this time it produced only a dry sucking sound. "Dagnabbit!" he grumbled. "It's out. This one doesn't count then." He snapped the metal cap back over the chamber, and returned the pipe to the pocket of his overcoat. "As I was sayin', things weren't so desperate back then. But now? Now, the goblin attacks get worse every day. Your old man's gone. And time's runnin' out to finish his quest."

"Not to mention we've got Captain Fist and her men trying to arrest us at every turn, and no wizard to help us!" Ed lamented. He jabbed anxiously at the fire with his stick.

"We're almost to Valley Top," Monty assured him. "The old coot will meet us there. That was plan B."

Still watching from the bushes, Hob hung on their every word. He'd known they were going on an adventure. But he'd never imagined that Ed's father and Monty had once been famous heroes, or that Ed and Monty were carrying on some kind of family quest, or that they were still going to meet the wizard—in Valley Top, of all places! Hob had just read about Valley Top in *The Ballad of Waeward the Wanderer*. It was the city on the mountainside from which Waeward had begun his journey west. Hob wondered what business Ed, Monty, and the wizard had there.

"Either way," Ed carried on, looking over at his friend, "I'd rather be out here with you, facing a million dangers, than stuck at home in a cage." He paused. "Thanks for coming to get me. I know you're risking your neck."

"Least I could do," said Monty. "Your old man risked his neck for me more times than I can remember, from the very first day we met."

Ed paused. "Now, that's one I've never heard," he said quietly. "I was always '*too young*.'"

"Well," said Monty, "I say fourteen's old enough." He stared into the fire for a moment, before looking back up at Ed. "It happened almost thirty years ago now, when my old clan and I were recoverin' some dwarvish artifacts from an abandoned mountain hold. Even in those days, it was easy to cross paths with goblins up in the mountains, and a particularly nasty troop got the drop on us. I got knocked out early in the fight, and I woke up in one of their cages. The rest of my clan was gone. To this day, I can only assume they didn't make it."

Monty took a deep breath.

"Left to rot in a goblin cage, I didn't know why fate had spared me. And, to be honest, I wished she hadn't. Then your father came along. He was a young man then, not much older than you are now, huntin' down artifacts that might lead him to a different sort of treasure. He rescued me, took me in, and hired me to help him with his quest. He became my *new* clan. And his quest became my own." Monty paused. "And if I can't finish the blasted thing with him, then it's only right I finish it with you."

"He's not gone for good, Monty," said Ed. "We'll find him."

"Mmm," said Monty, nodding. "For now, though, let's get some sleep. I'll take first watch. And if any goblins show up, I'll give every last one the chop."

"I sure hope they don't show up," said Ed, peering out into the darkness, as he lay down by the fire. "I could use a break from goblins."

Hob sank back into the bushes. Suddenly, his thoughts returned the Sorcerer's message, and he was glad he'd heard it. The forest goblins, like those of the Gobble Downs, would be sending their troops off that night. That meant they wouldn't be out patrolling the woods. Unlike his companions, Hob could relax, knowing that none would come.

He curled up between a couple tree roots under the bushes, and tried to get some sleep. Instead of obsessing over the threat of goblin attacks, his mind once again returned to the mysterious boy and dwarf. What had happened to Ed's father? What was his quest—the one Ed and Monty were trying to finish in his place? Who was this Captain Fist trying to arrest them? And why exactly were they meeting the wizard in Valley Top?

No answers came, so Hob fell asleep still wondering.

Even without goblins to worry about, that night passed as slowly and fretfully as only a night spent outside in the forest could. Hob awoke many times to the scuffling of hidden creatures roving in the underbrush, and to visions, real or imagined, of eyes peering at him out of the darkness.

Once, he even sat straight up, gripped by fear that a bear was about to eat him! His bat-like ears had picked out the sound of some huge beast plodding and sniffing far off in the forest, and had funneled it into his dreams. He could only guess at what was really making the noise. Eventually, he tired himself out so much worrying about it, that—against his will—he drifted back to sleep.

When Hob awoke the next day—alive and uneaten—he wasn't sure if he'd heard anything at all. He couldn't tell what had been a dream, and what had been reality. The morning was quiet, but for the familiar songs of the birds, and the familiar grumblings of one old dwarf.

Monty and Ed were picking and eating spring blackberries that grew on a small bush across the stream, and Monty was complaining about it.

"I'm just sayin'," he griped, "it's too bad eggs and bacon don't grow on trees!"

Hob's own stomach growled, eager for any kind of food it could get. It occurred to him he hadn't eaten anything since the hardtack biscuits two days before. Quietly, he scoured the bushes around him, and managed to find a few tiny, unripe blackberries to pluck and eat. They were small and sour, but better than nothing.

Ed and Monty departed moments later, having picked their own bush clean. Once they were out of sight, Hob emerged from hiding long enough to take a quick drink from the stream, and wash his hands and face. Then he slipped back into the trees, and followed after his companions.

The trio walked for hours, but seemed to make no progress. The forest continued to loom around them, just as dark and dense as it had been at the end of the day before.

Worse still, because Hob had to dart between hiding places behind Ed and Monty, for each step they took, he had to take three. And on the second day, this began to catch up with him. Hob grew increasingly weary and footsore, and increasingly hungry after the meager sustenance of the blackberries wore off. All of which made it difficult to focus on sneaking.

When he inevitably misplaced a foot on a crackling twig, he swore Ed caught a glimpse of him through the forest. But Hob slipped quickly behind a tree, and the boy just shook his head and carried on. After allowing a more comfortable distance to grow between them, Hob carried on too.

In the early afternoon, things finally began to improve. Ed and Monty stumbled off the tiny footpath and onto a wide dirt road that cut through the forest on either side of them.

Hob stopped just before he too stumbled into the open.

"Well, I'll be!" said Monty. "Old Foresters' Road!"

"Where does it go?" asked Ed.

"All the way to the mountains, where it meets the road to Valley Top!" said Monty. "It used to be a popular route among traders and woodsmen, before the goblins started robbin' them all blind."

It looked as if the road might have once been smooth and wide enough for two horse carts to pass abreast, but it had become bumpy and overgrown. Trees crowded both sides of it and leaned out over top, their leafy boughs meshing together to form the ceiling of what looked like a long green tunnel through the woods. Here and there, slivers of golden sunlight pierced this emerald canopy, spilling in dappled patterns on the road, but Hob could see little sky and no mountains beyond.

Still, Monty seemed confident he knew which way to go. He and Ed turned right, maintaining a general northwesterly direction, and marched straight up the middle of the road. Hob continued to follow them, creeping through the trees alongside.

Spirits buoyed by the discovery of the road, Ed and Monty chatted boisterously as they walked.

"Why don't you finish your giantess story?" Ed suggested.

"I thought you'd heard it already?" said Monty.

"I don't mind hearing it again," said Ed. "It's different every time."

"Hah!" With a laugh, Monty launched into his tale. "She was a hairy one, that giantess ..."

On one hand, this helped Hob. It meant he didn't have to try so hard to keep quiet. On the other hand, it made him uneasy. It was impossible to tell what else might be lurking in the forest, listening.

Before long, Hob quit paying attention to Monty's tale altogether, and took it upon himself to keep watch. It was a good thing he did. Something was wrong. No birds or small critters fled as they approached. It was as if something had already scared them all away.

Then—*swish*—something stirred in the bushes.

Hob's ears caught the sound just in time. He stopped short, as a shadow swept through the trees before him. It was a tall human, cloaked in black. There one instant, gone the next. Hob's pulse quickened. He knew an impending ambush when he saw one.

He peered up the road to see if his unwitting companions had heard anything. They hadn't. They still marched along, Monty telling his tale. Hob wasn't surprised; he'd been following them for nearly two days, and they hadn't discovered him yet, either.

The shadow appeared again, this time weaving through the trees close to the road, stalking Ed and Monty.

Hob followed it. He couldn't think of anything else to do. If he called out to warn his companions, it would only bring on the ambush sooner—and land him in trouble also. And he certainly couldn't stop the shadow by himself.

Then, suddenly, the shadow was gone again. Hob scanned the trees, but he'd lost it in the gloom.

He looked to Ed and Monty, as they continued their stroll.

"And her toenail was THIS BIG!" said Monty, sticking out his arms.

Then they got ambushed. Not by the shadow, as Hob had feared, but by two soldiers. The pair emerged from the trees, one on either side of the road, right in front of Ed and Monty.

The soldiers were big, burly men. One was noble looking with a thick wrap-around mustache, the other grim and squinting. They wore identical crimson cloaks and gold-plated armor with the same circular crest on the breastplates: a red crown on a golden sun. They held long swords in their gloved hands.

"Hello, gents," said the mustached soldier. "Glad you could make it."

"Aye," said his grim companion. "We've been waiting for you."

Ed and Monty stopped dead, Monty's tall tale cut short. Drawing their goblin sabers, they turned and fled back up the road—back in Hob's direction. But before they'd taken three strides, the shadow swept out of the trees in front of them, blocking their escape. They were surrounded.

In a flash, there was a sleek sword in the shadow's hand. In another flash, Ed and Monty's sabers were out of theirs—sent spinning to the ground. The shadow had disarmed them both with one swing.

The two soldiers then seized Ed and Monty from behind, pinning their arms back in tight, painful-looking holds. The mustached one took Monty. The grim one took Ed. Both Ed and Monty struggled furiously against their captors' grips, grimacing harder the longer they fought. Finally, they gave up. They'd been captured.

For a long time, they just stood there, glaring at the shadow in furious silence.

Then Ed spoke. "Captain Fist," he growled.

The Captain dropped the hood of her black cloak to reveal her stern, proud face. She nodded curtly to the boy.

"*Prince Edric,*" she replied.

CHAPTER EIGHT

A Wild Ride

*P*rince Edric!

Hob had to cover his mouth to keep from gasping aloud. The boy—Hob's savior, adventure guide, and unwitting companion—was not just Ed, but *Edric, Crown Prince of Yore!*

Hob was drawn forward by a sudden, unshakable curiosity. He felt like a fish on a hook. He crept up through the trees, took cover behind a large oak at edge of the road, and peeked out for a better look at the Prince and his captors. The two big soldiers continued to restrain Prince Edric and Monty, while Captain Fist circled.

"I knew you would come by this road," said the Captain, "if you survived the Gobble Downs, that is." She paused. "It was madness to go in there."

Her manner of speech reminded Hob of the great Wizards of the East. He'd read a lot about those powerful magicians who'd once helped defeat the Sorcerer, and who'd brought magic to Yore. They'd built their homeland of *Arcan* into the most advanced civilization in the world, and were thought to be the first to discover magic.

"You're the one who chased us in there!" snapped Monty. "You great *wit*—"

"Now, now, Master Montague," Captain Fist interrupted. "Don't be cross. You must have known you could not escape me forever. It is impressive you managed to sneak Prince Edric out of the palace at all, under the watch of my Royal Guards."

"I do what I can," Monty growled.

"Indeed," said Captain Fist. "But now, the fun is over. The Great Lords of the Royal Council have unanimously declared Prince Edric a *deserter*, in violation of the Royal Oath, and have ordered me to return him to the palace by *whatever means necessary*. And I will."

"They have no right to give that order!" Prince Edric spat. "I'm the Prince!" He struggled against the grip of the grim soldier—who must have been one of the Royal Guards—but he couldn't break free.

"They have every right," Captain Fist scolded him. "In your rush to forget who you are, have you also forgotten the laws of this land? The laws that dictate the powers and duties of both Crown and Council? The Kingdom may be united by its loyalty to your family, but the Great Lords of the Council still hold sway in their own regions. You cannot go against all of them at once. You need them."

"Not as much as they need me!" Edric countered. "Isn't that *really* why they won't let me leave? Why they tried to stop my father from leaving? They need us around to legitimize their power. Well, they can't make me smile for the crowds, and slap the royal seal on their crooked laws, if I'm not there to do it!"

Captain Fist shook her head. "They want you to stay, because they believe the Kingdom is only safe with a member of the royal bloodline on the throne. As do your people."

"Then they've *all* got their heads in the sand!" Prince Edric said. "The goblins are coming for us, and there's only one way to stop them. If I don't find my father, and help him finish his quest, the whole Kingdom's doomed, no matter what!"

Hob gaped. *That* was the purpose of the King's quest, of Prince Edric's quest, nothing short of saving Yore from the goblins?

"My men and I have been fighting goblins since before you were born," said Captain Fist. "I know all too well their strength. And I also know they can be defeated. That is why it should be the duty of our Prince, our future King, to stay here and fight the war at home!" She paused. "For all his own reckless-ness, your father was a wise enough ruler to see this. I am certain he left you here to keep your family's oath in case something went wrong. And I am certain he left me here to ensure that you do. To stop you from chasing after him on the same desperate, all-or-nothing quest that has surely claimed his life."

Hob gaped again, connecting yet more of the dots. Prince Edric's father, King Edgar of Yore, was not just gone, as Monty had alluded to the night before, he was dead? Did any of the other goblins know this? Did the Sorcerer?

"You don't know *any* of that!" Prince Edric shouted at the Captain, his voice full of pain and determination. "My father's *not* dead! And you'll *never* stop me from finding him!"

"I already have," said Captain Fist. She turned to her men. "Bind them!"

Hob watched, as the two guards holding Edric and Monty bound their hands behind their backs with short ropes, and then coiled a longer rope around their torsos, tying them together back to back. Meanwhile, Captain Fist led three horses onto the road from where they'd been hidden in the trees, two white ones and a massive gray charger. She looped their reins around three narrow tree trunks on the verge of the road—straight across from Hob's hiding place—and signaled to her men. Together, the guards hauled Edric and Monty over, and hoisted them onto the rump of the gray charger. The pair sat there, tied together, cursing and squirming, their legs dangling helplessly over the horse's sides.

"I will take them to King's Rock myself," Fist informed the guards. "Sir Deckard," she said to the grim guard, "you ride with me. Sir Reginald," she said to the mustached guard, "you return to Valley Top and call off the search."

But none of them got to do any of that.

Before the guardsmen could even answer, the Captain threw up a hand to silence them. She'd heard something. A huge creature was stomping to-ward them through the underbrush. The noise grew louder and louder, until—*CRASH!*—not fifty paces up the road, Carl the Troll burst out of the trees!

The troll appeared in a hail of leaves and branches, peering around and sniffing the air with all three of its heads. At first, Hob couldn't believe his eyes. Then it dawned on him. The sound he'd heard the night before—of some huge beast plodding and sniffing off in the forest—had been the troll tracking their scent. It had followed them all the way from the Gobble Downs.

With one last deep sniff, its heads turned in unison to stare at the guards, the captives, and the horses. The guards and captives stared back, stunned by the sudden arrival of the troll. Luckily, the horses were tethered facing the opposite direction, preventing them from getting spooked.

"Carl Two! Carl Three! Look!" exclaimed the troll's left head.

"I see 'em," muttered its middle head. "And I told you! I don't want to be Carl *Two!*"

"It's better than being Carl *Three!*" said its right head. "Besides, you're in the middle. You'd be Carl Two no matter which way we counted."

"Can we discuss this later?" snapped the left head, now apparently known as Carl One.

"Right!" agreed Carls Two and Three.

The troll raised its axe and charged.

"Attack!" shouted Captain Fist.

At once, she and her guardsmen rushed the troll. *CRASH! CLANG!* The guards met the troll's axe with their swords, and battled it back along the road.

It wasn't going to be an easy fight. Despite the guards outnumbering the troll three to one, the reach of the troll's long axe made it nearly impossible for them to land a blow, leaving them with no option but to dodge, deflect, and wait for an opening.

One finally came when the troll leveled a wild overhand swing at Captain

Fist. Unable to meet the force of it head on, she sidestepped it. The troll's axe blade sank a foot into the dirt. Fist then used her sword to pin it in place, adding her own weight to the troll's.

Seizing the opportunity, the two guardsmen charged in. *SLAM!* With one swipe of its free arm, the troll sent them both flying. They landed on their backs in the middle of the road, thoroughly dazed.

Fist was alone with the troll. It yanked its axe free, throwing her off balance. Then it attacked again. But the Captain wasn't to be outdone. Swift as lightning, she swooped and rolled, and nearly knocked the axe out of the troll's hands with her sword.

Hob watched in awe. He'd thought Edric and Monty were good swordsmen when he'd seen them fight in the Gobble Downs, but they were amateurs compared to Captain Fist. As skilled as any of the heroes from Hob's books, she was Captain of the Royal Guard for a reason. It was only because of the troll's sheer size and strength that she had her hands full.

Then Hob realized, *she had her hands full!* With Fist busy, and the other guards knocked senseless, Hob could try to free Edric and Monty. He dashed across the road to where they sat tied up on the charger's back.

At the sight of Hob reaching up and pulling himself into the saddle, Edric's and Monty's jaws both dropped.

"Hello," Hob whispered, sitting backward in the saddle to face them.

"So, I *did* see you in the trees!" whispered Edric.

"What're *you doin'* here?" Monty hissed.

"Saving you," said Hob, as he began tugging at the knots in their ropes.

"A likely stor*eeey*—" Monty sputtered. "Ack! Yer makin'em tighter! *Tighter!*"

Hob fumbled with the ropes some more, trying to undo the damage he'd already done. But he only made it worse.

"He's right. It's not working!" croaked Edric.

"Okay, okay ..." said Hob. He couldn't figure out the knots. "I guess we'll have to try something else."

He looked around for something to cut the ropes with, but all the sharp objects in the vicinity were in the possession of the three guards and the rampaging troll. Then Hob spotted the way the horse's reins were looped around the tree.

"*Oh no ...*" Monty groaned, anticipating Hob's next move. "Can't you just leave us alone?"

"Don't worry," Hob assured him. He spun sideways in the saddle and leaned over to the tree trunk to pull the reins loose. "*This* I can un-tie!"

"That's what I'm afraid of," said Monty.

"Would you rather stay here with *them?*" asked Edric, nodding back at the guards and the troll. "Because I wouldn't. Go for it, Hob!"

Hob un-looped the reins, and gave them a sharp tug. They slipped from around the tree and hung loose in his hands. Then he faced forward in the saddle and began snapping them up and down, which, as far as he knew, was how you got a horse to go.

The charger didn't budge. Instead, it just shook its head and neighed angrily. "*Neeheheheheh!*"

Uh oh, thought Hob.

The neigh was so loud that it caught the attention of Captain Fist, the Royal Guards—who'd finally returned to Fist's side—and Carl the Troll. Hob turned to see them frozen, mid-fight, staring back at him. Captain Fist and the Royal Guards looked confused, Carl the Troll giddy with excitement.

"The little goblin and the man-captives!" the troll's three heads exclaimed. "*Off with their heads!*"

The troll shoved Captain Fist and her men out of the way, and rushed toward Hob, Edric, and Monty.

With a new sense of urgency, Hob redoubled his efforts to get their horse moving. He snapped its reins wildly, bounced up and down in its saddle, and kicked his heels against its sides.

Again, the charger just shook its head and neighed.

In a panic, Hob dropped its reins, and started yanking right on its long mane, shouting, "Go, you stubborn old beast! Go!"

The charger *still* didn't move. Annoyed by the hair pulling, it merely turned its head sideways to glare at Hob with one dark, glassy eye. For an instant, Hob thought he was done for.

Then, with its head turned, the charger finally caught sight of the massive troll barreling up behind it. "*Neeheheheheh!*" Before Hob could give its mane another tug, the charger squealed and bolted!

The motion was so sudden that Edric and Monty were nearly thrown from the charger's rump. In a flurry, Hob used one hand to grab the ropes around Edric's and Monty's torsos and one hand to grab the front plate of the charger's saddle, just barely keeping everyone aboard. It was obvious they weren't so much riding the charger, as being carried off by it. Hob was just thankful it had been facing in the right direction—northwest, toward the mountains.

"What are you *doin'*?" Monty cried.

"I told you," Hob shouted. "Saving you!"

"Well stop it! We don't want to be saved! We don't want to be saved!"

"No, keep going!" hollered Edric, glancing back. "We've got company!"

Hob glanced back too. Carl the Troll was right on their tail. And the Royal Guards were mounting their two remaining horses to give chase, Captain Fist leaping onto one, her two men squeezing together onto the other.

What followed was a wild ride through the forest. With their arms and torsos bound, Edric and Monty could only grip the charger's rump with their legs, and if Hob let go of their ropes for even a split second, they were bound to fall off. So, the three of them jostled around together, as the charger galloped down long straightaways, clattered around tight corners, and leapt over deep potholes and fallen trees. Meanwhile, Carl the Troll, surprisingly fast on its troll-sized legs, and the Royal Guards, on their two horses, were never far behind.

Unable to steer the charger, Hob could do nothing to avoid the many slivers of sunlight that pierced the tunnel-like canopy over the road. *Flash, flash, flash!* They came at him faster all the time, making him squint and grow dizzy. Then, finally, a large gap opened in the trees overhead, bringing the world beyond the forest into full view. Hob shut his eyes to keep out the light. But seared into his vision was the silhouette of several great mountain peaks rising up before a bight afternoon sky.

The canopy closed in again quickly, and Hob was able to return to merely squinting. Still, it seemed the forest was finally growing thinner. In some twenty minutes of riding, Hob, Edric, and Monty had covered more ground than they had all morning.

Unfortunately, Hob had no idea where to go next, or how to get there without having any control over the charger. Even worse, with his head now swimming and his arms shaking from holding on to the saddle and Edric and Monty's ropes, he feared he wouldn't be able to keep things together for much longer anyway.

As the road began a series of tight, winding turns through a hilly area, it put the last of Hob's strength to the test. He and the others swayed dangerously from side to side.

"You have no idea what you're doing!" Monty shouted at him, quite correctly. "Let us off! I demand to be let off!"

After they came around the next bend, Monty got his wish. *WHUMP!* Appearing out of nowhere, a long oak branch swung toward them, catching Hob in the chest, and sweeping him back into Edric and Monty. Suddenly, all three of them were flying from their horse. Everything flipped and rolled, and they landed in a heap in the middle of the road.

Hob sputtered and wheezed as he tried to find his breath. When he opened his eyes, the whole world was upside down, and the charger was galloping off around another bend. A second later, someone grabbed Hob by his tunic, pulled him from the pile, and sent him stumbling away.

"Hide!" came a girl's voice—youthful, but full of authority.

Hob saw only her hand, tossing aside the oak branch. Too dizzy to think for himself, he ran on wobbly legs, and collapsed into a thicket of tall bushes at the roadside.

Edric and Monty were still tied together back to back, so the girl rolled them, like a log, off the road and into the bushes.

They crashed through after Hob, and the girl crouched down beside them, taking cover. The next instant, the troll rushed around the first bend, with Captain Fist and the Royal Guards riding immediately behind it. Hob watched through the bushes as they raced by—feet thumping, hooves clattering—hurrying off around the second bend in pursuit of the now rider-less gray charger.

CHAPTER NINE

The Wizard's Apprentice

Still hidden among the tall bushes, Hob stood up, dusted himself off, and turned to the mysterious girl crouched beside him. Who was she? Why had she knocked them off their horse? And why didn't she seem concerned about the little goblin standing next to her?

Hob opened his mouth to ask these questions, but she put a finger to her lips and shushed him. She must have wanted to make sure the guards and troll were really gone before speaking.

Hob had never seen a human girl up close before, and he stared back at her, intrigued. She was young and pretty—at least as far as he could tell—with light-brown skin, long ebony hair tied back with a kerchief, and bright, intelligent brown eyes. She was dressed for travel. She carried a heavy satchel over her shoulder, and she wore a green cloak over a skirt and bodice, leggings, and boots.

Hob couldn't explain it, but he had a good feeling about her. In fact, he'd already begun to forgive her for knocking him off his horse.

Edric and Monty weren't so easily won over. Although they hadn't taken a branch to the chest as Hob had, something much deeper in them had been wounded. Their *pride*. Still tied together on the ground, Monty on top, Edric facedown beneath him, they began to squirm and gripe.

"What's the meaning of this?" Monty growled.

"Are you trying to kill us or something?" Edric croaked, turning his head sideways so he could speak without inhaling mouthfuls of dirt.

"*Shh!* Calm down!" the girl pleaded with them. She grabbed their ropes and fought to hold them in place, while she pulled a small dagger from her belt.

"*Ahhk!*" Monty hissed. "She's got a knife!"

"What?" hissed Edric, squirming more violently than before.

"It's to cut you free!" said the girl. She slipped the blade under their ropes, and began hacking them away, first the ones around their wrists, and then the ones around their torsos. "I'm Stella, *Eldwin's apprentice.*"

She said it like it explained everything, but it only made Hob more confused.

Apparently, Monty understood, though. "Little Stella?" he exclaimed, wide-eyed. "You were smaller when I last saw you."

"I was ten," said Stella. "Now I'm fifteen."

"Aye," said Monty, nodding as he tallied the years in his head. "Prince Edric, this is *Stella.* She's on our side."

"*What?*" Edric scoffed. "She knocked us off our horse, and rolled us into a ditch!"

"I rolled you to *safety,*" said Stella, yanking up on her knife, so the last of Edric and Monty's ropes snapped and peeled away. "I rescued you!"

Monty flopped over onto the ground, while Edric burst to his feet.

"*Rescued us?*" he snapped, turning to face Stella for the first time. "You call that a ..."

But when he saw her, Edric trailed off. Clearly, she wasn't quite what he'd expected. He watched in silence, as she rose before him, staring back at him with a troubled expression on her young, pretty face. He softened.

"You know what?" he sighed, shrugging off the whole affair. "If Monty trusts you, I trust you." Then he flashed her one of his charming smiles, took her hand, and fell to one knee before her. "Thank you, fair maiden, for your brave rescue ... even if it *did* hurt a little."

Stella seemed caught off guard by this. "Y-you're welcome, Prince Edric, Your Highness," she stammered. "But *don't think*—"

"Just call me *Edric,*" the Prince interjected. "There's no need for all that palace talk out here."

"*E-Edric,*" Stella repeated. Then she yanked her hand away. "But, like I was saying, *don't think* you can charm me like one of those maidens who dote on you at court. I've got a job to do. I've got to be *tough* with you."

Edric straightened up, now looking truly worried. "I don't like the sound of *that,*" he said. "Where's *Eldwin?*"

"Aye, lass," added Monty, finally picking himself up off the ground. "Are you takin' us to him?"

Stella went quiet for a moment, refusing to make eye contact and looking more troubled than before. "Not exactly ..." she mumbled.

Even Hob could tell something was wrong.

"What do you mean, *not exactly?*" asked Edric.

"*Umm,*" said Stella, still averting her gaze. "Come on. Let's get away from the road." She fetched a wooden magician's staff from the bushes, where she must have hidden it earlier, and headed into the trees.

Nervous and confused, the others hurried after her. Stella led them a short distance through the forest, marching over a small rise and into a little gully on the other side. She stopped there, just out of sight and direct earshot of the road, and turned to face them.

"*So?*" said Edric, as he, Monty, and Hob gathered around.

"S-so," Stella mumbled, "I'm afraid I have some bad news." She met their eyes again, but looked no less troubled. "It's Eldwin. He's, um ... well, he's ... *gone missing!*"

"*What?*" Edric exclaimed, clutching his forehead. "Not him *too?*"

Stella cringed and nodded.

"Are you sure, lass?" asked Monty. "He is a *wizard,* after all. They do have a habit of disappearin'."

Hob gasped. Eldwin must have been the wizard Edric and Monty were searching for, the one they were hoping to meet in Valley Top!

"I'm *sure,*" said Stella, darkly. "Nearly a week ago, I went to meet Eldwin at his cottage, to join him on this quest. But, instead, I found him missing, and his cottage burned out, torn apart! I couldn't find any clues as to whether it was some sort of goblin attack, or just one of his experiments gone horribly wrong. I mean, he once spent a whole month transmogrified into a newt! All I know is there was no trace of him." She shook her head. "I waited as long as I could for him to return, but with no luck. Then I realized it would be up to me to guide the quest in his place ... at least, until he could find us. So,

I gathered up all his surviving notes and supplies, and set out to meet you."

Hob noticed Edric and Monty exchange horrified glances. Edric had gone completely pale. He looked as if he might be sick.

"I'm sorry to hear that, lass," said Monty, putting on a brave face, and turning back to Stella. "I'm sure he'll find us eventually."

"We're *doomed!*" cried Edric, showing no such tact.

"What? No! You can't think that way!" Stella admonished him. "We have to stay *positive!*" She sounded forcefully upbeat all of a sudden. "Take me for instance. For me, this is a chance to prove myself."

Edric shook his head in disbelief. "I'm sorry," he said. "I know you've been through a lot. But nothing about this is *positive!* The Royal Wizard is gone! And all we've got is, what, his *assistant?*"

"*Apprentice!*" Stella shot back, looking hurt. "And you could do worse! I'm organized. I'm motivated. And I'm capable of some pretty advanced magic for my age. I mean, I just saved your necks."

"You hit us with a stick," Edric groaned. "Thanks again and all, but that's not very *magical.*"

"It didn't *feel* very magical," Monty admitted, cracking his sore back.

"I had a *vision!*" Stella persisted. "That was the magic! I saw the three of you being chased down the road on horseback, and I knew right where to find you. Didn't you wonder about that? Didn't you wonder why I wasn't shocked to see this *goblin* helping you?"

Edric and Monty went silent. Everyone stared at Hob.

"I wondered!" Hob piped up. "You didn't try to run away, or kill me, or anything."

"No," said Stella, "because I'm a *seer,* just like Eldwin. Though, I can't control my visions like he can, yet. Certain things, events, just trigger them without warning." She pulled a crumpled piece of parchment out of her satchel, and unfolded it for everyone to see. "Look what triggered this one. The Royal Guards put them up all over."

WANTED
ALIVE and UNHARMED

EDRIC
CROWN PRINCE of YORE
1000 Gold Pieces

It was a wanted poster, with a woodprint of Edric's face on it. It read: *WANTED ALIVE AND UNHARMED, EDRIC, CROWN PRINCE OF YORE. REWARD, 1000 GOLD PIECES.*

Edric took the poster and examined it. "That doesn't look good," he grumbled. Then he smirked to himself. "I mean they could've at least made me *smile* in this thing. I look like a criminal."

"That's because they think you *are* a criminal," said Stella, taking back the poster, folding it, and returning it to her satchel. "Or at least a delinquent. Good thing I have a plan. We still have business in Valley Top, so we'll have to sneak you into the city. My hay cart's hidden near the edge of the forest, just off the road into the mountains. Let's go before anyone comes back to search for us." She paused. "Or don't you want my help?"

"No, no …" Edric sighed. "You might not be Eldwin, but we clearly need you. I guess we'll just have to make do."

"I guess *we* will," said Stella, pointedly.

"And what do we do with *him?*" asked Monty, glaring at Hob. "If we leave him here, he'll just follow us again."

"Then take me with you! For real this time!" said Hob. It was worth a shot. "I've been helpful so far. I rescued you twice before Stella did."

Everyone stared at him once more, Edric smirking, Stella biting her lip, and Monty turning tomato red.

"No way!" snapped the dwarf. "You're *still* a goblin!"

"Oh, come on, Monty!" Edric began. "I say he's—"

But Stella interrupted him. "Wait!" she said. "This could be important. As your new guide, I suggest we think it through very carefully." She tapped a finger against her chin. "On one hand, this goblin was in my vision. And I have reason to believe *Eldwin* may have foreseen him coming as well. All of which suggests fate has brought him here for some purpose."

Edric opened his mouth to offer his own opinion, but before he could, Stella carried on.

"On the *other* hand," she fretted, "I really don't know what purpose that could be. And it does seem awfully risky keeping a goblin around, with our luck running so thin."

Once more, Edric went to chime in, and Stella cut him off.

"On the *other, other* hand, we have to be very careful we don't jump to any—"

"We're keeping him!" Edric blurted out. "I want to keep him!"

Stella went quiet.

Monty gaped.

And Edric scrambled to explain himself. "I mean, he *has* helped a lot. And we can't just leave him in the woods with Captain Fist and that troll. And, Stella, you may be our guide, but I'm still the Prince. And that has to be good for *something*. So … Hob's coming!"

Hob's heart leapt. Had Edric just let him join the quest?

"I never *said* he couldn't come," Stella muttered, with a frown. "I just said we should *think it through*."

"And you did," Edric replied. "And I made the tough call."

"*Ugh*," Stella sighed.

"Don't worry, lass," Monty whispered. "He doesn't listen to *me* either."

Edric had only just accepted Stella into the company, and now the two were fighting again—because of *Hob*. Hob hoped Stella wouldn't hold it against him.

She took a deep breath. "Well, we know—*Hob*, is it?—may have a part to play in all this. But we don't know what it is yet. And we do have to get going. So, why don't we keep him with us until we understand more, and then make a final decision? Can we all agree to that?"

"Works for me," said Edric. "*Monty?*"

"*Fine*," Monty grumbled. "But if he so much as looks at us funny—"

"I won't!" Hob promised, suddenly unable to contain his excitement. "I'll stay in line, and carry my own weight, and follow orders, and—"

"*Be quiet!*" said Monty. "That's rule number one. Be quiet."

Using her staff as a walking stick, Stella led the others to the place where she'd hidden her hay cart. For almost an hour, they trekked straight through the trees and undergrowth, veering steadily away from Old Foresters' Road in the direction of the mountains. Edric and Monty used this time to fill Stella in on the events of their journey so far. And Hob did his best to follow orders and stay quiet.

Finally, they reached the hay cart. It sat hidden in a small glade surrounded by thick evergreens. As Stella had promised, the glade stood near the edge of the forest, right on the road to Valley Top. Below the curtain of dark branches on the far side, Hob could see a strip of golden brown, suggesting the wide sunlit road beyond. They merely had to wheel the cart through the trees, and they'd be on their way.

The cart itself was small and rickety and had two woolly mountain goats harnessed to the shafts. As the little company approached it, Stella plucked three wooden clothespins from her satchel, and distributed them.

"You'll be needing these," she said.

"*Why?*" Edric grumbled.

As soon as Stella pulled down the cart's back hatch, he got his answer. The hay pile inside reeked so badly of dung that it nearly made everyone fall over at first whiff.

"You've got to be kiddin'!" croaked Monty, fanning the stench away from his nose.

"You want us to get in *there?*" added Edric.

"That's what the clothespins are for," said Stella, pinching her nose to demonstrate. "You have to hide in the hay, or someone might see you. You're *wanted*, you know."

"I *know*," said Edric.

Seeing no point in arguing, he and Monty slipped the clothespins on their noses, and piled into the stinking hay. Hob went to follow, but Stella pulled him aside.

"Wait," she said. "Remember how I mentioned Eldwin may also have foreseen you coming? Here's why …"

She reached into her satchel, and pulled out a pair of strange old goggles. They had a small parchment tag tied to them with a string. It read: *For a new recruit.*

"They're yours," said Stella, pulling off the tag, and passing the goggles to Hob.

Hob turned them over in his hands, examining them closely. They had soft leather straps, intricate metal rims, and glass lenses so clear—yet oddly dark—he could see his reflection in them.

"They should allow you to see in the sunlight after we leave the forest," Stella went on. "Eldwin designed them mainly to see through magical illusions, but, as an added feature, he tinted the lenses to shade the wearer's eyes. At first, I couldn't understand what his note meant, but now I do. He foresaw you needing them."

"Wow," said Hob, trying on the goggles. "Thanks!"

The dark lenses made everything he saw only a quarter as bright—which was perfect for him, even in the shady glade. They felt like a cool drink for his dry, thirsty eyes.

A short time later, the little hay cart was on its way up the road to Valley Top. The road climbed a steep pass—a long, winding gap in the mountains, which was the only way through for hundreds of miles around.

Thankfully, the Royal Guards and troll were nowhere to be seen. And there was only one other tiny ox cart, miles ahead. Few travelers risked venturing through those goblin-infested lands so late in the day.

The hay cart bumped and wobbled as it climbed, with Stella driving and the mountain goats pulling. Edric, Monty, and Hob hid in the stinky hay, peeking out.

Edric and Monty parted the hay in front of their eyes, while Hob poked the lenses of his new goggles out in one direction after another, eager to test them on all the different sights.

Whether or not the goggles actually saw through illusions, they worked like magic for him. The same far blue peaks he'd often admired from his secret spot now soared overhead, shimmering under a late-day sun. And he could soak up every vivid, sunlit detail without dizziness or pain. He felt amazingly lucky to be in that place, wearing those goggles. He felt amazingly lucky for everything that had happened that day.

Hob continued to take in the sights as the journey unfolded. First, the pass climbed due west, up through tree-dotted foothills and smaller mountains. Then the pass curved northward around a much greater mountain, whose gravelly, scree-covered lower slopes were crowned distinctively by three craggy peaks. And finally, after making the turn around the great three-peaked mountain, the pass narrowed, and snaked down between walls of rock into a deep chasm.

For a few minutes, the rickety hay cart shook as it negotiated the steep bends. Then the road leveled out, the rock walls parted, and the cart emerged at the bottom of a great ravine cutting across the pass.

The ravine ran down, from west to east, between the mountain peaks, and was embanked by sheer, cliff-like slopes on both sides, forming a deep trench, effectively splitting the pass in two. At the bottom, the road crossed a small stone bridge over a trickling stream.

As the cart rolled over the bridge, Hob, Edric, and Monty peeked up the ravine and saw the stream's source. A few hundred feet above, barricading a gap between two opposing mountain peaks, there stood a towering dam.

"Once a wide river filled this ravine, fed by countless glaciers high up in the mountains," Stella said, stopping the hay cart on the bridge. She seemed unable to resist educating the others, even if it meant acknowledging they were probably peeking out of the hay. "But it's been reduced to a stream for an age, held back by that dam. *The Riven Gate.*"

The Riven Gate consisted of two stone towers and a massive steel gate slotted between them. The gate formed the wall of the dam, holding back a vast lake behind it.

"You see those towers?" Stella continued. "Those aren't bells hanging inside them."

Hob looked to the towers. Housed atop each one was not a bell, but a dark metal cylinder, hanging on chains from a great wheel.

"They're counterweights," Stella explained, "used along with a system of gears and pulleys to raise the gate. It's an engineering marvel. Any time an opposing army approaches, the weights are allowed to fall through the towers, pulling up the gate, flooding the ravine, and cutting off the pass with a deep river of rushing water."

"The gate's made of *ever-steel*, forged by the dwarves of old!" added Monty, his voice nasally due to the clothespin on his nose. "It's amazingly light, stronger than the hardest stone, and can never rust. The recipe's been lost for ages."

A thin sheet of water sloshed over the top of the gate and ran down its silvery face, gathering in a pool that fed the stream. Monty was right; the steel was untarnished, even after centuries of exposure.

"But what stops the armies from going *around?*" asked Hob, his voice just as nasally as Monty's.

"The mountains," Stella replied. "Most are too steep, too rugged, too disorienting to navigate without the pass. Perhaps a few seasoned mountaineers could do it, but not a whole army, unskilled in climbing and weighed down by weapons, armor, and supplies. Add to that, a frigid lake stretching back for miles behind the dam, and the fact that an army would be open to attack by archers at key ascents, and you have a hopeless task." She paused. "It's said, during the last war, the goblins did try tunneling *under* the ravine. But those attempts never met with much success."

Hob nodded. "Goblins base their tunnels on preexisting rock formations," he said. "They have a hard time hitting specific targets."

"And Valley Top's scouts scoured the slopes around the upper pass to find and destroy any small tunnels that did get through," Stella finished. "To this day, the pass remains the only way to reach Valley Top."

"So, why not cut it off again?" asked Edric, his voice nasally as well. "With all the goblin attacks?"

"Complacency," said Stella. "The people of Valley Top don't even post guards on the Riven Gate anymore. Their city has strong walls, which can easily withstand the occasional raid by mountain goblins. And, like the rest of the Kingdom, they refuse to believe anything worse is coming. They're more concerned with keeping the pass open for their *festival.*"

"*Festival?*" asked Hob.

"You'll see ..." whispered Edric.

Then Stella started the cart forward again.

On far side of the ravine, another snaking road brought them back up into the pass, and they left the Riven Gate behind.

By the time the little hay cart and its crew neared their destination, the sun was setting behind the mountains, and the western sky was dashed with red and gold. Hob marveled at the dazzling, fiery colors, awestruck by their beauty. Without Eldwin's goggles, he'd only ever seen sunsets through bleary, squinted eyes.

Finally, the hay cart wheeled around a tall ridge, and another astounding sight came into view. Framed by an opening in the pass ahead, there stood a high snow-capped peak overlooking the valley, with a small city perched on its eastern face. *Valley Top!*

Built strategically on the main pass through the Gloaming Mountains, Valley Top's thick outer walls were Yore's ultimate western defense. And while the city was nestled against alpine slopes to the west, beyond its eastern walls, a sheer cliffline broke away, plunging into the valley. Valley Top climbed this cliff-line to its peak, where a castle and tower soared against the blazing sky.

Completing this vista was a sea of clouds, which had swept in over the valley below—a common occurrence when the warmth of day gave way to evening's chill. Soon, it would fill even the pass, and Valley Top and the surrounding peaks would be left alone above the clouds.

"Stay well hidden," Stella reminded the others. "I've heard the Royal Guards are inspecting everyone who enters."

Edric, Monty, and Hob shuffled about under the hay, making sure they were completely covered. Still, they continued to peek out.

The world fell away around them as the cart climbed out of the pass, winding up a steep switchback road to the city. The cart then leveled off, and came to a sudden stop at the back of a long line of travelers, which stretched a hundred paces up the road, across a small plateau, and in through the city's front gate.

The gate itself was an imposing archway set between two sturdy watchtowers in the city's thick stone wall. Its spiky iron portcullis was raised, and, behind that, its heavy oaken doors were open. The dark figure of a Royal Guard stood beside it, inspecting every person, animal, and carriage seeking entry.

As their little cart lurched toward the gate, Edric, Monty, and Hob watched the travelers in line ahead of them. They saw only their backs, but overheard all of their gossip.

"What're they thinkin', puttin' up check points this time of year?" complained one man.

"We'll be here all night!" proclaimed another.

"Better just hope the goblins don't join us," added a woman.

"I could barely afford to come this year," said a farmer, "what with the goblins drivin' up the price of grain."

"Aye," said a second farmer. "But then, who can afford *not* to come? It's the Spring Chicken Festival."

"The *Spring Chicken* Festival?" Hob whispered to Edric.

"I've never been," Edric whispered back, "but I hear it's great."

An old peddler woman also stood nearby, telling a story to the captive audience in line around her.

From what Hob could see, she was frightening to behold. She had tattered black robes, a sunken face half-hidden behind stringy white hair, and a body so hunched that it seemed nearly bent in half.

"See that tower?" the old woman wheezed, pointing with a gnarled finger toward the castle tower above the city. "They say the Lady of Valley Top is trapped up there, a beautiful maiden, cursed by an evil spell to remain locked in her tower for all time. They say her parents, the former Lord and Lady of the city, made sure she had everything she could ever want, filling the castle with all the best servants, and even building her a library in the tower to rival that of the Royal Palace. But they say she can *never leave!* Indeed, no one outside the keep has ever seen her. And since her parents died, Valley Top has been left without a ruler."

The woman paused for effect, enjoying the stunned silence of the small crowd gathered around her.

"But if no one's seen her, how do you know she even exists?" one skeptic piped up. He nudged his travelling companion in the arm and whispered, "Crazy old bird!"

"I only know what *they say,*" said the woman.

"And who are *they?*" asked the skeptic.

In response, the woman made a rude gesture, and blew him a raspberry.

When their little cart finally approached the gate, Edric and Hob stole one look at the Royal Guard there—gruff, with a big chin and bored eyes—and lost all desire to keep peeking out of the hay. They sank as low as they could, and kept deadly quiet.

"Good evening, little lady," they heard the guard say, as the cart rolled to a stop beside him. "I don't suppose you'll mind if I take a poke around in that hay?"

"Go ahead, sir," said Stella, sounding forcefully cheerful. "I've got nothing to hide. Yep, there's nothing under there but a load of manure!"

She didn't make a very good liar, which worried Hob. He would fare worst of all if they got caught.

Hob, Edric, and Monty listened with bated breath as the guard's footsteps approached the back of the cart. The hay *rustled* overhead.

For a second, Hob thought they were finished. Then the rustling stopped, and they heard the guard cough, sputter, and stagger back, having caught a whiff of the cart's stench. Suddenly, Hob understood Stella's plan; the guard couldn't even get close.

Hob heard him struggling to speak. "On second thought ... *Cough!* You look harmless enough ... *Cough!* Go ahead, little lady."

"Why thank you, sir!" said Stella.

Once they were a safe distance inside Valley Top, Edric poked his face out the front of the hay pile to speak with Stella, or, more accurately, to gripe at her. "That was too close!" he whispered. "Couldn't you have just *magicked* us into the city?"

"What do you think I just did?" said Stella. "That was scent magic. And strong stuff too!"

"I mean like *POOF*, we disappear out there, and reappear in here," said Edric.

"Real magic doesn't work that way," Stella told him. "You can't just teleport living things. It's too dangerous."

"I guess it would be a little much for an *assistant*," Edric goaded her.

"*Apprentice!*" she snapped.

Hob peeked out of the hay again too. He took in every fascinating detail of their ride through town. The tight winding streets and tall crooked buildings were all constructed of the same weathered gray stone, which looked like it had been quarried from the mountain itself. Everywhere, townsfolk made their way home for the night, dressed in warm leathers, furs, and wools.

Hob also spotted a wanted poster, identical to the one Stella had shown them earlier, plastered to the inside of an archway that spanned the street between two shops. The woodprint of Edric's face seemed to stare back at Hob as it passed.

Beyond the archway, the cart rolled into a seedy part of town, where the buildings were black and grimy and even more crooked than before, and the people shuffled about with their heads down and their hoods up. It was there that Stella stopped the hay cart.

They pulled up in front of a dingy old inn crammed between row houses on either side. It was three stories tall, all of them slightly askew, and was alight with many glowing windows. It had a large wooden sign that hung out over the street, which, to Hob's horror, featured a grotesque relief carving of a *severed goblin head!* He couldn't help but notice it bore an uncomfortable resemblance to his own. The sign read: *The Headless Goblin Inn.*

"Hurry now," said Stella, dropping the back of the hay cart. "I'm told the innkeeper is a friend of Eldwin and Monty's. We'll be safe inside. Edric, give your cloak to Hob, so he doesn't cause a scene."

As Hob followed the others into the inn, shrouded in Edric's heavy cloak, he passed directly under the headless goblin sign. He glanced up at it, and then adjusted his hood so no one would see his face.

CHAPTER TEN

Underground Business

Together, Stella, Monty, Edric, and the walking mound of cloak that was Hob shuffled in through the door of the Headless Goblin Inn.

After the previous days spent in the quiet wilderness, the wall of sound that greeted them was overwhelming. Mugs clinked and dishes clattered. Rowdy voices chatted, laughed, and sang, belting out tone-deaf renditions of two separate but equally rude drinking songs.

From beneath his hood, Hob surveyed the wide tavern before him. It was a smoky room, with walls and floors of gray stone, and wooden beams supporting a low slanted ceiling. The only light came from a great fireplace in the middle, around which many strange and shady-looking customers had gathered. They were an exotic lot, brought together by the Spring Chicken Festival from around the valley and the lands beyond. They filled every chair and barstool, and none of them were inclined to break away from their drinks, tales, or songs to pay the newcomers any mind.

Only the innkeeper noticed the little company enter, and she hurried over to greet them. She was a bouncy old dwarf lady, who sported *both* a frilly pink apron and a black eye patch. She gave Monty a big hug, and then stepped back to examine him with her one good eye.

"It's been too long, you old scoundrel!" she said.

"I'm the scoundrel?" Monty scoffed. "Look at this place. It's quite a pirate's den you've got here, Marta."

"I like to think of it as a place for the *misunderstood* ..." said Marta. Then she leaned forward to whisper in his ear. "Still, I can't say I'm too fond of havin' *royal* guests nosin' around." Her good eye scanned Prince Edric.

"Don't worry," said Monty. "The lad's as *misunderstood* as anyone."

Marta straightened back up, grinning. Then her eye shifted to Stella, and finally to Hob.

"Now *him* I like the look of!" Marta said.

"You wouldn't, if he took that hood off," Monty warned her.

Marta laughed. "And tall, dark, and bearded, where is he?"

"Eldwin's gone missing," Stella replied sadly.

Marta looked disappointed. "I'm sorry to hear that. Still, he always turns up."

"This is Stella, his *apprentice*," Monty explained.

"Apprentice, eh?" said Marta. "Never knew the old coot to have any patience for teachin'. You must have chops, lass!" She paused, her tone turning serious. "But can you honor his *agreements?*"

"I can pay," said Stella.

"Perfect!" Marta clapped her hands together. "Follow me then. No need to worry about your cart. Once you're settled in, I'll have it taken to the stable out back."

She led them across the tavern and in behind the bar. A line of pewter tankards hung on hooks under the counter. Checking to make sure no one was watching, Marta chose the third from the left, and pulled down on it. Hob heard a faint *click* sound, and was surprised when the top of the wine barrel next to him popped open like a trapdoor. Inside, there was no wine, but rather a well-like shaft delving into the earth, and a ladder leading down into darkness.

"Where does it go?" Edric whispered.

"To a place for customers who *value their privacy,*" Marta answered. "Now, hurry on. They're waiting."

"Who's *they?*" asked Edric.

"The *crew*," said Stella, knowingly. "Eldwin arranged to meet them here. But, be warned, these are great mercenaries we're dealing with. They don't mess around. They even swore Eldwin to complete secrecy about them. All I could find in his notes was one vague correspondence. And all he could tell me was that we *need* them. So, please, no missteps."

"Don't worry," Monty assured her. "I've treated with a mercenary or two in my day."

"And *most* people find me charming," Edric added.

Stella held up a finger in front of his nose. "No missteps."

Hob was the first into the barrel and down the ladder. As he reached the bottom, he stumbled backward onto the floor. The darkness around him was so thick he could barely see. Then he remembered his goggles. He pulled them up onto his forehead, and his vision returned.

He found himself in a gloomy, underground hallway, which stretched about ten paces from the base of the ladder to a small door. The hallway doubled as a cellar of sorts, its drippy stone walls lined with shelves full of bottles, casks, and crates.

Edric, Stella, and Monty joined Hob at the bottom of the ladder, and together they started toward the door. As they got close, Hob could hear muffled, high-pitched voices coming from the other side. Could they have been coming from the crew of great mercenaries?

The company stopped outside the door, and Stella opened it, revealing a strange stone chamber within. It had a low vaulted ceiling hung with a crude chandelier, a weapon rack in one corner, shelves of books and maps in another, and a large circular table in the center, ringed by old barrels put to new use as stools. Strangest of all, though, were the room's occupants. A dozen tiny men sat three to a stool around the far side of the table, chattering away in high, squeaky voices. As the door opened, they stopped talking and looked up at the newcomers.

"These are your *mercenaries?*" Edric whispered to Stella. "*Gnomes?*"

The gnomes were all slightly shorter than Hob, with rosy faces, long white beards, and pointy hats quite a bit taller than themselves. The only way Hob could tell them apart was by the numbers on their hats: *one, six, eleven, thirty-seven*—to name a few.

"Shh! Don't insult them!" Monty hissed, before Stella could even answer. "Why didn't you say Eldwin got us *The Gnomes?*"

"I didn't know," Stella whispered back. "Are they really any good?"

"They've scored some of the biggest treasure hauls of the past twenty years!" Monty replied. "Highly secretive, though. No one knows how they do it. And they almost *never* take outside jobs." He shook his head in disbelief.

Edric studied the gnomes with new eyes. Hob looked again too. The gnomes stared back at them blankly.

"Greetings, esteemed, er, gnomes!" Stella piped up.

She took a tentative step into the room, and bowed. Edric, Monty, and Hob copied her. An instant later, the gnomes were all squeaking at them.

"*Eindelijk!*"

"*Je bent laat!*"

"*Laten we beginnen!*"

And so on.

"Oh, and did I mention they only speak *Gnomish?*" Monty added, as he and the others straightened out of their bows.

"No," Stella groaned, looking skyward. "DO ... ANY ... OF ... YOU ... SPEAK ... COMMON ... TONGUE?" she asked the gnomes, sounding out one word at a time.

They all cocked their heads in confusion, except for one fellow with the number *thirty-seven* on his hat, sitting front and center in the crowd. He raised his hand.

"I translate," he squeaked, proudly.

"Thank goodness," Stella murmured. "I ... AM ... STELLA ... ELDWIN'S ... APPRENTICE. DID ... HE ... SET ... THIS ... MEETING ... WITH ... YOU?"

Gnome Thirty-Seven held up a finger for her to wait, and then whispered a translation to the gnome sitting next to him. This gnome had the number *one* on his hat. Hob guessed he must have been the troop's leader.

"*Ja, we zijn hier om Eldween te ontmoeten,*" replied Gnome One.

"Yes, vee here to meet Eldveen," Gnome Thirty-Seven translated.

"May we sit, then?" asked Stella, gesturing to the empty seats around her side of the table.

This required no translation. Gnome One frowned, but nodded anyway.

Stella didn't wait for a better invitation than that. She made straight for the stool directly opposite Gnomes One and Thirty-Seven, while Monty made for the stool to her left, and Edric and Hob the two stools to her right. Before they even sat down, the gnomes spoke up again, Gnome Thirty-Seven translating for Gnome One.

"But varr is Eldveen? Vee are supposed to be meeting Eldveen."

"W-what? Oh, him?" Stella stammered, as she sat down. She must have known the question would come up, but she didn't seem ready for it so soon. "It's a long story …"

The gnomes all scowled. They could see she was stalling. Then, just when it seemed tensions couldn't get any higher, Hob settled onto his stool between Edric and the gnomes, and mistakenly dropped his hood.

"Gobleen! Gobleen!" the gnomes all squeaked in terror, forgetting about Eldwin's absence for a moment. "Gobleen!"

"So they know *that* word," Hob groaned.

Monty glared at him across the table.

"It's okay!" Edric shouted at the gnomes. "*Nice goblin! Nice goblin!*"

"Right!" said Stella. "*Friend!*"

"*Vriend?*" repeated the gnomes, in their own language.

Apparently, they knew that word too—even if they didn't believe it. They shot Hob sideways glances, and collectively shifted one seat away from him around the table. Again, Gnome One began nattering at Gnome Thirty-Seven.

"Eldveen better have a *good* explanation for this!" Gnome Thirty-Seven translated. "Varr is he? Vee demand to see him *now!*"

"W-well, that's the thing," Stella began again, cringing before the words even escaped her lips. "Eldwin's *missing*. He's *not coming*."

"*Niet komend!*" squealed Gnome Thirty-Seven.

The whole troop gasped at once. And Gnome One began squawking directly at Stella.

Gnome Thirty-Seven rushed to translate. "Liars! Gobleen-friends! How do vee know you are Eldveen's apprentice? An impostor, most likely! Vee make deal only veeth Eldveen! No Eldveen, *no deal!*"

Then, without another word, Gnome One hopped off his stool and marched for the door. Gnome Thirty-Seven and the rest of the troop followed in a long line.

"Didn't you say we *need* them?" Edric muttered to Stella, rather unhelpfully.

Stella panicked. "But I really am Eldwin's apprentice!" she said, jumping to her feet. "You can trust me!"

The gnomes ignored her.

"Lass!" Monty whispered, suddenly. "Eldwin must've offered somethin' *big* to get them to the table. Somethin' they couldn't get any other way. What *is* it?"

Stella thought fast. "Oh! I know *that!*" she cried. "The *Vuurhart!* The *Vuurhart!*"

The gnomes had gathered at the door. Gnome One was reaching for the handle. But, upon hearing that word, they stopped and looked back.

In a flurry, Stella fished a big leather-bound journal out of her satchel, and leafed through the pages. "Ah ha!" She held the book open for all to see. In the middle of a page covered with pasted-in notes, there was a small piece of parchment with a message written on it in tiny handwriting. *Terms accepted. Crew and transport for the Vuurhart. Meeting set to confirm. Signed, Number One.*

The gnomes stared agape. One and Thirty-Seven even scurried over for a closer look.

"*Het is mijn schrijven,*" said Thirty-Seven. "It is my writing."

"*En mijn handtekening,*" said One.

"And his signature," explained Thirty-Seven.

Stella nodded. "And you can't get the *Vuurhart* without us." She slammed the book shut in their faces. "Only we know where it is."

"What's a *Vuurhart?*" Edric whispered to Monty.

"*No idea,*" whispered Monty.

"*Shh!*" Stella hissed at them. "Only *we* know where it is."

"Oh, right!" they said.

Taking the hint, Hob held back his own questions. He also wanted to know what the *Vuurhart* was, but he was going to have to wait with the others, until Stella found a good time to clue them in.

Meanwhile, Gnomes One and Thirty-Seven hurried back to their companions to deliberate. Tiny voices whispered back and forth. Tiny fists pounded palms. Tiny feet stamped the floor. And finally, tiny heads nodded in agreement, before turning back to Stella and the others.

"You tell us everything you know," declared Gnome Thirty-Seven. "And if vee believe you are truly Eldveen's associates, vee consider helping you still. Until then, vee speak no *secrets,* make no *promises.*"

"A-agreed," said Stella, sounding relieved. "I assume that was always the purpose of this meeting? To fill you in on the details? I know Eldwin could keep secrets with the best of them."

Gnome Thirty-Seven nodded on behalf of the others.

"Well, let me show you I have the answers," said Stella. "They're all in here." She held up her leather-bound journal again, and leafed through the pages. Parchment notes and scraps filled every page, many burnt and torn, but all pasted in neatly and labeled with her tidy handwriting. "I compiled every note, list, and receipt I could find in Eldwin's abandoned cottage. I call it *The Quest Master's Guide.*"

"And I call it a *scrapbook,*" Edric whispered, jokingly.

Stella shot him a threatening look, and he went quiet.

"Sorry," he mumbled. "*Not the time.*"

Gnome Thirty-Seven translated everything Stella said in a hushed voice, causing the other gnomes to react with a slight delay. Finally, they all nodded, and Gnome One led them back to the table. As they settled in again, Hob noticed they continued to leave the stool beside him empty.

"So, let's start with the basics," Stella began, sitting back down, laying her journal open on the table, and surveying Edric, Monty, Hob, and the gnomes. "The purpose of our quest is fairly straightforward. Nearly one year ago, with the Kingdom on the verge of war with the goblins, King Edgar snuck off, against the will of his Lords, to finish his lifelong quest to drive the goblins back underground. Only, he never returned. We must find the King, if he's anywhere to be found, and help him finish his quest. Or, *if necessary,* we must finish it in his place."

"We'll find him," said Edric, with a familiar tone of determination.

Stella nodded sympathetically.

Gnome Thirty-Seven continued to whisper a running translation, trying to keep his companions up to speed.

"Now, King Edgar kept his plans a total secret until the day he left," Stella went on, "not only from those trying to stop him, but from *everyone,* including my master Eldwin. It seems the King was afraid Eldwin would insist on joining him. And he wanted Eldwin to stay behind and watch over Prince Edric. This meant there was a lot to piece together after the fact. We know, however, that Valley Top is the last place the King was ever seen. That's why our journey starts here. And we've always known the object of the King's quest—the lost *Sunflame of Yore.*"

Hob gasped. He couldn't believe he hadn't guessed that himself! What *else* could the King have been searching for?

Stella turned to him with an amused smile. "You've heard of it then?"

"Oh, yes!" said Hob. "There's a whole chapter on it in *From Bloody to Bloody Boring: A Painfully Detailed History of Yore.*"

This really seemed to catch Stella off guard. She went quiet for a second, staring at Hob with raised brows. "You mean, you *read* it? In *that book?*"

"Hah!" Monty scoffed. "Goblins can't read."

"*Most* goblins can't read," Hob corrected him. "Because most goblins think it's a waste of time. But some of us can read just fine."

"Prove it then," Monty grunted.

"That is, if you wouldn't mind …" said Stella. She sounded more polite than Monty, but still plainly skeptical. "Why don't you refresh our memories?"

"Yeah, show 'em, Hob!" cheered Edric.

Suddenly, all eyes were on Hob—including the gnomes'.

"O-okay," Hob stammered, feeling put on the spot. "Well, um, let's see … A long time ago … an evil man, known as '*the Sorcerer,*' returned to Yore from a journey to *Arcan* in the East, where he had delved into forbidden magics. Back then, Yore was divided into six small early kingdoms, and no one here had any knowledge of magic, making it an easy target for the Sorcerer's treachery."

Hob stopped and gauged his audience's reaction. This was the longest he'd ever discussed history without getting punched. Everyone seemed interested enough, though. Gnome Thirty-Seven whispered a hurried translation.

"Now, the Sorcerer had only one weakness," Hob went on. "Sunlight is the bane of *all* dark magics, and the Sorcerer could only use his powers at night. So, one night, he used those powers to cover the entire valley in an eternal black cloud, which permanently blotted out the sun. After that, he began a campaign to take the valley for himself, and its people for his slaves. And when the people resisted, he enlisted their ancient enemies, *the goblins,* to act as his army, promising them a share of the lands and spoils, in exchange for their unending service. The valley was plunged into darkness for a very long time."

Hob paused for effect, and to let Gnome Thirty-Seven's translation catch up.

"After a hundred years of despair," Hob continued, "one of the six original kings of Yore, the King of the Middle Lands, Prince Edric's *ancestor,* had finally had enough. He fled the valley to seek the aid of the Wizards of the East. At first, his people feared he had abandoned them. Then he returned with the Wizards! They flew in on their legendary airships, bringing with them their greatest invention, the *Sunflame*: a magic fire that, when lit in its enchanted cauldron, burns with the purest light of the sun! Once the Middle King placed the Sunflame in its cauldron, high upon the peak overlooking his city at the center of the valley—a city now called *King's Rock*—it was as if the whole valley was filled with magic, unseen sunlight, even at night and under the clouds. The goblins were driven underground for good. And the Sorcerer's powers were broken, except inside the very darkest chambers of stone, completely closed to outside light. Finally, the six armies of Yore marched together on *Shadowguard,* the Sorcerer's great fortress at the north

end of the valley, where he was holed up in the darkness. Fearing his own destruction, he fled, and his clouds parted."

Hob took a deep breath, preparing for the grand finale.

"For the Middle King's great heroism, it was proclaimed that he and his heirs had been chosen by fate as the saviors and protectors of all of Yore, and as the eternal keepers of the Sunflame. And so, he was made High King, while the other five Kings became his Great Lords, agreeing to rule their old kingdoms in his name, so long as they might advise him as a Royal Council. As for the Sorcerer? No one knows where he went. But it was said that as long as the Sunflame burned over Yore, he would never return."

There was a long pause.

"*Whoa!*" said Edric, at last, staring at Hob with what looked like a mixture of awe and pity. "Did you have all that memorized?"

Hob shrugged. "I didn't have many books."

"*Hmph!* Nice trick, goblin!" Monty snorted. "I met a horse who could do math once too."

"Well, I couldn't have said it any better myself," Stella cut in. "Sorry I doubted you, Hob."

The gnomes all whispered to each other in amazement.

Hob blushed, turning a rather darker shade of green than normal.

"Unfortunately, the story of the Sunflame doesn't end there ..." Stella went on.

Quickly forgetting his self-consciousness, Hob shifted to the edge of his seat to listen. All goblins knew the Sunflame had disappeared—it had allowed them to go back above ground at night—but Hob had never met any goblin who knew what had happened to it.

Stella flipped through her journal again, stopping at the relevant page. "This is taken directly from Eldwin's notes," she began, before reading aloud. "*For two hundred years, our Kingdom was at peace. But no longer. It isn't known how word of the Sunflame reached the dragon, whom we've come to call Ma-rauder, but once it did, nothing could have stopped him from possessing it. Drag-ons are creatures of fire, famed for their love of rare treasures, and the Sunflame was both. Marauder flew in, concealed in a storm cloud, and fell upon King's Rock without warning. And being a dragon, he consumed the Sunflame, swallowed it whole, and flew off with it in his belly.*"

Stella paused to let that sink in.

"*In the thirty-five years since, nothing has been the same. The edges of the valley have grown wild and dangerous, and the goblins have begun raiding night after night. Worse still, dark clouds have begun to linger over Shadowguard in the north, giving us reason to suspect the Sorcerer of old may have finally returned to his fortress—*"

"He *has!*" Hob interrupted. His mind raced. In all the excitement of the past few days, it hadn't occurred to him that the humans *didn't know*. Finally, he had a clear chance to prove to them just how useful he could be.

All eyes were on him once more. But this time he welcomed them.

"How do you know that?" asked Edric and Stella, together.

"Aye ... *how?*" growled Monty.

"The Sorcerer called upon all the goblin hordes to send troops to his army!" Hob exclaimed. "I was there. I heard his voice in my head. Of course, I missed the try-outs, and they found the books I stole from the treasure pile, and I had to run away, but—"

"GET TO THE POINT!" Monty barked.

"Well, the Sorcerer is back!" said Hob. "And he wants revenge! His army will be ready 'when the first leaves of autumn fall.' That's when he's going to attack."

Edric, Stella, and Monty fell silent. After a brief translation, the gnomes began to murmur nervously amongst themselves. This was not news anyone wanted to hear.

Then Monty shook his head. "Hold on!" he said. "Don't any of you find it odd that we just happened to get saddled with the one goblin who's ready to spill all the beans? I still don't trust him!"

"But if he's against us, and this is a lie, it's not a very good one," Edric countered.

"Right," Stella agreed. "It would only scare us into working harder and faster to defeat his side. No. I think Hob's telling the truth. And, if so, then there's no longer any doubt … This quest is the Kingdom of Yore's last hope!"

Edric nodded in dire agreement. Monty grumbled something about Hob under his breath, but eventually nodded as well. Even the gnomes joined in. No one wanted to see the Sorcerer come to power again.

"And where are we goin' on this quest, may I ask?" Monty wondered aloud. "I searched with King Edgar for years, and we never found a single clue that might lead to that blasted dragon."

"You weren't alone," said Stella. "Until recently, *no one's* been able to determine the location of Marauder's lair. That's why the gnomes can't find the *Vuurhart*, the *Dragon Heart Stone*, without us …"

"*Oh!*" exclaimed Edric, Monty, and Hob.

Suddenly, it all made sense—what the gnomes were after, how it related to the larger quest, and why they couldn't get it by themselves. As far as Hob knew, dragons were exceedingly rare and dangerous. If the gnomes wanted to find one, *and* slay it, they'd need all the help they could get. The whole troop perked up at the mere mention of finding the dragon and the *Vuurhart*.

"In fact," Stella went on, "it's likely that only two people know how to find the dragon. King Edgar, if he's alive, and Prince Edric."

"The lad?" Monty gasped.

"M-me?" asked Edric.

Hob and the gnomes gaped at him.

"Yes, you," said Stella. "Remember that old book Eldwin told you to read?"

"Sure."

"Well, it holds the key to finding the dragon. After your father disappeared, Eldwin did some digging. He heard from the Royal Librarian that the King had been obsessed with a certain book, and had been making secret trips to scour the Kingdom for a copy. Eldwin came to believe this book held clues as to the whereabouts of a mysterious Lost City, which was home to a dragon matching Marauder's description. Unfortunately, the Royal Council had Eldwin barred from the palace before he could find the book. Apparently, the Great Lords felt he was a bad influence on the Prince."

"You don't say?" said Monty, winking at Edric.

"Fair enough," said Stella. "But that's why Eldwin sent cryptic instructions for Edric to find the book and read it. It will lead us to Marauder and the Sunflame."

For a moment, Edric said nothing.

"You *did* read it, didn't you?" Stella persisted. "Before your things were stolen by the goblins? If not, this quest is over."

More silence followed.

The gnomes and Monty leaned forward, staring at Edric in suspense.

Hob held his breath. Unfortunately, he was pretty sure he knew what book Edric and Stella were talking about *and* what had happened to it. But he didn't know what to do about it. If he admitted *he* was the goblin who'd stolen the book, it was sure to destroy all the trust he'd built with them. It made his stomach feel all twisted up in knots, but he had to keep quiet and hope it wouldn't matter.

"Yes," Edric replied. "I read it."

"Hooray!" cheered Monty and the gnomes, clapping their hands.

Stella nodded her approval.

And Hob exhaled, letting out a quiet sigh of relief. Everything would be okay.

"But I'm not saying any more than that!" Edric added. "That information's our only guarantee the gnomes won't run off without us!"

Hearing this translated, Gnome One said something to Gnome Thirty-Seven, and laughed.

"Smart boy," said Gnome Thirty-Seven.

The meeting lasted a while longer, with Stella asking for input as she made a list of things they might need, encounter, or *experience emotionally* on their quest. Then after a brief discussion about teamwork—and how there was no "I" in team, but there was a "me," but it didn't count because the letters were out of order—she called for Marta to bring dinner.

Hob had never had such a fabulous meal in all his life. Nothing in the Gobble Downs even compared. There was warm beef stew braised with red wine gravy, roasted potatoes, beets, spring peas, and sweet cider by the mug. Hob's mouth sang a new tune with each flavor, all in harmony. He ate plate after plate, until, for the first time in ages, he was full.

As dinner wound down, Stella went over to speak with Gnomes One and Thirty-Seven at the far side of the table. A few minutes later, she returned.

"Good news," she announced. "They're willing to proceed. They still won't tell me much. But they want me to accompany them, in Eldwin's place, to inspect the rest of the crew, and sign some sort of contract. Then, hopefully, they'll let us in on their secret arrangements, and join our quest."

"So you're leaving?" asked Edric.

"Tomorrow at dawn," said Stella. "I hope to be back for you in the evening, one way or another. Until then, you're safer here. Promise me you won't leave the inn?"

"*What?*" Edric protested. "You can't expect me to just hide in my room all day?"

"Promise!" said Stella.

"Okay, okay," Edric grumbled.

"Thank you," said Stella, before turning to Monty. "Keep an eye on him?"

"No way!" said Monty. "I'm not lettin' you go off by yourself with a bunch of strange gnomes. They could rob you blind! And *my* face isn't on the wanted posters. I'm comin' with you, lass, whether you like it or not."

Stella sighed, and turned to Hob. "Looks like you're on guard duty."

A short time later, Hob and Edric lay in their beds, talking. Marta had shown them to the cozy chamber they would share for the night. It had two small beds with a nightstand between them, a fur rug on the floor, and an empty wardrobe in one corner with a broomstick propped up beside it. Moonlight streamed in through the dusty window at Hob's bedside.

"… Talk about living proof three heads aren't necessarily better than one!" Hob concluded.

"Not when they're attached to the same dumb troll!" Edric agreed.

They laughed and laughed, until the laugher died down and was replaced by contented silence.

"Uh … Edric?" Hob began again.

"Call me *Ed*."

"*Ed*," Hob repeated, proudly.

He'd been thinking about *The Ballad of Waeward the Wanderer*. A tiny voice called up to him from deep inside his twisted-up stomach, begging him to say something about it. This was as good a chance as he was likely to get, and he really wanted to. Unfortunately, the words just wouldn't come out.

"Sorry about your father," he finished instead. It occurred to him he hadn't had the chance to tell Edric that yet. "Is he your *only* family? Captain Fist made it sound like you two are the last of the royal line."

More silence followed.

"Yeah, we're it," said Edric. "I have no brothers or sisters. And my mother died when I was born. It's always been just me and my father."

Hob nodded. No wonder Edric wanted to find the King so badly. "If it helps," Hob said, "in stories, the best heroes never have both parents."

"It doesn't really," Edric muttered.

"Oh, sorry," said Hob. "I don't know my father. And my mother's a giant monster who tried to have me beheaded. So I'm not exactly an expert."

"That was your *mother?*" said Edric. "Man! What am I complaining about?" He shook his head, and stared up at the ceiling. "I didn't have it *that* bad, really. Not until my father left."

There was another long silence.

Edric broke it with a sigh. "I guess I just miss him, you know? I understand why he had to leave in secret. He couldn't let anyone stop him. And he wouldn't have wanted to risk anyone else's life on his quest. He's like that. He's a *real* hero. But I wanted to go with him, *not* take his place at the palace." He shook his head again. "I don't know how he made it look so *easy!* Filling in for him was a nightmare. Everyone either tried to control me, or avoided me completely. Even my so-called friends. And they all wondered why I kept sneaking out to hang around with commoners! *Hah!*" He laughed darkly, and looked back over at Hob. "The only thing that kept me going was the thought of this quest, of finding my father ..."

"We will," said Hob. "Tomorrow, we'll be on our way."

For a second, Edric went silent, like he wasn't so sure about that, like there was something more he wasn't saying. Then he nodded, and rolled over to go to sleep. "G'night, Hob," he said.

"Good night, Ed."

Hob blew out the candle on the nightstand, and rolled over in his own bed, curling up beneath the blankets. He had a hard time believing where he was, whom he was with. It occurred to him this was the first human bed he'd ever slept in. It wasn't lumpy, scratchy, cold, or hard; it was like being tucked into a warm cloud. Hob fell asleep at once.

CHAPTER ELEVEN

A Goblin About Town

Hob awoke with a painful buzzing behind his eyes, and a mouth that tasted more than a little like goblin gruel. As he lifted his head from the pillow, he discovered the problem. Sunlight streamed in through the window beside his bed. He was lying in a bright patch of it.

Squinting hard, Hob swatted at the shutters, trying to close them. Then he remembered Eldwin's goggles. He fumbled around on the nightstand until his fingers found their leather strap. He pulled them onto his face, and fastened the strap behind his head. As he reopened his eyes, he felt his headache begin to dissipate.

Hob glanced around the room. Edric's bed was empty.

"He must have gone for breakfast," Hob assured himself, though he secretly worried Edric and the others had decided to leave without him after all.

Luckily, he was distracted from these fears, and what remained of his headache, by the music piping up outside his window. It didn't sound like the goblin music he was used to, full of banging drums and clanging metal. It was much softer and sweeter.

Hob stood on his bed, opened the window, and leaned out of it.

Outside, the Spring Chicken Festival was underway. A parade of musicians marched up the street below, playing strange instruments—silvery mouth

110

tubes, and wood with strings. And, all around them, crowds of humans of every shape and size—some even smaller than Hob—wandered about. Looking across town, Hob saw tents and banners, tables and signs, flags and stages, all in bright hues. He wasn't sure he'd ever seen so many colors in one place.

Goblin holidays existed mostly as an excuse to hit things, like *Whack-a-Snake Day*, or hit each other, like *Clubmass Eve* and *Bruise Morning*. But a Spring Chicken must have been a wonderful thing to have inspired such a party.

Looking between two buildings across the street, Hob could see a small courtyard where the townspeople had erected a stage. They seemed to be putting on some sort of a play. Onstage was an old man in black armor. He was obviously the villain. He laughed maniacally and raised his sword to the throat of a pretty woman in a white dress. From off stage, a young man in a puffy white shirt swung in on a rope, drawing his own sword. He was obviously the hero.

Hob could tell this was the final showdown between the two. The audience members seemed to know it as well. Their cheers echoed all the way up to Hob's window. The actors' swords flashed as they dueled back and forth across the stage. Hob quickly lost himself in the action.

A few minutes later, Edric returned to find Hob jumping between the two beds in their little room, swinging a broomstick like a sword, and making quite a mess of the covers. Realizing he wasn't alone, Hob froze, and let go of his pretend sword mid-swing. It spun toward the doorway.

Smack! Edric ducked the broomstick just in time, and it struck the wall in the hallway outside.

A tense moment passed. Hob worried Edric might send him packing.

Then Edric burst out laughing. *"Hah hah!"*

"Sorry!" Hob squeaked. "I was just …" He searched for the right word.

"Practicing?" ventured Edric, with a smirk. He stood in the doorway, carrying a tray of food in one hand and a big canvas sack in the other. A sheathed sword and a coil of thin rope hung from his belt, and a crossbow was slung over his back. He must have paid a visit to the weapon rack in the secret cellar. "I brought us some lunch," he said, entering the room. "Or, *breakfast* for you."

Edric was right. Outside, the sun was already high in the sky. If anything, it was *past* lunchtime.

"I'm usually *nocturnal* …" Hob mumbled.

"I'm not judging," said Edric. "Hope you like bread and honey."

He passed Hob a plate of bread and a small bowl of honey, and sat with him on the edge of the bed.

"Eat up!" said Edric. "We've got a lot to do, and not a lot of day left to do it in."

"I though' we were wait'n' fer Stello?" Hob mumbled, his mouth already half-full of food.

Regardless of what happened on the rest of the adventure, the meals at the Headless Goblin had made everything worth it. The bread was warm and soft, the honey sticky and sweet.

"We *are* waiting," said Edric, tucking into a plate of his own. "Just not in here. Remember that tower-Lady the old woman was talking about? The pretty one?"

"The Lady of Valley Top? A beautiful maiden, cursed by an evil spell to remain locked in her tower for all time?" asked Hob. It wasn't a story he'd soon forget.

"That's the one," said Edric. "Well, I've been thinking about her. Actually, I can't stop thinking about her. I have to see her for myself!"

Hob bit his lip nervously. "I don't know, Ed. Isn't that exactly the sort of thing Stella said *not* to do?"

"Stella says a lot of things," said Edric. "But what does *she* know?"

"She knows the Royal Guards are in town, and there's a huge festival going on," said Hob. "Maybe we should just do what she asked. She saved us from them once already, after all."

"And you're not the least bit curious about the mystery of the Lady in the tower?" Edric pressed him. "About the world outside that window?"

"It doesn't matter," Hob replied, firmly. "I can't just do whatever I want. I'm not a rebel, like you."

"But you *are* a rebel like me!" Edric exclaimed. "An *adventurer* like me! You skipped out on your own execution, ran off with a human and a dwarf, and even followed us when we told you *not to.* What do you call that?" Edric laughed, reached in his sack, and drew out a small sword, complete with a scabbard and sword belt. With a flourish, he freed the blade from the scabbard, and turned the hilt toward Hob. "Here. Every adventurer needs one of these."

"*Whoa,*" Hob whispered, taking the sword and holding it up in the beam of sunlight. It wasn't much longer than a dagger, but it was the perfect size for him. The bronze hilt was fashioned after a falcon, and the blade was made of shining steel.

"It's just lucky I found one in your size," Edric went on, setting aside the belt and scabbard. "It's a dwarvish short sword, I think."

"Thanks!" Hob exclaimed, still in awe. It was a gift to match even Eldwin's goggles. His very own sword!

"You're welcome," said Edric. "No more practicing with broomsticks for you. It's time for a real lesson!"

"Huh?" said Hob. "A lesson?"

An image flashed in his mind's eye of Grunt handing him a clobber-stick and dragging him into the practice ring in the Great Cave. And Hob fretted for a second that Edric's lesson might be like that one. This was followed by pang of guilt and worry. Hob knew that Grunt, his brother, his first friend, had only been trying to help him—had only wanted what was best for him. Had Grunt been punished for Hob's supposed crimes? Had he made it through the Clobbering? Been shipped off to join the Sorcerer's army? Hob hoped he was all right.

"Yes, a lesson!" Edric went on, bringing Hob's attention back to the present. "If you're going to be part of the quest, I'm going to have to teach you a thing or two about *real* adventure."

"Wow!" said Hob. Edric's lesson did sound much better than clobbering practice.

"And you know what's the greatest adventure of all?"

Hob thought back to all the stories he'd ever read. "The search for the Heavenly Chalice of—?"

"That's right. *Life!* I'm going to teach you how to live."

"Oh!" said Hob.

"And real life is out there," Edric went on, pointing out the window. "You can't find it in here, or in some book, or by following every dumb rule. You have to go out and *live it*. And that means going to see the Lady!"

"But *why?*" Hob sighed, suddenly feeling more conflicted than before.

Edric hesitated. "Well, I ... Oh, maybe you wouldn't understand ... Maybe it's human stuff. Just, please ... It's *important.*" He stared at Hob, with big, hopeful eyes.

Hob groaned. "Oh, all right," he said. He still wasn't sure it was a good idea. But he didn't want to disappoint his new friend, especially after Edric had given him such a great gift, and promised to teach him about a life of adventure. It was everything Hob had ever wanted and more. How could he refuse?

"Excellent!" said Edric, clapping his hands, and standing up from the bed. "Now, we're gonna need some disguises." He looked Hob up and down. "*Especially* you. Luckily, I borrowed some clothes from the cloak room." He emptied his sack's remaining contents onto the floor.

A short time later, a tall figure appeared in the doorway of The Headless Goblin Inn. He wore a dark burgundy cloak and a black patch over his left eye. The hood of his cloak was pulled up, leaving his face barely visible under its shadow.

A much smaller figure waddled up next to him. His boots were too tall for his short legs. His little winged sword and scabbard bounced awkwardly against his hip. And his green cloak trailed behind him along the ground. Even more peculiarly, his face was hidden under a thick brown scarf, a tight hood, and a green hat with a long feather and wide brim. All that could be seen were his eyes, which appeared abnormally large behind the odd tinted goggles he wore. He promptly banged his head on the doorframe, and stumbled sideways into his friend.

"No peripheral vision," Hob explained, adjusting his goggles with hands hidden in floppy elbow-length gloves. "But I'll get used to it."

"Just follow me," Edric encouraged him. "You look great."

The next thing Hob knew, he was waddling along beside Edric as they made their way through the winding streets of Valley Top, heading for the castle tower that loomed over every part of the city.

The mountain sky above them was clear and blue. And Hob felt the sun's gentle warmth on his skin, and admired its light where it fell, golden, on the stone walls of the buildings and on the many different faces of the people in the crowds. This was just the sort of sunny day Hob had always longed to experience for himself, but had never been able to without Eldwin's goggles.

Still, as the streets grew increasingly congested around him, Hob began to feel overwhelmed. It was one thing to overlook the festival from the safety of his room; it was another thing to be squeezing through the teeming human masses himself!

It didn't help matters that Edric's face stared at him from every wall and street corner. There were wanted posters of the Prince up everywhere!

"Oh, look, the market!" said Edric, ignoring the crowds and the posters, and pointing dead ahead. "What do you know? It's on the way."

Without warning, he dragged Hob up the street, through a tall archway between the buildings, and into the city square.

Really more of a *circle*, the square was a round area, paved with cobblestones, and ringed so seamlessly by shops and apartments that the only roads in or out passed through four identical archways. It housed the marketplace at the heart of the Spring Chicken Festival, and was filled with a sea of people milling about between the many tents and stalls.

Hob was more nervous than ever. But, as he followed Edric through the marketplace, he couldn't help but get caught up in the wonder of it all. Edric too seemed to be enjoying the sights, sounds, and smells. He made an excellent guide. He led Hob from stand to stand, explaining what sort of goods they were selling or just how delicious their treats were.

Some sold clothing, or toys, or jewelry, or cookware; others sold meats, or cheeses, or breads, or cakes. One man was serving whole roast chickens, just for the occasion. His sign read, *Mortimer's Spring Chickens, Official Chicken Vendor of the Spring Chicken Festival.*

It was a good thing Hob had just finished lunch; looking at all the delicious things to eat made his mouth water.

Occasionally, they encountered local city guards on patrol, dressed in half-helms, simple chainmail armor, and surcoats bearing the mountain crest of Valley Top. Edric paid them little attention, and they paid him none.

Only once, when he spotted the crimson cloaks and gilded steel armor of three Royal Guards, did Edric panic. He turned away and pretended to examine whatever the nearest merchant was selling *very* closely. Hob copied him. When the guards had passed, the pair moved on.

The crowds were most dense around the performers. At every turn, there were musicians and bards, actors and acrobats, dancers and jugglers. One man wearing a big three-eared hat with bells on it attracted a great deal of attention by jumping about, doing handstands, and making rude noises at passersby. There was also a woman breathing fire out of her mouth like a dragon, and another man swallowing a whole sword while balancing on a strange one-wheeled contraption.

"That looks dangerous!" Hob worried.

"Relax. I'm sure he knows what he's doing," said Edric. He stopped at a gap in the crowd around the man, and watched with fascination.

Hob wasn't convinced. One slip, and the man would be riding the sword instead of the wheel. When he pulled out three daggers and began juggling them, Hob had to look away.

Distracting himself, Hob tried to study the festival-goers around him. But he was too short to see their faces very well. At his eye level, he saw a few small children run by, waving colored ribbons. And he noticed three large crows fighting over a chunk of fallen bread near a baker's stand. They bobbed and weaved like tiny swordsmen, jabbing and thrusting to steal crumbs from each other. One paused for a second to scan the crowds, making sure the coast was clear, and then returned to the duel.

The audience around the sword swallower broke into applause as he finished his act—thankfully, still in one piece. Edric turned his attention elsewhere.

"Hey, you like books, right?" he asked Hob.

"I, uh ..." Hob felt his throat tighten. Was Edric subtly accusing him of stealing *The Ballad of Waeward the Wanderer*? If Hob said "yes," would it confirm his guilt? If he said "no," would Edric know he was lying? Maybe he needed to—

"Then we should check out the bookshop!"

Edric took Hob's arm and led him toward the edge of the square. There, tucked between two much taller buildings, was a tiny bookshop with a bright red door. It looked like it had been squeezed in and had gotten stuck. A wooden sign hung at the front, black with gold lettering that read: *The Paper Sparrow.*

Inside, a single patron browsed, while the owner sat by the door, reading. Or, perhaps he was sleeping. Hob couldn't quite tell. The four short walls were lined with bookshelves. Tall stacks of additional books were scattered around the floor. The air smelled of musty parchment and binding glue.

Hob was in heaven. He could have happily moved in and spent the rest of his days there. He wandered the store, letting his gloved fingers trail across the book spines as he read their many titles. He was amazed that so many had even been written! And on such a variety of subjects: *On the Dancing of Heavenly Spheres; The Art of the Duel: An Illustrated Guide to Swordplay; Paul and John's Book of Songs ...*

After a while, he reached out and grabbed a thick leather-bound volume titled *The Lost People of the Wild: The Legend of the Ancient Elves.* But, as he did, he felt a hand fall on his shoulder.

"Welp, I think that's enough of these dusty old tomes," said Edric, losing interest. "Better get going."

Hob didn't even have enough time to put his book back before Edric whisked him toward the door. Instead, the book joined one of the stacks at the front of the shop.

"Sorry we couldn't help you find what you were looking for, sirs," said the owner, not bothering to look up from his book. "Come again soon."

"You know what," said Edric, pulling open the door, "I think we should grab one of those roast chickens on the wa—"

Then he froze. Together with Hob, he stepped back into the shop, closed the door so it was only open a crack, and peeked outside.

Two tall figures stood there with their backs to the door, scanning the marketplace. One wore a crimson cloak, the other a cloak of black. The crimson cloaked man turned to his companion, revealing his profile. He was ruggedly handsome, with a chiseled jaw and a steely gaze. His thick hair and trimmed beard were of a fiery orange color that Hob had never seen on a person before.

"Don't be so hard on yourself ..." the man said. "Yes, the boy gave you the slip, but what else could you have done? Sometimes complications arise."

His companion turned to him, revealing her profile as well. It was Captain Fist! "Where the boy is concerned, complications *always* arise."

"Still, a three-headed troll!" the man replied. "It's not every day you fight one of those and live to tell about it!" He shook his head in amazement.

"Let us just say, it was not so *three-headed* when I was done with it," Fist growled.

The man laughed darkly. "At any rate, Captain," he said, "I don't think he's here. Even Prince Edric wouldn't be foolish enough to come to the festival when he knows we're looking for him."

"You would be surprised," said Captain Fist, peering around. "But, very well. Have guards posted at every entrance to the square, and meet me at the gates."

And with that, the two parted and left.

"Who was that?" Hob whispered, as soon as they were out of earshot.

"Sir Lance Buckler, Captain Fist's Lieutenant," said Edric, pausing. "Can you believe she defeated the troll?"

"I know!" said Hob.

"Good thing she's on our side." Edric shook his head in admiration.

Hob stared at him, confused.

"Well, I mean, *normally*. Not so much at the moment." Edric scowled. "She seems to think letting my father and me search for the Sunflame is against her oath to protect us or something. Right now, I wish she were a little less impressive."

"So, I guess we should be getting back to the inn, then?" said Hob.

"Yep," said Edric, "right after we pop up to the tower." Then he was out the door, dragging Hob back into the marketplace.

They made their way straight across the bustling square, heading for the tower in the distance. Before long, the crowds around them grew so large and dense that Hob had to cling to Edric's cloak so they wouldn't be separated. Hips and knees buffeted Hob. All he could see were people's bottoms!

Finally, at the very heart of the square, the pair passed through the largest crowd of all, and emerged in a wide circular clearing at its center. They paused at the edge of the clearing to get their bearings.

In the middle stood a tall stone fountain. Cool spring water gushed from its many spouts to fill a raised pool at its base. And a ring of people held hands and danced around the pool to the same music Hob had heard earlier. Off to one side, the musicians from the parade played their strange instruments while a drummer kept the beat.

Tall posts displaying bright banners stood here and there around the clearing's edge. And long ropes strung with colorful little flags and pennants ran between them, crisscrossing overhead as they circled the clearing. Again, Hob noticed three crows. They were perched on these flag lines, looking out over the crowds, no doubt searching for some dropped food to eat.

Soon, a man in a giant white chicken suit bounded out from behind the fountain, holding hands in the spinning chain of dancers. He had a feathery body, skinny legs in bright yellow tights, floppy chicken's feet shoes, and an oversized chicken head that bobbled around on top of his own—with his face sticking out of the beak.

"Who's *that?*" asked Hob, wide-eyed.

"Why, that's the Spring Chicken, o' course!" interjected a fat man standing next to him at the edge of the crowd. "What? Have ya been livin' in a *cave* yer whole life?"

Hob nodded. "Yeah, pretty mu—"

Edric's hand clamped over Hob's mouth. "*Shhh!*" he whispered. "It's just an expression!"

Thankfully, the fat man wasn't listening. "Hey, Chicken, these two blokes could use a dance!"

The Spring Chicken looked over at them with a wily grin. "Could they now?" he said, as he flailed toward them around the clearing.

"Yes, sir!"

Before Edric and Hob could escape, the fat man shoved them forward to meet the Spring Chicken. Feathery hands clasped their forearms and pulled them into the ring of dancers. The fat man and the Spring Chicken started laughing their heads off.

"C'mon, lads! Join the fun!" exclaimed the chortling face inside the chicken beak. It was long and horsey, with beady eyes and a pointy mustache and goatee.

"Don't be shy, boys!" yelled an old woman who streaked by in the crowd.

The trio was quickly swept off in the dance, Edric first, followed by the Spring Chicken, followed by Hob.

The Spring Chicken even began to sing with the music:

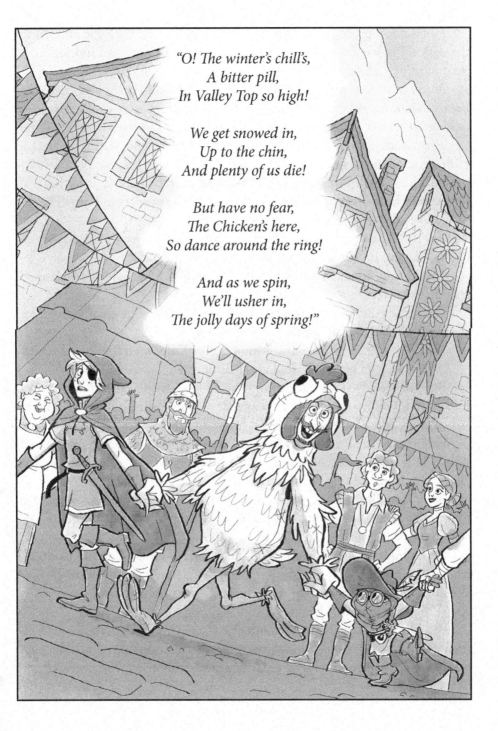

"O! The winter's chill's,
A bitter pill,
In Valley Top so high!

We get snowed in,
Up to the chin,
And plenty of us die!

But have no fear,
The Chicken's here,
So dance around the ring!

And as we spin,
We'll usher in,
The jolly days of spring!"

Hob knew he and Edric were in trouble the instant they got pulled into the dance. He looked past the white feathers to his right, and spotted Edric bobbing along ahead. Edric looked worried too.

As the music moved faster and faster, Hob could barely keep pace. He began to alternate between running as fast as his big boots would allow, and pulling up his feet so he'd be carried along by the dancers to either side of him.

Then, suddenly, the Spring Chicken's feathery hand jerked away, and Hob tumbled to the ground. He looked up to see what had happened. It appeared a little boy in front of Edric had tripped and fallen, causing Edric to topple over him, and the Spring Chicken to topple over them both. The rest of the line stumbled to a halt behind Hob.

As Edric stood back up, Hob noticed something was wrong. Edric's hood had fallen, and his eye patch was askew!

The Spring Chicken noticed as well. "Your Highness!" he exclaimed, leaping to his feet.

The rest of the dancers around them gasped. Everyone recognized Edric at once—no doubt from all the wanted posters.

"I've found Prince Edric! The reward is mine!" declared the Spring Chicken. "Sorry, Your Highness." He dove at Edric, trying to tackle him.

But Edric dodged the tackle, and the flailing chicken man flopped onto the ground. Unfortunately, there were many others waiting to take his place. When Edric turned to run, he found himself trapped.

Shouts of, "The Prince! The Prince! He's mine! He's mine!" came from all sides, as the nearby dancers rushed to surround him, and a dozen spectators charged in from the front of the crowd.

"*CAW!*" Spooked by the shouting and the sudden commotion, the crows took flight from the flag lines overhead, and flapped out of the square over the roofs of the buildings.

In the midst of it all, Hob stood, and glanced around, trying to decide what to do. He quickly spotted a pair of golden helmets and crimson-cloaked shoulders pushing forward through the front rows of the crowd.

"Ed! Royal Guards!" he cried.

But Edric was already in the clutches of as many townsfolk as could get their hands on him—including the very persistent Spring Chicken. They were eagerly awaiting the Royal Guards' arrival, hoping to share in some part of the reward.

Hob panicked. He could think of only one way to save Edric, and it would be risky at best. But what choice did he have?

Hob hopped onto the rim of the fountain pool, and removed his long gloves. Then, making sure to leave the goggles over his eyes untouched, he grabbed his hat, his scarf, and his cloak by its clasp, and tore off his disguise for all to see! "*RAAAHHRRRG!*" Doing his best Brute-impression, he scrunched up his face and let out his *goblin-iest* roar!

The heads of Edric's captors and the people in the crowd turned to stare at Hob in shocked silence.

"*AAAAAAAAAAHHHH!*"

They all started screaming. Edric's captors scrambled over each other to flee, allowing him to slip from their grasps. And the crowd around the fountain burst and scattered, buffeting away the Royal Guards.

Hob's gambit had worked!

Unfortunately, it had also set off an instant riot. Men, women, and children who hadn't even seen Hob were now shouting, "The goblins are coming! The goblins are coming!" By the time this news spread across the square, it told of a full-blown goblin invasion.

All of the townsfolk, and even some of the city guards, took off running. And the remaining guards were too busy trying to avoid getting trampled by their fellow humans to worry about whether there was really a goblin attack underway.

In less than a minute, the fleeing crowds had managed to overturn so many food carts and flatten so many tents that, if goblins *had* been attacking, they would've found much of their work done for them.

Meanwhile, Edric grabbed Hob's hand and pulled him down from the fountain. Together, they ran. Hob kicked off the clunky human boots he wore over his own, trying to keep up. But even so, he struggled to match Edric's speed. Hob's legs were so much shorter, and he wasn't used to a sword bouncing awkwardly against his hip.

They didn't get far before they heard an angry voice call out behind them. "The reward—I mean, *the Prince*—is getting away!" It was the Spring Chicken. He and his followers had begun to regroup.

Trailing Edric through the chaos, Hob lost all sense of direction. Ahead, two herds of fleeing townsfolk crossed paths, blocking the way forward. Edric and Hob stopped in their tracks.

Hob became frantic. But Edric kept his cool. He drew his sword, cut an opening in the back of a nearby tent, and dragged Hob inside.

The tent's shelves were lined with wooden toys, and an elderly couple cowered behind the counter.

"Sorry," Hob said to them, as Edric yanked him through the tent and out the front flap.

They emerged in a deserted walkway between two tightly packed rows of tents and stalls, most of them still unharmed. A butcher's stand stood directly across from them. It had a wooden roof and counter, and it displayed many strings of smoked sausages and large cuts of salted meat.

"Where to next?" asked Hob.

"Not that way," said Edric, pointing with his sword.

Twenty feet to their left, the stampeding crowds had knocked the *Olive's Oils* tent into the *Toasty Goat BBQ Shack*. A rising wall of smoke and flame blocked the walkway. No wonder the area was deserted.

Hob felt horribly guilty. He certainly hadn't meant to cause such destruction; he'd only been trying to save Edric.

"There they are!" yelled the Spring Chicken. "There they are!"

Hob and Edric looked to their right. An angry mob of townsfolk from the fountain and a few city guards stood just ten feet up the walkway in that direction. The townsfolk had managed to arm themselves with torches, pitchforks, and other weapons both proper and improvised. Musicians brandished their instruments like clubs. A blacksmith swung his hammer. And they were all led by the Spring Chicken, who'd gotten his feathery mitts on a sword.

"Great, now they've got torches and pitchforks," Edric groaned. "That's *never* a good sign."

He raised his own sword, assuming a defensive stance. Hob drew his little sword too, although he had no idea how to use it.

"See, I told you!" said the Spring Chicken. "He's *with* the goblin!"

"That's probably why he's wanted!" said a pitchfork-wielding man. "He's a goblin-loving traitor!"

"The whole *'teen rebel'* thing was cute for a while," said an old woman, smacking a rolling pin into her palm. "But this time he's gone too far!"

"The royal backstabber!" said one of the musicians, jabbing the air with a large string instrument. "Forget the reward. Let's make him *pay!*"

The mob began to advance.

Hob's scheme had backfired! Now the townsfolk were convinced that Prince Edric was a goblin sympathizer! Even the promise of reward money for his capture might not spare him from their wrath.

"HALT!" a voice cried out. "By order of the King's Royal Guard!"

Suddenly, Captain Fist appeared on the roof of the butcher's stand, having climbed up from behind. Sword drawn, she leapt down into the walkway, landing between Edric and Hob and their attackers.

"The Prince is under my custody. He will *not* be harmed!" she continued. "He may be a foolish, foolish child. But he is no traitor!"

Unfortunately, the crowd was too worked up to listen to reason—even coming from the intimidating Captain Fist.

"She's lying!" spat the Spring Chicken, stopping before her.

"It's a royal conspiracy!" declared a city guard.

"Why, she's probably a *goblin herself!*" added the angry musician.

It seemed to Hob there would be no talking their way out of the situation. Apparently, Captain Fist agreed.

"*Run!*" she shouted at Edric, without taking her eyes off the mob.

Wasting no time, Edric and Hob clambered right over the butcher's counter, scattering sausages, and exited through a curtain at the rear of the stand.

Before Hob closed the curtain, he glanced back at Captain Fist. She was quickly being overwhelmed. She seemed reluctant to strike any of the innocent townsfolk with her sword. And though she sent several flying with well-placed kicks and punches, there were always more ready to swarm her. The Spring Chicken rushed in, and caught her in a feathery headlock. She elbowed his beak so hard that his chicken head spun backward, blinding him. Then she rolled free.

Hob had seen enough. He turned and followed Edric out of the square.

CHAPTER TWELVE

Truth and Illusion

The pair avoided any further encounters as they fled the square through one of its tall archways. But the streets outside were packed with frightened townsfolk.

Edric yanked Hob into a nearby back-alley, and led the way up the narrow gap between buildings, weaving around piles of refuse and empty barrels.

"Thanks ... Hob ..." Edric panted, as they walked. His eye patch had managed to get so twisted around that it now looked like he was missing an ear. He slipped it off, and pocketed it.

"I'm ... just glad ... that worked," Hob panted back. "At least ... *sort of.*"

While in the shadows of the buildings, he lifted his goggles to wipe the sweat from his brow, and then slipped them back over his eyes.

For quite some time, the pair pressed on through a zigzagging maze of similar back-alleys, until Edric brought them back to the edge of a wider street.

"So, are we looping around to the inn then?" asked Hob, as he joined Edric at the end of the alley. "*Ed?*"

The street outside was empty, and Hob found Edric staring up it toward the castle tower. They were closer than ever.

"You can't be serious?" Hob groaned. "We're still going?"

"We have to!" said Edric. "It's the whole reason we came!"

"But now there's an angry mob after us!" Hob protested.

Edric looked like he was about to reply, when the sound of thumping boots and jangling armor stopped him. He grabbed Hob and pulled him behind a stack of barrels at the edge of the alley. Hob peeked through the cracks between the barrels and saw the source of the noise. A whole troop of city guards went marching by.

"I wonder what all the panic's about?" said one.

"Who knows?" said another. "But, if it means a chance for us to get out of the castle and see the festival, then I'm all for it!"

"My ol' lady's birthday's comin' up," said a third. "Maybe I'll get her a pot."

"Don't get her *cookware*," interjected the first. "Women hate that."

"Oh … well maybe a nice broomstick."

A second later, they were gone, headed in the direction of the town square.

Edric waited for the thumping and jangling to fade, before emerging from behind the barrels.

"Did you hear that?" he said. "The angry mob is drawing the guards away from the castle. If anything, that'll make things easier for us. Let's go, before they come back."

"But, Ed," said Hob, following him out into the street, "this *makes no sense!*"

"Look, I know you don't get it," said Edric. "But this is happening. You can either come with me, or go back to the inn on your own."

Hob sighed. He didn't want to be left alone in a town screaming for goblin blood, so he followed Edric up the street to the tower.

Edric wasn't wrong about things being easier with the castle guards called away. Soon, he and Hob were sneaking in through the castle's open gate, with not a watchman in sight.

The castle was made of the same weathered gray stone as the rest of the city, but cut stronger and thicker. And, while it was modest by castle standards, it was impressive to Hob, who'd only read of such things.

As he and Edric passed through the gate in the outer wall, they entered a vacant cobblestone courtyard with a small keep on the far side. The keep's main hall rose up only four stories under a gabled roof, but the tower next to it added at least another three. The tower was round and topped by a wide room with a conical spire. Ivy snaked up and down its stonework, stemming from a little garden at its base.

The whole place gleamed with the red light of the sinking sun. But, unlike the evening before, Hob was in no mood to admire its beauty. It was a bad sign. They'd wasted too much time at the festival. Dusk drew near, and, soon, Stella and Monty would return to find them missing.

Edric gestured for Hob to follow him as he led the way around the courtyard. Nestled along the inside of its walls were stables, workshops, and storehouses, which the castle relied on for its daily needs. Sitting next to them were piles of timbers, stacks of barrels and crates, and two large hay carts. Edric and Hob edged their way around these buildings and supplies, and crept over to the base of the tower. They took cover in the garden there, huddled behind some shrubs.

"See?" Edric whispered. "Easy as pie."

"Now what?" asked Hob, glancing around. He saw no entrance to the tower anywhere.

Edric smiled. He pulled the crossbow from his back and the coil of thin rope from his belt. He began to tie the end of the rope to a loop near the bottom of a thick bolt already loaded in the crossbow.

Hob gaped. "I don't think that's going to work, Ed. Maybe we should try the castle door? Or call up to her? Or, better yet, we can leave a note, go back to the inn, and you two can be pen pals!"

Ignoring Hob and finishing his work, Edric raised the crossbow to his eye, took aim at the top window of the tower, and—*twang!*—loosed the bolt. *Thock!* It buried itself deep in the upper part wooden window frame. Edric gave the rope a sharp tug to see if it would support their weight. Satisfied, he tossed his crossbow into the bushes to lighten his load.

"Fine. Just a *quick* hello then," Hob went on. "I don't think we should be pushing our luck."

"That's the plan," said Edric, as he began to climb the rope. "Just a quick hello."

The Prince was tired and sweaty when he reached the top of the rope a few minutes later. Carefully, he climbed through the open window into the tower room.

Hob followed immediately after him. Being small and spry, the climb had given him much less trouble. He hopped down softly from the windowsill, and joined Edric on the stone steps below, where the Prince stood trying ever so quietly to catch his breath.

They found themselves in a vaulted, circular chamber that appeared to serve as both a bedroom and a library.

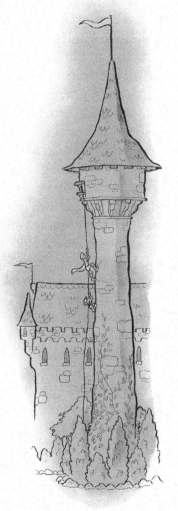

Massive floor-to-ceiling bookcases covered every inch of wall inside, except where they'd been built around the window and door. Fashioned of dark wood, trimmed with polished bronze, and packed with thick tomes, the shelves ran up easily a dozen feet, and a long ladder slid around them on tracks. Hob couldn't believe how many books they held—easily twice as many as had been in the little bookshop on the square.

On the bedroom side of things, most of the furnishings had been built right into the shelves, including a desk, a wardrobe, and a chest of drawers. However, standing separately on a dais at the center of the room was a huge four-poster bed draped in rich purple curtains.

The only thing that suggested any sort of curse or imprisonment was the door. It looked like that of a dungeon, with its thick black wood, great iron braces, and tiny hatched window.

As Hob looked around the room, he caught a flash of movement. A single eye peeked out through the curtains of the four-poster bed. It disappeared with a swish of purple cloth. The Lady of Valley Top!

Edric must have spotted her too, because he stepped forward and fell to one knee to address her. "My Lady of Valley Top, why dost thou hide? I have come to look upon thy beauteous face!"

Hob shot Edric a quizzical look. "*Beauteous? Dost thou?*" he whispered.

"That's how you talk to *Ladies*," Edric explained.

From behind the curtains came a muffled reply. "I hide when I see arrows strike my window," said the Lady, who sounded more like a girl to Hob. "I don't like visitors. Now go away! You aren't allowed to see me!"

"Fear not, my Lady, for I am *Prince Edric of Yore!*" said Edric, with flair.

"*Ahhk!*" screamed the Lady. "Then you *really* can't see me! *Go away!*"

Hob and Edric exchanged baffled glances.

Hob turned back to the window. Looking out over Valley Top, he spotted the city square and, beyond that, the shady district where their inn was located. It looked much farther away than he would have liked. And the sun was dipping dangerously low behind the mountains.

"Well, that's it then," he said, feigning disappointment. "Guess we'd better get going!"

Edric didn't budge. "Come on, Hob," he said. "She obviously needs our help." He gazed absentmindedly around the room. "See what you can find out about her, while I take a look around."

"W-what?" Hob stammered. "B-but you ...?"

It seemed like Edric should have been the one talking to the girl, while Hob played lookout. But Edric wandered away before they could discuss it.

"O-okay ..." Hob finished.

He watched as Edric circled the room, taking stock of the bookshelves. This wasn't at all how Hob had pictured things unfolding. Still, if he wanted to get out of there as soon as possible, he would have to try talking to the Lady himself. He left the window, sidled up to the edge of the bed, and gave the curtains a little tug.

"My Lady," he said, "what's wrong? Why won't you show him your face?" He added softly, "*He'll leave if you do.*"

A long silence followed, before the Lady's timid voice answered from behind the curtain. "B-b-because I *can't.*"

"Why not?" asked Hob. "Is it *the curse?*"

"Yes."

"Oh, wow. I thought you were just stuck in the tower. I didn't know you were stuck in *bed.* What if you have to, you know, GO?"

"No!" replied the voice. "That's not the curse. Neither is being stuck in the tower. That's just a rumor my father started as an excuse for me to hide in here, to save me the embarrassment of people knowing the truth!"

"What truth?"

"That I *refuse* to leave." The voice hesitated for a moment. "You see, one day, while I was brushing my hair before bed, a wicked fairy appeared in my room. She said something about inner beauty, waved her wand, and turned me into a *horrible monster.*" The voice paused. "And, I get it. As a little girl, I spent days in front of the mirror, trying on dresses and brushing my hair, making sure I was pretty, just like a Lady should be. It was all I cared about. Maybe I deserved to be cursed ... But that was years ago. I've learned my lesson. And yet the curse won't break!"

Hob felt awful for her. As much as he envied her extensive library, he knew how miserable life could be having *only* books for company.

"I'm sorry ..." he said. Then he paused. "What kind of monster are you?"

"What do you mean, 'what kind?'" she asked. "An ugly monster!"

"Well, I'm sort of a monster too," said Hob, getting an idea. "So, maybe you could show your face to me?"

"You're a monster?" the voice replied, as one eye peeked out from behind the curtains. "*AHHHK!*"

The curtains closed again, tightly.

"*Shhh!*" Hob hissed. "I *told you* I'm a monster!"

"You didn't say you were a *GOBLIN!*" the Lady replied.

"A goblin's a kind of monster," Hob muttered, "and not the worst kind, either! Just wait till you meet a troll."

"*A troll!*" squealed the Lady.

"Don't worry, my Lady!" Edric chimed in from across the room. "Hob's a *nice* goblin. And we haven't seen a troll since *yesterday.*"

"Thanks, Ed," said Hob.

"Don't mention it."

Hob tried again to reason with the Lady behind the curtain. "So, are you going to let me see you?" he asked.

"Is *he* looking?" the Lady replied.

"Nope, he's busy checking out books … for *some reason.*"

It was true. Edric had started picking through the bookshelves, inspecting the spines, and pulling the odd one out to peek inside it.

"Okay then …" said the girl behind the curtain, "but promise you won't scream."

"I promise."

A hand emerged, and slowly, reluctantly, pulled back the curtain. There,

through the gap in the veil, Hob saw a normal looking teenage girl, kneeling on her bed. At least, as far as he could tell, she was normal looking. She had long auburn hair, soft freckles on her face, and big hazel eyes, which, had they not been so mournful, might have been quite pretty. She wore a rich green dress, which brought out their color.

"Huh?" said Hob. "You don't look like a monster to me."

"That's what my parents always told me!" the girl complained. "But they were just trying to make me feel better. I can see the *truth* right here."

From under her covers, she pulled out an old silver hand mirror. She held it up and examined herself. Then she tilted it, directing her reflection at Hob.

"See?" she said.

"Looks the same to me," said Hob, more confused than ever.

"I knew it!" she cried, yanking the curtains shut again. "But at least you tell the truth!"

"*Hob!* What's the matter with you?" snapped Edric, as he rolled the bookshelf ladder around from behind the bed. "You're supposed to be helping!"

"I told her she looks fine," said Hob.

"Well, that's clearly not what she wanted to hear," said Edric, beginning to climb the ladder. "Don't you know *anything* about Ladies?"

"No," said Hob. "I've never met one before."

"It's all right," the Lady sighed. "Maybe goblins just can't see *ugliness.*"

"I can too see ugliness!" Hob insisted.

"I'm surprised you can see anything at all, really," said Edric, stopping halfway up the ladder, "with those goggles on inside."

"The *goggles!*" Hob exclaimed. He gave the curtain another tug. "Let me see you once more, my Lady. Ed, don't look."

Without saying anything, the Lady of Valley Top parted the curtains again to reveal herself. Hob took off his goggles, and studied her. She looked the same as before.

"So far, so good," he said. "Now, the mirror …"

Again, the Lady angled her mirror toward Hob. This time, reflected on its surface was a *horrible monster!* It was wearing the same green dress as the Lady, but its face was completely different: purple and pocked, with crooked fangs, stubby horns, a bulbous nose, and a mane of bristly, matted hair.

"Just as I suspected!" Hob declared. "It's not *you* that's cursed. It's your *reflection.* Maybe your ability to perceive yourself altogether. I don't know. But, either way, it's just an illusion!"

For a moment, the Lady went silent. "What? How can that be? I know what the fairy said! I know what I see and feel! How can I believe you, or my parents, when you tell me not to trust my own senses?"

"Because I can prove it," said Hob. "These goggles see through illusions."

He held out his goggles for the Lady, and she took them tentatively. She looked through them into the mirror, and let out a small gasp.

"That's *me?*" she asked.

"Yes," said Hob.

The Lady smiled at him. Then she took another long look through the goggles. Hob made sure not to rush her. Finally, when she was satisfied, she handed the goggles back to Hob, leaned down, and kissed him on the cheek.

"Thank you, nice goblin," she said. "You may call me Isobel."

Hob blushed, turning his accustomed shade of dark green. "*Don' mention it*," he mumbled, turning away to wipe the goggles on his tunic. He put them back on, but left the lenses tilted up on his forehead. "Sometimes we just need to see things through someone else's eyes ... or goggles ... or whatever. If you know what I mean?"

Hob wasn't sure he even knew what he meant, but that wasn't important. The curse was as good as broken thanks to his goggles. Now, perhaps he and Edric could finally get out of there.

"Will you show yourself to him now?" Hob asked Lady Isobel.

"O-okay ..."

Lady Isobel climbed down off her bed, and stepped out from behind the curtains. She straightened her dress, ran her fingers through her long hair, and turned to Edric.

Edric was completely oblivious. He'd come down from the ladder, and he stood there, tearing books from the shelves. He gave each one a glance, and then tossed it haphazardly into a growing pile on the floor.

"Hey, Ed!" Hob exclaimed.

"What? Huh?" muttered Edric, turning to look at them.

Hob pointed emphatically to Lady Isobel.

"Oh! Hey, you *are* pretty!" Edric remarked, before turning back to the books.

Now, it was Isobel's turn to blush.

Hob was ecstatic. "Great! So can we *please* go?"

"Not yet ..." said Edric, tossing another book on the pile.

Hob gaped. He was about to ask, "Why in the world not?" when his bat-like ears picked up on muffled sounds originating outside the tower window. There were hurried footsteps, shuffling bodies, and whispers of, "This way … Over here …" The mob was closing in.

Hob dashed to the window. The sun had finally set, and night had come to Valley Top. With his goggles on his forehead, Hob's eyes adjusted quickly to the gloom, but he still couldn't see anyone. No torches lit the courtyard or the street beyond. The mob must have passed them by. Hob was certain, however, that he and Edric were running out of time.

"That's it!" Hob said, marching over to confront his friend. He grabbed Edric by the arm and jerked him around. "You saw her. Let's go!"

"Take it easy!" said Edric, pulling his arm free.

"No!" said Hob. "I want the truth. If you didn't come to *see her*, why *did* you come?"

Edric stared at Hob stubbornly. "What does it matter?"

"It matters because we're *both* risking our lives to be here. I want to know why!"

Edric finally broke. "It's *the book*, all right? I came for the stupid book!"

Hob had a sinking feeling he knew exactly what book Edric was talking about.

"I meant to read it," Edric continued, "just like Eldwin told me to. But his message never said what it was *for*. So I put it off, and put it off. And then it was gone. Stolen in the Gobble Downs! I thought Eldwin might have understood. I thought he might've known what to do. But when we got stuck with Stella instead … well, she would've just freaked out. She couldn't know. No one could."

Hob gaped. Suddenly, everything made sense.

"And when I heard that old woman mention the library here in the Lady's tower," Edric went on, "well, I thought maybe no one would ever have to."

"So you made up a story about wanting to see Lady Isobel so you could come look for a copy of the book?" Hob surmised. "And you dragged us through the festival so you could check that bookshop on the way?"

"Yes," Edric admitted. "It was the perfect cover. You believed it. And if anyone else on the quest ever found out, they would have too. It'd just be me being a crazy teenage screw-up, as usual. I'd rather have everyone think that, than know I almost doomed my entire Kingdom … *my father*."

Hob's palms went clammy. It had all been *his* fault. He cursed himself for not telling Edric about the book the night before. If only he'd known that

Edric hadn't actually read it. Now, it was too late. If the Prince found out that Hob had stolen his book—and had tried to cover it up!—there was no telling how he would react. Hob had only one option. He had to find Edric another copy fast, so he'd never have to tell him the truth.

"Well, let's find your book then," said Hob, in a strange, overly loud voice. He turned to Isobel in desperation. "We're looking for a book. Do you have it? *The Ballad of Waeward the Wanderer?*"

Hob realized his mistake as soon as the words escaped his lips.

Isobel thought for a second, and then shook her head. "Sorry, I've never heard of it. And I know every book in here."

But Hob wasn't listening. He turned back to Edric.

The Prince had a disturbed look on his face. "I don't think I ever told you what the book was *called* ..." he said, in a quiet, empty tone. "And neither did Stella."

Hob had no words. There was nothing for him to say without either blatantly lying, or admitting his guilt—and he couldn't bring himself to do either.

"It was *you* ..." Edric whispered, finally.

"I ... uh ..." Hob stammered.

"No! It *was you!* You said more than once that the other goblins wanted to execute you for stealing books!"

"Well, you see ..."

Suddenly, Edric lunged forward and grabbed Hob by his furry collar, lifting him up so they were face to face. "Mine was one of them, wasn't it?" he shouted, giving Hob a shake. "*Wasn't it?*"

Hob could see the anger and pain in Edric's eyes. It broke his heart. "Yes ..." he admitted, hanging his head.

"You let me believe this was all *my* fault!" Edric railed at him. "But it's *your* fault! Your fault my Kingdom is doomed. Your fault my father is lost for good. You're a liar and thief, just like every goblin ever!"

Hob opened his mouth to protest, to beg forgiveness, but no sound came out.

"I thought you were different," Edric finished, his voice turning quiet, yet hard as stone. "But you're *not.*"

He lowered Hob, almost gently, and then let him fall the last few feet to the floor. Hob's legs gave way, and he dropped to his knees. He looked up at Edric, his mouth still opening and closing wordlessly.

An uncomfortable silence filled the room, until Lady Isobel broke it.

"I thought you said he was a *nice* goblin?" she said.

"Stay out of this!" Edric snapped at her. Then he rounded on Hob once more. "Go! Get out of here! I *never* want to see you again."

"No!" Hob pleaded, finally finding his voice. "No, please … It's okay …" He had an idea. It was bound to make everything right. "I read it! I read the book! I can get you to the Lost City!"

Edric paused. "*What?*" he asked, as though he'd misheard. He shook his head. "No! I'm not following *you* anywhere."

"But … but … I …" Hob stammered.

"I can't *trust* you!" Edric drew his sword, and pointed it at Hob. "You've been lying to me ever since we met. You'd say anything to trick me into letting you stay. I don't know what your deal is … You might be a spy, a saboteur, or just a *freak*. But Monty was right. You're a *threat*. You can't be part of this quest. So leave! And don't come back!"

It was over. Hob had told the truth; he *could* lead Edric to the Lost City. But if Edric didn't believe him, then it didn't matter.

"Go!" Edric finished, with a thrust of his sword.

They stared at each other for one last moment, Edric's blade hanging between them. Then Hob could take no more. Fighting back tears, he turned, rushed to the tower window, and climbed outside.

CHAPTER THIRTEEN

Up a Tower Without a Rope

Hob felt numb, empty, as he lowered himself back down the tower, using the rope hanging from the crossbow bolt in the window frame.

The soft thuds of yet more falling books and the protests of Lady Isobel emanated from the tower's top room. And out beyond the castle walls, another blanket of evening cloud had spread over the valley, breaking around the mountain slopes below the city and glowing white under the nearly-full moon in the clear sky above.

But Hob hardly noticed any of that. All his thoughts were focused on keeping moving, getting out of there. As his feet touched ground, he released the rope, and stood for a moment in the garden at the base of the tower, hidden by tall shrubs and the tower's dark shadow. He turned and gazed across the moonlit courtyard toward the castle gate.

Hob didn't know exactly where to go from there. But he couldn't stay. There would be no "*adventuring along*" anymore. And there was no way he could carry on the quest alone. So far, neither Waeward nor King Edgar had made it back from their excursions to the Lost City alive, which meant Hob stood no chance. If by some miracle he managed to escape Valley Top, then he supposed he would head into the wilds, and find somewhere quiet to live out his days, far from both humans and goblins, the way he was clearly meant to be.

In that instant, Hob felt the weight of it all. He was angry at Edric for not understanding, for not listening. He was angry at himself for lying about the book, for believing he could ever be friends with someone like Edric in the first place. The pain was so much worse than it would've been had Hob never joined the adventure at all. It wasn't a dream he was losing; it was something real.

Hob shook his head. He'd have plenty of time for regrets later. First, he had to escape. He started toward the gate.

Then, suddenly, something stirred in the bushes around him, and the darkness itself seemed to leap out at him. An arm wrapped around his neck, preventing his escape, and a hand clamped firmly over his mouth to stop him from screaming—a hand gloved in black.

Jerked around by his captor, Hob could see more dark figures emerging from the bushes and from behind the base of the tower, crowding the shadowy garden. Hob spotted handsome Lieutenant Buckler, grim Sir Deckard from the forest, five city guards, and a dozen crazed villagers led by the Spring Chicken—no longer wearing his chicken head. It was an ambush!

Hob tried to call up to Edric in warning, but the hand over his mouth stifled his cries. He writhed against the strong arm restraining him, but it only constricted more tightly around his neck.

Then a familiar voice whispered in his ear. "That is enough, *goblin*. Be silent now, or I will silence you myself."

Hob's worst fears were confirmed. He was being held by Captain Fist. He went limp. It was no use fighting *her*.

"Gag him," whispered the Captain.

The Spring Chicken approached, raising a cloth gag. Without his chicken head, his long, horsey face could be seen fully for the first time. It was clear that his pointy goatee attempted to compensate for his lack of a chin. And a mop of sandy hair lay matted down on his head, greasy after a day spent under a hot costume.

Fist's arm tightened briefly around Hob's neck, choking him so he couldn't make any noise. She removed her hand from his mouth, allowing the Spring Chicken to gag him.

Hob couldn't believe what was happening. The last time he'd seen Fist and the Spring Chicken, they'd been locked in hand-to-hand combat. Now they were working together?

With the gag in place, the Spring Chicken set about tying Hob's hands behind his back with a length of rope. Meanwhile, Captain Fist reached around with her free hand, unbuckled Hob's sword belt, and took it from him with the sword and scabbard still attached, stuffing them under her arm. Hob's goggles were next to go. Fist slipped them off his head, and tucked them into one of the pouches near the back of her belt, hidden beneath her cloak. Though both the sword and goggles were relatively new to Hob, he already felt naked without them.

"Looks like you were right," the Spring Chicken whispered, as he fastened his knot around Hob's wrists. "They *were* here."

"I told you they would be," Fist whispered back. "I've had this tower watched day and night since we arrived. Sir Deckard saw them enter." She peered up to the window above. "My Prince never could resist a damsel in distress."

It was almost as if part of her *admired* Edric's impulsiveness. Or, perhaps, she just admired her own ability to predict it. Either way, Hob knew she was off the mark. The Captain had simply gotten lucky; Edric was up the tower because of its library, not its Lady.

The Spring Chicken gave Hob a quick pat down. Fist stopped him, jabbing a finger into his chest feathers.

"It is time for you to hold up your end of the bargain, Chicken Man," she hissed. "I deliver the gold and the *creature*. You allow me to leave with Prince Edric, alive and unharmed."

"You have my word," whispered the Spring Chicken, crossing his heart. "The boy's all yours." He looked down at Hob with a maniacal grin. "Now give me what's *mine!*"

"Take him," Fist replied, thrusting Hob into the clutches of the Spring Chicken.

Hob fought to escape the Spring Chicken's grip, hoping he would find it less resilient than Captain Fist's. But the wiry man inside the chicken suit was surprisingly strong. And with Hob's hands bound behind his back, he was easily overpowered. Soon, the Spring Chicken had one arm around Hob's neck just as Fist had, forcing Hob to stop squirming unless he wanted to strangle himself.

"Now, stay quiet until I'm inside," Fist ordered the Spring Chicken and his companions, quickly strapping Hob's sword belt on above her own. "I'll not have you alerting the Prince."

The Spring Chicken nodded obediently.

And with that, Captain Fist climbed the rope up the tower. Her movements were smooth and powerful, and she reached the top in no time at all. Like a dashing hero from Hob's books, she slid stealthily onto the window ledge and perched there, ready to pounce on an unsuspecting enemy. Before she did, she drew a knife, and cut the rope right under the crossbow bolt. It slithered down into the garden, preventing any escape through the window.

The movement must have caught Edric's eye, because his voice called out from inside. "Hob! I told you never to come back!"

This was followed by one of Lady Isobel's screams. "*Aaahh!*"

"*Captain Fist!*" Edric shouted.

"Are you not pleased to see me, my Prince?" asked the Captain. "I am very pleased to see *you*."

Then she swooped into the tower room. Sounds of struggle echoed from within, crashing, clanging, and yet more books falling to the floor. Moments later, the sounds died out, leaving the crowd at the base of the tower staring up in silent anticipation.

"Come on," Hob heard Lieutenant Buckler say to Sir Deckard. "Let's fetch the horses."

"Aye, Lieutenant," said Sir Deckard.

Footsteps signaled their departure, but Hob didn't look. Part of him hoped that if he kept his eyes fixed on the tower window, he might somehow will Edric to appear there, miraculously free, and ready to climb down the vines and save him.

But it wasn't to be. Hob's view of the tower was quickly wrested away, as the Spring Chicken spun him around to face the mob.

"He's ours now!" declared the Spring Chicken. "And you know what we do with goblins here in Valley Top?"

"Burn them!" cried the mob.

"That's right. We *burn* them!" cried the Spring Chicken. "So, get to work!"

The Spring Chicken forced Hob to watch from the center of the courtyard as his pyre was built. Pitchforks, shovels, hammers, and axes reduced one of the hay carts by the stables to kindling, while strong arms hauled over a beam from the timber pile by the workshops, and planted it upright in the hay and debris. The townsfolk crowded around. Many of them lit torches, chasing away the cool moonlight and tinting the yard almost as red as it had been under the setting sun.

Finally, the Spring Chicken dragged Hob forward. The crowd parted ahead of them, clearing an aisle to the pyre. A city guard stood at the far end, waiting with a length of rope to bind Hob to his post.

The crowd chanted as the Spring Chicken marched Hob up the aisle.

"Villain!"

"Spy!"

"Green scum!"

"*BURN HIM!*"

All eyes were on Hob. They seemed almost goblin-like, wild and blood-thirsty. Their excitement grew with every step he was forced to take.

Then—*BANG!*—just before Hob reached the pyre, the tall oaken doors of the keep's main hall burst open. The Spring Chicken halted the march, as everyone looked toward the doors.

Captain Fist strode out of the darkness within, her black cloak billowing.

She dragged a struggling Prince Edric in her wake. Like Hob, Edric was gagged, with both arms bound behind his back. Captain Fist kept a tight grip just above his left elbow, twisting whenever she needed to force him on.

The pair headed directly for the castle gate. As she walked, the Captain wedged forefinger and thumb between her lips and let out a shrill whistle. Seconds later, Lieutenant Buckler and Sir Deckard rode in through the gate on horseback, leading the Captain's gray charger between them. Both guardsmen held torches to light their way.

Hob stamped, squirmed, and tried to scream. He wanted to call out to Edric, but the gag in his mouth prevented it.

"Shut up, *goblin!*" snapped the Spring Chicken, giving Hob a shake.

Hob's exertions proved to be unnecessary; the large crowd was more than enough to draw Edric's attention. As Fist hauled him past, Edric stared up the aisle at Hob. For a moment, their eyes met, and a strange mixture of emotions flashed across the Prince's face—fear, anger, and something else. He obviously blamed Hob for their situation, but maybe, just maybe, he also felt sympathy for him.

Edric began to struggle against Fist's grasp more determinedly than before.

"Be still!" snapped Fist, jerking him on.

As Lieutenant Buckler and Sir Deckard approached with the horses, the Captain looked up at them.

"Quickly now!" she said. "Our journey leaves us no choice but to spend one night on the road. If we ride tonight, then we can get away from this accursed place, and arrive safely in King's Rock by sundown tomorrow."

She threw Edric up onto the charger's shoulders, and, with a swish of her cloak, seated herself in the saddle behind him. Then she took the reins from Lieutenant Buckler, and a freshly lit torch from Sir Deckard, and pulled the horse around. She rode for the castle gate, followed by her two guardsmen.

The Spring Chicken turned back to Hob wearing a nasty grin. Hob knew he should have been panicking, searching for a way out. But with Edric leaving, there simply wasn't one. Hob went limp—ready to let the Spring Chicken drag him the rest of the way to the pyre.

Yet, they got no farther. Nor did the three riders and Edric reach the gate. Instead, four more horsemen galloped through into the courtyard—the remainder of the Royal Guards. Attention returned to Captain Fist, as the newcomers rode to a halt in her path.

"What is the meaning of this?" Fist demanded, stopping her horse. "Why have you abandoned your posts?"

Sir Reginald, the mustached guard from the forest, was first to answer. "Captain!" he said. "An *army of goblins* marches up the pass! The lookouts from the city guard say it's as though it appeared out of nowhere. They say when they were called to the riot in the marketplace, the length of the pass was empty. Yet, when they returned to their towers, the goblins were somehow *past* the Riven Gate."

Fist cursed under her breath. "How many?" she asked.

"Nearly a thousand," said Sir Reginald. "More than this city can handle, should they decide to attack."

"And if they are already past the Riven Gate, there is nothing to stop them," Fist finished. "How long do we have?"

"A few hours, at most."

She cursed again.

Several of the nearby townsfolk overheard the exchange, and the news spread quickly. Cries of terror rose up, even as the message grew increasingly distorted.

"The goblins are here!"

"The Headless Goblin's *out of beer?*"

"They're at the gates!"

"They poured it down the *grates?*"

Hob knew this wasn't going to help his prospects at all. Sure enough, the crowd soon turned on him, looking more malevolent than before.

A feathery arm gave Hob another shake. "What do you know about this, *goblin?*" growled the Spring Chicken.

"Nff'n!" Hob cried through his gag.

"All part of your evil plan, no doubt. Well, I'll make sure you don't *live* to see it through … Light 'er up, boys!"

Suddenly, a dozen torches streaked through the air, thrown by townsfolk onto the pyre. They *sizzled* and *spat* as they plunged into the hay. The ruined hay cart burst into flames, which *roared* and leapt ten feet into the air. And the Spring Chicken dragged Hob toward the blaze.

This time, Hob resisted. "Moh! Mhon't!" he screamed, kicking and squirming.

All around him, eager faces swam in the red light. As the wall of fire neared, Hob could feel its sweltering heat on his skin.

"This is it, *goblin,*" said the Spring Chicken, lifting Hob up to heave him into the inferno.

Then, at the last second, something blotted out the light. A horse galloped in at the end of the aisle, and stopped there, blocking the pyre. Captain Fist and Edric were silhouetted on its back.

"There has been a change of plans, Chicken Man," Captain Fist said. "The goblin is needed for questioning."

CHAPTER FOURTEEN

At the Gates

"It was one of the men who lights the beacons in the pass," Lance Buckler explained, as he climbed the twisting stairwell. "He spotted the goblin army from the last beacon, and ran all the way back to town to give us as much time as he could."

"So, the fools weren't even first to spot it," Captain Fist growled.

She trailed Buckler up the stairs, dragging Hob along with her, his furry collar clutched in her gloved hand. Two more Royal Guards followed. One was the big-chinned, bored-eyed guard who'd inspected Stella's hay cart at the city gate, the other a grizzled guard with a thick beard. They had Edric sandwiched between them. Both Hob and Edric remained gagged, with their hands tied behind their backs.

"To be fair, Captain, the lookouts were *ordered* to the square," said Buckler, pausing at a door partway up the stairwell.

"To deal with *one* goblin," Fist reminded him.

"It seems their commanders thought there was an invasion."

"Well, there is *now.*"

Buckler sighed in agreement, and pushed open the door.

The party entered a stone guardroom built atop the city wall, directly over the main gate. A wide archway in the room's front wall led out onto the ramparts. The stairwell door they'd just come through was set in a side wall, opposite an identical one at the far end. Both stairwells climbed the watchtowers that flanked the gate.

The guardroom was unadorned, except for a set of table and chairs in the middle, a row of empty weapon racks lining the back wall, and flickering torches mounted beside each entrance.

A pair of city guards sat huddled at the table with their backs to the door. When they heard people enter, they jumped up, and spun around. One of them nearly dropped his spear.

"Hey! You can't bring *him* in here!" said the guard who wasn't fumbling with his spear. "He's the enemy! He's a—"

Captain Fist stepped forward, dragging Hob with her, and nearly strangling him in the process. The effect on the guards was the same as if she'd drawn a sword. They retreated as fast as they could, backing right into the table.

"The goblin is an *asset*," the Captain scolded them. "Which is more than I can say for you and the rest of your so-called *guard*. If you had not been so concerned with hunting down one little goblin, and had kept your watch on the pass, we would not be in this mess."

The guards shifted where they stood, doing their best to avoid meeting Fist's gaze.

"It was the clouds what did it, ma'am," said the clumsy guard, who finally had his spear under control. "You can't see a thing down there."

"I promise you, the clouds had not yet rolled in when the goblins arrived in the pass. And *that* was when they should have been spotted. Before they reached the Riven gate. While there was still time."

The guards flinched. Fist had yet to truly raise her voice, and she had them shaking.

"Now, get out of my way, and go find something useful to do," she ordered them.

The first guard opened his mouth to speak.

"*Elsewhere*," Fist finished.

The guards exchanged a look, and then scurried out the front archway onto the ramparts.

Fist turned to the pair of Royal Guards holding Edric. "Tie the Prince to a chair. He'll be safest in here."

The men nodded. They lowered Edric into a chair in front of the table, and bound his legs and torso to it with strong ropes.

"Mm-mph!" Edric protested, through his gag.

Then two loud voices echoed out of the stairwell behind the company.

"Let me through! Let me through!" cried the first, belonging to the Spring Chicken.

"What business do you have here?" demanded the second, belonging to grim Sir Deckard. "We're trying to organize the defenses."

"I have a goblin to keep an eye on!" the Spring Chicken replied. "He's still *my* prisoner, you know. I only loaned him out because we're under attack."

"Right, we're *under attack*," said Sir Deckard, with disgust. "Don't you have better things to do than to harass one little goblin? Haven't you learned *anything?*"

The Spring Chicken ignored Sir Deckard and called up directly to Captain Fist. "Captain! We had a *deal!*"

Fist let out a noise somewhere between a sigh and a growl. "Let him pass!" she called down to Sir Deckard.

Moments later, the Spring Chicken marched in through the stairwell door. His formerly-white feathers were gray and disheveled. His hair clung to his forehead in sweaty clumps. He was panting from exertion and overexcitement. In the relative calm of the guardroom, he seemed a madman.

He glared down at Hob, and then up at Captain Fist. "Remember … he's *mine* once you're done with him," he said.

"Once I'm done with him," said Fist.

The Spring Chicken grinned smugly.

Hob swallowed hard. He hadn't really been spared—just granted a stay of execution, negotiated by Captain Fist. She'd said she needed him for questioning. The problem was, Hob didn't *know* anything. He racked his brain for something he could tell her that might keep him alive.

"Follow me, everyone," said Fist. "Except you, my Prince."

Edric wasn't going anywhere, having been tied securely to his chair. He and Hob could only exchange glances, as the Captain dragged Hob out the wide archway at the front of the room, with Lieutenant Buckler, the two other Royal Guards, and the Spring Chicken in tow.

The group emerged on a broad wall-walk over the city's main gate, set between the flanking watchtowers. This great walkway ran right through open archways in the sides of both towers and onwards the length of the wall. Within the archways, Hob could see further entrances into the tower stairwells. Every feature was constructed of thick stone.

City guards and townsfolk rushed back and forth along the wall, preparing for the coming attack. Some carried torches to fend off the darkness—though the moon was large and surprisingly bright—while others followed with arms full of weapons and armor, wheelbarrows full of rocks, and anything else that could be used to fend off the goblins.

Half the city had answered the call to arms, while those unable to fight had either barricaded themselves in their homes or joined the mothers and children in evacuating through the west gate at the back of the city. Captain Fist had taken charge with remarkable efficiency, setting these plans in motion before she'd even left the castle yard. And over the past nearly three hours, the townsfolk had worked valiantly to carry them out.

The Captain dragged Hob to the front of the wall, before finally releasing her grip on him. The others gathered around.

The parapet there was almost too tall for Hob to see over, but he managed to peek through one of the square crenels that were indented in it every few feet. Battlements like this ran the entire length of the wall.

With his hands still tied behind his back, Hob pressed his chest against the stonework, and craned his head through the crenel. His eyes traveled to the top of the tightly closed gate and portcullis in the wall below, then out across the wide plateau before the city, and finally down the steep switchback road into the mountain pass.

The road zigzagged down a short distance from the plateau before it disappeared. Though the plateau was clear, the evening clouds had closed in not far below, filling the pass most of the way up the road. The nearby mountain peaks jutted out of this misty sea like towering islands of stone and snow.

The short stretch of road visible above the clouds was empty. There were no goblins to be seen. But they could be *heard*. The clanking of their armor, the thunder of their boots, and the rumble of their voices all rose out of the mist, echoing off mountain walls.

"They are getting close," Captain Fist whispered to herself.

"Bad news, Captain!" a voice exclaimed. Another Royal Guard rushed out through one of the tower archways, and joined the group at the battlements. He was a younger man with a scruffy chin. "They still haven't found Lady Isobel. They searched the tower and castle, but she's not there. They don't know where she went. Some keep swearing she doesn't exist."

Captain Fist and the rest of the company turned to face him.

"Well, Sir Fredrick, tell them she *does* exist!" said the Captain. "Tell them to keep searching! The Lady *must* be escorted to the west gate, and evacuated with the others. Make certain they understand this. Then get to your post."

"Yes, Captain!" Sir Fredrick was off and running again.

Captain Fist shook her head, and addressed her other men. "Lieutenant Buckler," she said, "make sure everyone is in position on the wall—city guards at the front, townspeople at the back. Sir Paddrick, Sir Wilhelm, go find Sir Deckard and Sir Reginald, and get to your posts as well. Get armor on as many townspeople as you can. Get weapons in their hands. Organize them. Encourage them. Our defenses *must hold* long enough for the evacuees to get out and take cover in the mountains." She paused. "And if the goblins see enough resistance, perhaps they will think twice about attacking in the first place."

The guards were about to reply, when Hob interrupted them.

"M'ey migh'd!" he exclaimed, forgetting his gag, and nearly choking on it.

Everyone turned to stare at him.

"Go," Fist instructed her men, without taking her eyes off Hob.

Buckler and the other Royal Guards departed to help organize the defenses. Captain Fist, meanwhile, reached down and loosened Hob's gag. It fell slack around his neck.

"*Phtt, phtt, phtt ...*" He struggled to spit the stray fibers from his mouth.

"*Speak!*" Fist demanded.

"Yeah, tell us what you know!" added the Spring Chicken, stepping up beside her to take part in intimidating Hob. "That's why you're still alive, isn't it?"

"S-sorry!" Hob sputtered. "I was only saying I think the Captain's right. They *might* think twice before attacking." He paused to sort out his thoughts. "This so-called army of theirs, I'm sure it's nothing but a mismatched troop of goblins cobbled together from nearby hordes, marching north to Shadowguard. They're thugs and raiders, but they're not soldiers yet. None of them have fought a real battle in their lives. If the defenses hold, they might back down."

Captain Fist studied him carefully. "Perhaps," she said. "But then why come at all? That is what concerns me."

Hob had no answer for her. "I don't know," he sighed.

"He's holding out on us!" growled the Spring Chicken.

"I should hope not," said the Captain, staring at Hob, "or I may begin to doubt his usefulness."

The Spring Chicken grinned. He was practically licking his lips with anticipation.

Hob tried to think. "It just doesn't make sense," he muttered aloud. "I heard the Sorcerer order his troops to march *straight* to Shadowguard. They shouldn't be here."

The two humans stared at him incredulously.

"I mean, I don't think the Sorcerer's the type who likes to be disobeyed," Hob clarified. "The goblins wouldn't come here against his will."

The Spring Chicken stopped him there. "What do you mean, '*the Sorcerer?*'"

"Are you telling us the Sorcerer has *returned?*" demanded Captain Fist.

"Oh, yeah, I guess I am ..." said Hob, realizing the information *would* come as a shock. "He's back! And he sent crows to all the valley hordes telling us to have a Clobbering and send troops to Shadowguard an—"

"Shh!" Captain Fist held up a hand, silencing him. "Even if I believed you ... and I'm not saying I do ... that does not answer my question. Why have they come *here?*"

"That's what I'm trying to tell you," said Hob. "I *really don't know.*"

"Then we're getting nowhere!" shouted the Spring Chicken. "I say we kill him right now!" He drew his sword, and advanced on Hob.

Captain Fist stepped between them. "No!" she said. "If there is any truth to what he says, he may still be of use to us."

"But he's clearly lying!"

"We don't know that yet."

"Oh, come off it!"

The Spring Chicken grabbed Fist's arm, and tried to force her aside. It was a mistake. In a flash of black, the Captain had him pinned facedown on the stone wall-walk, with a knee jammed between his feathery shoulder blades and his wrist held back in a painful-looking grip.

"*Enough!*" she hissed. "You are here as a courtesy only. The goblin will be returned to you when I decide. And no sooner."

The Spring Chicken nodded, his cheek rubbing against the stones.

Hob tried not to smile. Though it was satisfying to see the chicken man put in his place, there was still a chance Hob would end up his prisoner, or worse, before the night was done.

"And if you ever lay a hand on me again," Fist warned, "I will toss you over the ..." But she trailed off.

BOOM! BOOM! BOOM!

Goblin war drums sounded in the pass, drawing the Captain's attention away from the Spring Chicken. She released him, stood up, and returned to the battlements. The Spring Chicken joined her a moment later, nursing a sore wrist. Hob peeked back through his crenel.

The goblins appeared below. They streamed out of the cloud sea, marching on foot up the top of the switchback road, looking like a dark river of armored bodies, swords, spears, axes, and pikes, flowing eerily up hill.

Turning away, the Captain scanned the watchtowers flanking the gate-platform until she spotted Lieutenant Buckler. Along with a number of city guards, he surveyed the defenses from atop one of the towers.

"You two," he said to a pair of guards, "go shore up that gap in the east line."

"Are we ready, Lieutenant?" Fist hollered up at him.

"As ready as we'll ever be, Captain!" Buckler hollered down.

"Good!" replied the Captain. "Then return to my side. We defend the guardroom together."

With that, she turned back to the Spring Chicken. His face was suddenly as pale as his feathers.

"You want to kill goblins, Chicken Man?" Fist said darkly. "You're about to get your chance."

BOOM, BOOM, BOOM! The war drums kept a steady beat.

Hob wouldn't have thought they could be so frightening, but somehow they were, like thunder approaching before a violent storm.

The goblins' numbers grew quickly as they climbed out of the mist and up the switchback road, filling the plateau before the city.

Hob remained standing at the battlements over the gate, his hands tied behind his back. Captain Fist stood beside him, Lieutenant Buckler and the Spring Chicken a step behind her.

The entire length of the wall now bristled with armed humans. The city guards were scattered along the front parapet, each section under the command of one of their royal counterparts. They stood armed and ready, waiting for what was to come. The townsfolk were lined up nervously behind them, outfitted with whatever they could find. For every *real* sword, spear, and shield in the crowd, there were two cooking-pot-helms, two broom-handle-pikes, a carving-knife-dagger, and a table-leg-club. One portly woman even wielded a crude mace, fashioned from an iron kettle strapped to a tree branch.

Hob spotted Marta the innkeeper and a gang of tough-looking patrons from the Headless Goblin posted not too far from the gate. At least *they* looked ready for a fight! They were all armed to the teeth with weapons from the rack in the inn's secret cellar.

Hob wondered, in passing, where Monty and Stella were. He'd been expecting them back hours ago. They might have been somewhere in the city, searching in vain for Edric and him. Or they might have been stuck outside, cut off by the goblins in the pass. Hob hoped not, for his sake as much as theirs. He was desperate for their help.

Again, he peeked through his crenel in the battlements. As the army closed in, it became obvious that it was a goblin pack like no other. The usual variety of shapes and sizes was gone, replaced by one dominant combination, big and brawny. *These* were fighters!

Finally, the front lines clattered to a stop a few paces back from the wall. Hob sank low behind his crenel, taking care to stay out of sight even as he continued to peek through. If the other goblins saw him there, it would only make matters worse.

In the center of the plateau, a gap appeared in the goblin ranks, breaking around a lone figure approaching the gate. Though the rest of the goblins were on foot, this one seemed to be riding a strange beast. The rider was too big for his mount, causing him to sway awkwardly with each step it took. Swaying with the rider was a huge black crow perched on his shoulder.

Only when this lead goblin broke through the army's front lines did Hob finally recognize him. It was *Brute!* He slowed to a stop at the head of the army, just before the gates of Valley Top.

Brute's mount turned out to be some sort of wild pig, woolly and brown, with a coarse mane running down its spine, and extremely long tusks jutting out from its snout. Mismatched armor plates hung from its back. Beads and decorations were woven into its fur. And iron bands connected its tusks to leather reins, which Brute held in hand.

"A *war-hog*," Hob whispered.

He'd never seen one before, but he'd heard them described in songs and stories. Found in the mountain forests bordering the valley, they were a species of monstrous pigs that goblins once rode to war.

It was said that some war-hogs grew bigger than bulls, but this one wasn't even five feet tall at the saddle. It struggled not to collapse under Brute's massive weight and that of its own makeshift armor. Hob wondered where the goblins had found the poor creature.

"What did you say?" asked Captain Fist, prying Hob from his ruminations.

"It's a war-hog," he repeated.

She didn't look impressed. "And what of the *goblin riding it?*" she pressed. "That is the sort of information you're here for."

"Oh," said Hob. "That's Brute. He's … trouble."

"Trouble?" asked Fist.

"Let's just say, I doubt *he'll* think twice before attacking."

Hob returned his attention to Brute. The mighty goblin dismounted, and stood before the gate. He had the war-hog beside him, the army at his back, and the crow still perched on his shoulder.

Hob noticed a roll of parchment clenched in the crow's beak. But before he could puzzle out what might be on it, another goblin pushed his way out of the crowd behind the war-hog. This one was *much smaller*. He stumbled, but quickly regained his footing. A few of his fellow troops sniggered. Ignoring them, he straightened his oversized helmet, and stood proudly at Brute's side.

"And that one's Snivel," Hob groaned. "Don't waste your time on him."

Hob was surprised to see Snivel there. Only the biggest, meanest goblins seemed to have earned places in the Sorcerer's army. Brute must have literally carried Snivel through the Clobbering for him to have made the cut.

For a moment, the human and goblin lines faced off in tense silence, bracing for what was to come. Then Captain Fist leaned out over the battlements and addressed Brute directly.

"Turn back now!" she warned. "Or face the full might of Valley Top!"

Her voice echoed across the plateau, sending a stir through the goblin ranks. Some of them were nervous.

Brute, however, wasn't nervous at all. "We'll turn back, once we've got what we've been sent for!"

He grabbed the roll of parchment from the crow's beak, unfurled it, and held it aloft. Edric's face stared up at everyone over the gate. It was one of the wanted posters!

"*The Prince!*" Brute bellowed. "We know he's in there! Hand him over, and we'll leave! Don't, and we'll flatten the city and everyone in it!"

A collective gasp rose up from the humans along the wall.

Hob slipped completely behind the battlements. Everyone nearby stared at him in shock, including Captain Fist. She grabbed him, and pulled him back from the edge of the wall, so they were both out of sight of the goblins below. She knelt, bringing them face to face.

"What is the meaning of this?" she hissed.

"*You* tipped them off, didn't you?" growled the Spring Chicken, rushing over to join them.

"How could I have?" Hob snapped. "I've been with Edric since we got here. Just ask him."

The trio turned to the guardroom. They saw Edric still inside, gagged and bound to his chair. The distressed look on his face told them he'd heard Brute's demands too.

"I do not need to ask," said the Captain, finally. "But if it was not you, then *how*? How did they get that poster? How do they know he's here?"

Hob wasn't sure. He understood why everyone suspected him; the goblins would've needed a spy inside the city to spot both a wanted poster *and* Edric himself. But how could any goblin have made it back to the army so quickly? Then it dawned on him.

"The crow!" Hob gasped. "The crow must have taken them the poster! Told them Edric was here! Told them the city was unprepared, open to attack!"

Once more, the humans stared at Hob incredulously. But he was sure he was right. Suddenly, he remembered the crows perched on the flag lines around the fountain in the marketplace. They'd flown off right after Edric's identity had been discovered! And they must have seen all the wanted posters in town! If even one of those crows had been the Sorcerer's pet—the one now sitting on Brute's shoulder—it could have flown a poster straight to the passing goblin army, told them of the Prince's whereabouts, and even delivered a message from its master.

"The Sorcerer has special crows that act as his messengers," Hob explained to Captain Fist. "Some must also be his *spies!* And that's one down there! I think, in one way or another, the Sorcerer ordered this attack! He must want Edric as a hostage! Or worse!"

Captain Fist stared at him in stunned silence. She pulled him close so their eyes locked. Her gaze was piercing. But, as much as Hob wanted to look away, he would not.

"Tell me the truth," she said.

"I am."

Fist stared a moment longer, and then released him. She stood, and strode back to the battlements.

"We will never surrender our Prince!" she called down to Brute and the goblin army. "We will fight you to the last!"

A nervous murmur rippled through the human line along the wall. Down on the plateau, the sound of shifting feet and clinking armor signaled the goblins were growing restless.

"Hear that, boys?" Brute hollered with glee. "They wanna fight!"

"*YEAHH!*" the goblins roared.

"So, what are we waitin' for?" Brute finished. "*ATTACK!*"

"*ATTACK!*" the goblins roared.

And just like that, the battle began. No level of resistance could have scared the goblins off. They were bound and bent on capturing Edric or destroying Valley Top.

As Captain Fist, Lieutenant Buckler, and the Spring Chicken prepared to meet the first wave of attackers, Hob returned to his crenel. The goblins streamed toward the wall in a howling, black mass.

While they had no ladders with them on their march, many hurled up large grappling hooks fixed to the ends of long ropes. The hooks caught in the battlements faster than the human defenders could throw them back down, and the goblins began to climb.

A team of goblins also attacked the gate below Hob. Some pried up the portcullis with strong arms, while others hustled forward carrying a heavy old log they'd found, and used it as a battering ram. *BANG! BANG! BANG!* The makeshift ram shook the oaken doors.

All around Hob, townsfolk rushed out of the tower archways and up to the battlements to drop rocks on the battering ram goblins. The rocks *clanged* off their helmets, sending half of them stumbling away dazed. The rest dropped the log and fled. The townsfolk cheered, and hurried back to their posts along the wall.

By then, the first goblin climbers had reached the top of their ropes.

Hob was helpless. His sword had been taken from him, and his hands were bound behind his back. He crouched behind the battlements, trying to stay out of sight and out of harm's way.

Luckily, the human defenders on the gate-platform drew all the attention. Captain Fist and Lieutenant Buckler sprang into action, crossing swords with every one of the goblins who climbed onto the platform, knocking a series of them back off the wall, and kicking down their shared grappling hooks. Hob had never imagined a pair of fighters could work so quickly and efficiently. They moved together with practiced ease, covering each other's blind spots and attacking in concert. The Captain, especially, made her opponents look as though they were standing still. For his part, the Spring Chicken rushed about, finally given an outlet for his rage, but never succeeded in reaching any goblin before the Captain or Lieutenant had already dispatched it.

Hob looked up and down the length of the wall through the archways in the watchtowers. The city guards at the front parapet met the goblins sword to sword. Scattered archers shot arrows into the sky. And brave towns-folk rushed forward to drop rocks on the ascending goblins. As the rocks struck helmet or breastplate, they sent many climbers crashing back into the throng. But more always rose to take their place. Soon, hundreds of goblin warriors were mounting the wall.

The city guards fought them valiantly and managed to knock a few more back down. But, eventually, the guards were overwhelmed and forced away from the parapet, allowing the goblins to pile onto the wall-walk.

Beside Hob, Captain Fist spun, kicked a goblin in the chest, and sent him screaming from the wall. When she turned away, ready to engage the next attacker, she found Lieutenant Buckler there instead. They had cleared the gate-platform for the moment.

"Take the Prince, and run," Buckler panted. "We'll hold them as long as we can!"

Without hesitation, Fist hurried for the guardroom.

Just as quickly, she stopped.

One look through the archway told Hob why. Edric's chair was empty, and his ropes lay split upon the floor. He was gone!

Hob searched the length of the wall for any sign of the Prince. But all he saw were signs of impending human defeat. The city guards could retreat no farther from the parapet, having backed into the lines of townsfolk behind them. The townsfolk brandished their makeshift weapons in an effort to look intimidating, though their faces betrayed their fear. And the goblins stalked forward, clutching their own crooked weapons, ready for a fight. The two sides were only a sword-length apart. In seconds, there would be bloodshed.

Then a voice cried out from somewhere above. "*Stop! I surrender!*"

Everyone froze.

Hob's eyes followed the voice to the top of the watchtower on his left. Edric stood there, perched on the battlements, an abandoned grappling hook caught in the crenel between his feet, and bewildered city guards lurking a few paces off to either side.

"*Hold!*" Brute cried. "It's him! It's the Prince!"

Both lines on the wall held. A confused silence settled over the battlefield, as everyone wondered what to do next.

Captain Fist broke it. "Grab him!"

The city guards tried to catch Edric, but they weren't fast enough. As they lunged, he dropped from the side of the tower.

Hob's stomach leapt into his throat. But as Edric fell, he caught the rope attached to the grappling hook. He swung to a stop halfway down the tower with his feet braced against the stones, out of reach of the guards above and the goblins below.

"If I turn myself over, you'll leave Valley Top unharmed?" Edric called down to Brute.

"*No!*" Fist shouted in horror. She tore across the wall-walk over the gate, into the archway in the left watchtower, and up the stairwell inside.

Buckler followed at her heels.

Everyone else anxiously awaited Brute's response. Taking care to remain hidden, Hob peeked through his crenel again, toward the spot where Brute still stood before the gate. Brute exchanged glances with several other large goblins gathered around him. Most of them nodded. A second later, Brute turned back to the Prince.

"We came for you, not the city!" Brute declared, clenching his jaw as he struggled to contain his disappointment at having to cut the battle short. "Orders 're orders!"

"Then, here I am," said Edric, allowing himself to slide the rest of the way down the rope.

As soon as he came within reach of the goblins below, they seized him and dragged him down into their midst. He vanished for a second, and then reappeared in the arms of two burly goblin warriors, who marched him straight over to Brute.

That was when Captain Fist emerged on the watchtower. It was all Lieutenant Buckler could do to keep her from swinging down the rope in a fatal attempt to go after Edric.

"No!" she screamed. "No!"

Brute smiled as the two goblins holding Edric stopped before him.

"Put him on the war-hog," Brute said. "And tie him up good and tight. We've got a long way to go."

The goblins worked fast. One held Edric in place on the war-hog. The other pulled out a rope, and tied Edric's hands behind his back, looping the rope through an iron ring on the back of his crude saddle. Finally, Brute took the war-hog's reins, turned, and began to lead it away across the plateau.

"MARCH!" he bellowed.

Once more, the army on the plateau parted before Brute and closed in behind him. And Hob, Fist, Buckler, and the rest of the humans over the gate could only watch as Brute, Edric, and the war-hog were swallowed up by the ranks.

At the same time, goblin attackers poured back over the battlements along the wall, rappelling down their ropes, and rejoining the great mass on the ground. And, with a great deal of clatter, the whole army managed an about face, marching off again down the switchback road. In minutes, the last lines had passed into the clouds and out of sight.

CHAPTER FIFTEEN

After the Goblins

Edric was gone. In his place, he left only crushing silence and stillness.

The night, by then many hours old, had taken on a harsh chill. Hob shivered, unable to so much as cross his arms for warmth with them tied behind his back. Yet, his mind was elsewhere. He couldn't make sense of what had happened, couldn't accept it. He felt sick, almost faint.

At some point, Captain Fist returned from the tower, stepping up to the battlements between Hob and the Spring Chicken. Lieutenant Buckler and the rest of the Royal Guards returned next, gathering behind her, anticipating her next command. But Fist said nothing. She just stood with her eyes fixed on the sea of shifting clouds below.

After a time, the city guards and townsfolk along the wall began to stir. The initial shock was wearing off, and they grew restless.

The Spring Chicken leaned out past the Captain to glower at Hob. Though he had enough sense to remain silent, his eyes spoke for him: *This was YOUR fault!*

Hob averted his gaze.

"*How?*" hissed Captain Fist, breaking her vigil at last.

She swept around to peer back into the guardroom. The broad archway at the front framed Edric's empty chair perfectly, almost mockingly. It was the only thing you could see in the dim light within.

"I freed him."

A figure stepped into the archway, facing Captain Fist. It was Lady Isobel! She had been hiding around the corner, just inside. In her hand was the knife she'd used to cut Edric's ropes. She dropped it, and it rattled on the stonework at her feet.

"He asked me to," Lady Isobel went on, stepping out onto the wall-walk. "I *had to!* For Valley Top! For my people! No more hiding up a tower. This city needs a leader."

Instinctively, Lieutenant Buckler and the other Royal Guards moved to arrest her.

Captain Fist stood still. She stared at Isobel, seething, but was forced to swallow the better part of her rage. "Stop!" she said, before Isobel was arrested. "This is the Lady of Valley Top. We shall not lay a hand on her."

Honor bound the Captain. She'd been up the tower; she knew who Isobel was. The Royal Guards had no clear authority to punish the Lady in her own city. It would have divided the Kingdom and done nothing to bring Edric back.

The Royal Guards retreated, forming a circle around Captain Fist, Hob, the Spring Chicken, and Lady Isobel.

Meanwhile, the voices of the townsfolk rose up:

"The Lady of Valley Top?"

"Can it be?"

"The curse is broken?"

Those within earshot were quick to abandon their posts along the wall. They squeezed in through the archways in the watchtowers above the gate, and gathered behind the perimeter set by the Royal Guards. All were eager to catch a glimpse of their mysterious Lady, suddenly free.

"The curse *has* been broken!" declared Lady Isobel, from the center of the crowd. "By that goblin!" She pointed to Hob.

This declaration caught Hob off guard. His instinct was to look away, as if he were being accused of something unpleasant. It took him a second to realize what she had said.

"Oh, yeah," he admitted. "I guess it kind of was."

Low gasps and hushed chatter emanated from the crowd.

"Foolish children," growled the Captain, turning her back on the scene. "Reckless."

Again, she stared out into the clouds where her Prince had disappeared. A change had come over her. She leaned forward, almost hunched, on the battlements. Though she remained proud and strong, she seemed deflated— like a stately flag on a windless day.

Hob wouldn't have thought it possible, but he actually felt for her. After all, Hob too mourned Edric. The Prince had given his life to save the city—a heroic act. But Hob couldn't see the glory in it, only the loss. Edric had spared Valley Top a single battle, but in the process had surrendered his life, his quest, and possibly the larger war. Fist was right; he *had* been reckless.

A disturbing thought entered Hob's mind then, unwelcome and unbidden. Had Edric's sacrifice actually been a desperate means of escape—a way to go out a hero, instead of a "screw up," as he'd feared? Had it all been about the loss of the book? If so, then Hob deserved the Spring Chicken's scornful glances—it *had* been his fault!

More secret doubts followed. Was Hob every bit the evil monster the humans thought him to be—and perhaps worse, for not recognizing it? In his selfishness, had he sent Edric straight into the clutches of the Sorcerer? Was there any way for him to set things right?

"You have to let me go!" Hob blurted out, before he could stop himself.

Roused from their chatter, all the humans turned to stare at him. By the looks on their faces, they seemed to think he was either rude for interrupting them—or completely *insane.* Hob didn't care which. His words were meant for Captain Fist alone. It was to her he would have to plead his case.

"I don't mean GO go," he said, rather unhelpfully. "I mean, GO save Edric! I can do it. Or at least I can try. I'll get closer than any of you. They'll see you. They'll smell you. You'll never get anywhere near him. I'm the only chance he's got!"

At first, Hob's claims were met with silence. There seemed to be a collective holding of breath as everyone waited for the Captain's reply. Fist straightened up, and stared down at Hob, once more the imposing figure he'd come to expect. Her dark eyes seemed to see everything and reveal nothing. Hob had no idea what she was thinking ... but she wasn't saying "no."

"I'll join the army," he continued. "I can still catch up, if I leave now." He paused, suddenly realizing the inherent, *fatal* risk involved. "I-I just need something to hide my face. If the other goblins recognize me, they'll kill me."

More silence. Captain Fist continued to stare. Hob met her gaze stubbornly. If he wavered at all, she wouldn't believe him.

It was Fist who broke. She knelt, drew her knife, and cut the ropes that bound Hob's hands. Then she stood and scanned the crowd. Her eyes stopped on a small, scrappy figure—a young man who had answered the call to arms in what were clearly a few pieces of hand-me-down armor. His helmet, breastplate, and shield were all ancient and beat-up, but they would suit a goblin nicely.

"You! Your armor, now!" Fist demanded. "Give it to him."

The boy obeyed without question, stepping out of the crowd, through the ring of guards, and toward Hob. Off came his helmet, revealing shaggy brown hair and ruddy cheeks. By the looks of it, the boy was even younger than Prince Edric.

He dropped the helmet into Hob's arms. It was basically a rusty bucket with the lower half of a visor still attached. The half-visor was rusted in place, permanently covering the wearer below the eyes. It would disguise Hob's face well.

The boy then set down his shield, and began fumbling with the straps of his breastplate.

"Here, let me help you," said Isobel, stepping in.

"Thanks," mumbled the boy, obviously surprised to be receiving help from the legendary Lady of Valley Top.

"You can't be serious!" snapped the Spring Chicken, looking on. "You're not setting him *free?*" He raised his sword, and tried again to push past the Captain to get to Hob.

Fist held the Spring Chicken back with an outstretched arm, but Hob flinched just the same—nearly dropping his new helmet.

The Spring Chicken raged. "That creature's not going to save the Prince! He's going to run away! You'll never see either of them, ever again!"

"It is possible," admitted the Captain, her voice measured but forceful. "Still, it seems he did help Lady Isobel. And I fear he might be right. He's now our only hope."

"No, I won't let you. He belongs to *me!*" The Spring Chicken tried desperately to force his way past the Captain.

The Captain grappled with him. "*Not* until I'm done with him!"

"Be done with him then!"

The Spring Chicken finally broke loose, lunging at Hob, and raising his sword for a killing blow.

Tonk! This time, Hob did drop his helmet.

A second later, it was all over. With a sharp kick to the back of his knee, Captain Fist took out the Spring Chicken's leg. He stumbled before he could strike. In a flurry, he twisted around, and slashed at her. Her hand shot out and seized his arm at the wrist, arresting his sword mid-swing. Then with her other hand, she grabbed the feathers of his chicken suit, and flipped him over the battlements.

With a shriek, the Spring Chicken tumbled down the front of the city wall. *Plop!* He landed in a mound of horse manure piled beside the gate. He was lucky; the manure had broken his fall and spared him serious injury. But he was left stuck upside down in dung, with only his skinny chicken legs poking out, flailing up at the sky. Hob craned his head through his crenel for a better look. The Spring Chicken would bother him no more.

"Here," said Lady Isobel.

Hob turned to see her approaching with her arms full of the boy's donated gear. She strapped the breastplate around Hob's torso, and looped the shield over his arm.

"You may also need these," said Captain Fist, turning to Hob with the items she'd confiscated from him in the castle yard. In one hand, she held his goggles. In the other hand, she held his little sword, wrapped in its scabbard and sword belt.

Lady Isobel took the items from the Captain one at a time, strapping the sword belt around Hob's breastplate, so the sword and scabbard hung at his hip, and strapping the goggles around his head, leaving them flipped up on top. Finally, she picked up the rusty helmet, and tried to fit it on him. It slid neatly over his goggles, but became stuck on his large ears.

"Ooo! Ooo!" Hob squeaked.

"Sorry!" said Lady Isobel. "It just needs a bit of a twist."

"*Oooooo!*"

As Isobel worked the helmet down the rest of the way, Captain Fist took charge.

"Prepare to ride, men!" she ordered the Royal Guards. "We follow the high ridge road from here to the Riven Gate. We must open the Gate as soon as the army crosses the ravine. If Prince Edric *is* rescued, the goblins may try doubling back to take revenge on the city."

At last, Lady Isobel had Hob's helmet on him. She stepped back, nodding her approval. The helmet was too tight, leaving Hob's ears folded down uncomfortably inside. Still, all that could be seen of his face were two big eyes peering out of the darkness between the visor and the brim. This, in conjunction with his breastplate—which hung like a giant bell from his shoulders to his knees—meant he was well covered, even if he didn't look very *inspiring*.

Hob was ready to go.

Captain Fist turned her attention back to him. "Find him," she commanded.

Finally, Lady Isobel knelt down, and kissed him on the forehead of his helmet. "Thanks again, nice goblin," she said. "And good luck."

CHAPTER SIXTEEN

Into the Clouds

Hob ran heedlessly down the switchback road from the city into the mountain pass, his ill-fitting armor jouncing and jangling as he went. Soon, great bands of mist swept across his path—luminous in the pale moonlight—and he came to a stop on the shoreline of the vast cloud sea. It churned past the mountain, flooding the road ahead.

Tentatively, Hob took his first step into the clouds. They engulfed him, becoming fog, endless and all encompassing. Even inside, their vapors glowed with pale moonlight, brightening up the night, and yet hiding more from him than night ever could.

Alone and out of view, Hob could have abandoned his mission right then, just as the Spring Chicken had predicted. He could have turned and fled into the mountains where no one would ever find him. But he wasn't going to. Not while Edric needed him.

He ran on.

The fog grew thicker and thinner in waves, as Hob hurtled down the rest of the switchback road and south into the pass. Mysterious shapes swam in the haze. Towering mountainsides, rock outcroppings, and scraggy trees were all reduced to shadows. It was a world of ghosts.

Finally, Hob heard the percussive clatter of the goblin march growing louder in the distance, signaling he was catching up. After a while, it echoed all around. *THRUMP-THRUMP, THRUMP-THRUMP.*

Then, new phantoms materialized ahead. Shadowy figures, hunched and heavy, tromped up and down in the mist, passing no more than ten abreast between the murky mountain slopes to either side. Hob had reached the army's rear-guard. Though he couldn't see very far, he knew the army stretched out almost endlessly before them, marching south down the pass.

THRUMP-THRUMP, THRUMP-THRUMP.

Was it the march or Hob's heart that pounded so? He could feel the blood coursing through his veins. And, though the air was cool, his skin felt clammy with sweat.

After escaping the Gobble Downs, he'd hoped never to see another goblin again. Yet, there he was, about to venture into the heart of a whole army of them.

Hob slowed his pace, but didn't turn back. Instead, he crept to within a few yards of the trailing goblin ranks.

Taking a deep breath, he shook himself loose. For his plan to work, the other goblins would have to believe he was one of them. He would have to look the part. He drew his sword, raised his shield, hunched his back, and stuck out his elbows.

Then something else occurred to him; he'd have to smell the part too! He gave his armpit a quick sniff and recoiled. It had a proper goblin stink to it. Luckily, Hob had been too distracted to bathe since fleeing the Gobble Downs. He decided that if he survived the night, a wash would be his first order of business the next morning.

Finally, he hurried forward, and fell in at the back of the army.

"Oi!" growled a husky goblin, as Hob shuffled up beside him. "Where'd you come from?"

Hob panicked. "Uh ... well, the fog, I guess ..." he stammered. "Which is to say ... Where'd *you* come from?" He growled that last part, in his *goblin-iest* voice, and pointed his sword.

The big fellow merely shrugged, as if to say *fair enough*, and then refocused his attention ahead.

Hob didn't linger there. He knew Edric—the Sorcerer's prize—would be at the center of the army, where he'd be hardest to reach. So, with muscles tensed, shield squared, and sword tucked firmly at his side, Hob scuttled ahead, plowing through the narrow space between the two goblins in front of him.

The interior of the march proved disorganized at best, full of goblins bumping, shoving, advancing, and falling back.

Being small and sprightly, Hob found every opening that presented itself in the chaos. He ducked, dodged, and darted through a fog-bound obstacle course of tromping legs, clanking armor, and swaying swords and shields.

Several times, he thought he saw familiar faces from the Gobble Downs, but he didn't stop to be sure. What mattered was that none of them seemed to recognize *him*.

Though most of the goblin warriors towered around him, Hob also encountered a few smaller goblins nestled among the ranks, who hadn't been visible from his distant vantage point above the gate. While these little goblins made Hob's own stature seem less conspicuous, they also frightened him. Each was a jittery blur of fangs, spiked armor, and wild eyes. Hob supposed any small goblin who'd made it through the Clobbering was bound to be extra mean—if not completely crazy.

Hob was fleeing one of these little terrors, when he ran into a much larger goblin.

"Watch it!" snarled the great hulk, grabbing Hob by the shoulder.

Hob thought fast. He growled and hopped madly from leg to leg, bashing sword against shield. If he could seem half as dangerous and unpredictable as the other goblins his size, the big fellow might just leave him alone.

It worked. The goblin backed off with an apologetic grunt, and Hob went on his way.

For more than two hours, Hob worked his way forward like this, until the rear-guard was finally behind him, and he was closing in on the middle ranks. Then the army reached the ravine. As the road constricted and snaked down between the rocks, it jammed up the goblins, halting Hob's progress.

Suddenly, he could do nothing but keep his shield squared in front of him and shuffle along with the rest of the pack, trying to hold his position.

As he stepped onto the bridge at the bottom of the ravine, the rocks receded into the mist. It was as if the bridge were floating there, unanchored on either end. Hob could hear the shallow stream trickling underneath, but could see only a short stretch of its dark waters on either side. Up in the western mountains, he thought he may have glimpsed the faintest specter of the Riven Gate, but it was likely just his imagination.

After the road climbed back out of the ravine, it widened again, allowing Hob to continue advancing. It also began to curve steadily eastward around the gravelly, scree-covered slopes of the great three-peaked mountain that bordered the lower half of the pass. All three peaks were now lost in cloud.

Eventually, the goblin army came around to the south side of the mountain, where the pass straightened and descended due east into the valley. It was then that the Riven Gate opened.

The goblins couldn't see it happen. They'd left the ravine behind in the cloud. But they heard it—felt it! A tremor shook the earth, sending bits of debris *clacking* down from on high, and forcing them to stop and shield their heads. A dull *screech* of metal on stone split the air. The *roar* of rushing water echoed down the pass.

Hob alone understood the source of the phenomenon. The Royal Guards had released the massive counterweights on either side of the dam, which had, in turn, hauled up the ever-steel gate in its moorings, and flooded the ravine. There was no going back.

Hob took advantage of the goblins' confusion to make up more ground. He hurried on while the others stalled.

"Move it, you lugs! Dawn's a-coming!" came the call to resume the march.

Hob recognized the voice at once. It was Brute's! Though Hob couldn't see him, he sounded close by.

"That's it! *MARCH!*"

The goblins began shuffling forward again.

Hob pressed on with new determination, swerving around them, squeezing past them, and moving in the direction of Brute's voice. If Hob could find Brute, he was sure to find Edric as well!

Soon, Hob fell in behind a wall of broad-shouldered goblins, all square to each other like enormous bricks marching in step. He got stuck there for a moment. Then, finally, a crack opened between them. He prepared to dash through, but checked himself at the last second. Framed in the space between the goblins was Edric, swaying along, slumped and beleaguered, atop the war-hog. His hands remained bound behind him, tied to the iron ring on the back of his crude saddle.

The sight filled Hob with hope—and *dread.* Brute and a posse of other thuggish goblins guarded Edric, forming two lines, one on either side of the war-hog, with Snivel at the beast's rear end. They marched along as if in their own private parade, backs straight, chests out, and spears held high.

"*CAW! CAW!*"

Hob looked up. The Sorcerer's crow was there too. It drifted languidly through the mists above, rarely bothering to beat its wings, a dark and watchful spirit at the edge of sight.

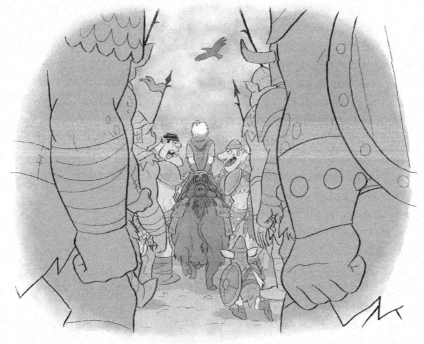

The goblins argued over what to do with Edric.

"Why *can't* we kill him?" demanded a hulking mountain goblin with a face like a shark. "We've got the troll with us. He could give the boy the chop right now!"

The shark-faced goblin was almost as big as Brute, so his words carried almost as much weight. He and Brute led the escort, opposite each other at the front of the war-hog.

The only goblin ahead of them was the old fellow who led the beast by the reins. With his hunched back and protruding jaw, he looked a great deal like a war-hog himself. "I'm with Gnasher!" said the war-hog keeper. "Think how happy the Master'll be, when he finds out we didn't just capture the boy, we *killed* him!"

"You numskulls!" countered a gorilla-browed goblin, marching behind Brute. "He won't be happy. He'll kill *us!*"

"Right!" Brute declared. "The Master said to bring him the boy *alive*. So that's what we're gonna do!"

"*Yeah!*" added Snivel.

"Oh! 'Cause you're the Master's *best buddy*, and you know *just* what he wants?" Gnasher grumbled, scowling at Brute with his shark-like face.

"No! I'm *in charge*, so we do what I *say!*" said Brute, glaring back at Gnasher over the top of the war-hog.

Edric reclined in his saddle, trying to stay out of the line of fire.

Hob felt terrible. He had no clue how to help his friend. Edric's guards were large and agitated, and there was no getting around them.

"I don't 'member the Sorcerer puttin' you in charge!" Gnasher protested. "I don't 'member him puttin' *anyone* in charge!"

"He's right, the Master didn't say," confirmed the war-hog keeper.

"So maybe *I'm* in charge!" Gnasher declared.

"Fat chance!" scoffed Brute.

"What's that?" said Gnasher.

"He called you fat," said Snivel.

"I'm not fat!" said Gnasher. "*He's* fat!"

"Hah!" Brute laughed. "I'm all muscle! Lemme show ya!" He drew back a fist, intending to put it straight through Gnasher's face.

It was proof of Hob's desperation that he actually wanted Brute to follow through. A brawl might have created an opening to get to Edric—as long as Edric *survived* long enough, that was. Hob prepared to make a break for it.

Then the ranks came to an abrupt halt, causing the goblins to crash into one another, and distracting Brute and Gnasher from their fight.

Brute straightened up, and raised a palm. "Hold!" he shouted.

Ahead, Hob could just make out the long line of the goblin army turning off the eastward road into the valley, and doubling back northward up the scree-covered slopes of the great three-peaked mountain. The line ascended into the mist.

"This is the spot!" Brute finished. He drew up a cattle horn trumpet, which hung at his hip, and blew into it. *BAROOOM! BAROOOM!* Then he turned to the rest of Edric's escort. "If we don't get back into the tunnels by sun up, it won't matter *who's* in charge!"

Even Gnasher nodded in agreement.

Only then did Hob realize, with horror, what he should have known all along. The goblins were headed underground!

CHAPTER SEVENTEEN

Strange Apparitions

Surrounded by the brick-like goblins trailing Edric's escort, Hob scrambled up the steep lower slopes of the three-peaked mountain, through mist and over loose, gravelly scree. Hundreds of small stones slid and shifted with every step the goblins took, erasing their footprints as fast as they made them. This, Hob guessed, made the three peaks an ideal place to hide a large tunnel entrance.

The Sorcerer had ordered his troops to stick to the tunnels under Yore wherever possible on their march. In fact, his crow had likely found them in one of the nearby mountain tunnels, intercepting them as they traveled north from their gathering place at High-Hole toward Shadowguard. And if a tunnel had brought them as far as the three-peaked mountain, it explained why they'd been able to appear nearly halfway up the pass with so little warning.

Now, they were headed back below, with Edric in their clutches. Hob cursed his lack of foresight. If he and Edric were taken underground, there would be no escape for either of them. The passages would be too tight, too congested. And it would be impossible to tell where they'd come out again. For all Hob knew, some combination of ancient tunnels might take them all the way to Shadowguard!

Not far up the slope from Hob, the war-hog was putting up a fuss. It stamped and squealed, slipping on scree, and causing Edric to wobble precariously on its back. The beast had to be tugged at and prodded by Edric's guards, until it finally got so high up that it became afraid to go back down. Only then did it begin to cooperate.

Hob followed the whole escort closely. Despite his bulky armor, he had little difficulty keeping up with the big, clumsy goblins around him, as they labored up the slope.

Eventually, the roots of two of the mountain's three peaks appeared in the cloud ahead.

Between these peaks, a steep gorge opened up. It climbed between diverging walls of rock and into the mist. The army funneled up it, no more than five goblins abreast.

The climb with the army proved harrowing for Hob. The gorge was dizzyingly steep and full of rubble and melting snow. A fall backward would have been deadly. So too would have been capture by Edric's guards. Even in the gorge, the same two lines still flanked the war-hog, led by Brute and Gnasher, trailed by Snivel, and watched over by the crow.

Out of necessity, Hob followed them more closely than ever. The brick-like goblins were soon forming their familiar barricade alongside him, and if they overtook him in those tight confines, he'd never get back through. Hob yielded most of the gorge to them, and took to scaling the massive snowdrifts and fallen boulders that lined its edges and ascended its walls.

A fork appeared mid-way up the gorge, at the crux where all three mountain peaks met. Between the peaks, the main gorge veered east, while a much steeper, tighter channel continued almost straight north. The goblins turned east with the main gorge.

Hob made the turn with them, and kept picking his way up over the snowdrifts and boulders, hoping that some brilliant plan to free Edric would spring to mind. But none did.

Then time ran out.

Without warning and with much clatter, the march drew to a halt again. Peering ahead, Hob saw the cause of the commotion. A narrow path split from the floor of the gorge and cut up through the rocks along the south wall. The line of goblins followed the path, vanishing not into the cloud, but into a towering crevice in the mountainside. They had reached the tunnel entrance.

The mass of goblins began to squeeze in around the base of the narrow path. Soon, Hob would get cut off from Edric, and they'd both be forced underground. Hob became frantic. He had to do something—right away!

"*SQUEEE!*"

At the first sight of dark tunnel, the war-hog resisted again. It twisted itself around at the start of the narrow path, and was soon taking up all the space between the rocks. Its keeper heaved on the reins, trying to get the beast back in line, while everyone behind it was forced to stand and wait.

This was the opening Hob had been waiting for, and he knew it would last a matter of seconds at most.

He glanced around in desperation, considering his options. He'd been hoping to find some way of delivering both himself and Edric to safety, but it was impossible. Finally, Hob understood. There was only one way to make things right. He could give Edric a chance to escape—but only by giving up his own.

Hob edged closer to the struggling war-hog, squeezing through a narrow gap between the rock to his left and the brick-like goblins to his right. He was suddenly calm, entirely focused on what he had to do. He let his shield fall to the ground. He tightened his grip on his sword. And he gave his head a quick shake, to check that his helmet remained on snug. It was imperative that his face stay hidden. Timing would be everything, and if his identity caused the goblins to catch on a second too soon, or Edric to hesitate a second too long, all would be lost.

Hob then crept up behind Snivel at the war-hog's rear end. The beast had been subdued and straightened out again, and was about to be hauled up the path to the tunnel. This was as close as Hob would get. He crouched down low, took a deep breath, and lunged!

It all happened in a matter of seconds. Hob shoved Snivel aside and leapt into the air. He landed on the rump of the war-hog, dug his fingers into its fur, and pulled himself into a standing position behind Edric. He raised his sword over the Prince's head, and let out a loud war cry.

"DIE, HUMAN!" Hob screamed. He hadn't planned on saying anything. It just came out. A last second stroke of genius, and luck.

"*SQUEEE!*" The war-hog panicked again, kicking and bucking once more.

This surprised its keeper, who lost hold of the reins. The rest of the escort recoiled from the rampaging beast.

Somehow, Hob managed to keep from falling just long enough to act. *Swish!* He brought down his blade. By design, it missed Edric's body and found its true mark, the rope between his hands. The rope burst apart.

At the same time, Brute's spear swung in from the side, and its wooden shaft connected with Hob's breastplate. *CRACK!* A shockwave rattled through steel, flesh, and bone. The war-hog kept running. And Hob dropped from its back.

Hob hit the ground, winded and in pain. Only his big, folded-down ears kept the helmet from flying off his head. Still, he kept his wits. He gave his sword a quick flick, as though the impact had jarred it from his hand, and sent it skittering across the dirt.

A second later, Edric landed crouched in the sword's path. It slid to a stop before him, and he seized it—just as Hob knew he would. Sword in hand, the Prince exploded to his feet.

The rest was up to him.

Hob watched from the ground as Edric fought. *Swish! Clank! Shwing!* Goblins rushed in from all sides, and Edric skillfully parried their blows. But they didn't back down, and he was soon surrounded. Even free of his bonds, escape would not be easy.

"You idiot!" Brute hollered, not at Edric, but at Hob. Brute stomped toward him, casting aside his spear, and clenching and unclenching his fists. "Who do you think you *are*, takin' a swing at the Sorcerer's prize? I'll wring your scrawny neck!"

Hob crawled backward along the ground, but came up against a rock. He had nowhere to go. Brute reached down with a giant hand, jamming his meaty fingers into the visor of Hob's helm. Hob was about to be unmasked!

Then—*whump!*—Brute got shouldered aside.

"Leave him alone!" growled Gnasher, taking Brute's place above Hob. "He's a *hero!*"

A second later, Brute tackled Gnasher outright. They slammed into the ground in front of Hob, and began pounding each other.

Hob was distracted from the fight by another loud, "*squeee!*" The frightened war-hog continued to buck, even as its keeper regained hold of its reins.

Edric, who was caught in a constricting knot of goblins, heard the noise as well. Noticing his momentary distraction, two goblins attacked. Edric moved fast, ducking the club of the first, while batting away the sword of the second. Then he rolled free between them.

Edric broke into a sprint, and launched himself at the war-hog. He caught hold, clambered quickly onto the saddle, and balanced there, standing, knees bent.

With one swing of his sword, he cut the beast's reins. It fled its keeper again, charging away from the tunnel and scattering Edric's attackers.

Unfortunately, the war-hog soon came up against the wall of brick-like goblins. The line did not break, forcing the animal to turn and run in circles. Edric was stuck. Goblins closed in from both sides—though, hesitantly now, for fear of catching one of the war-hog's flailing hooves.

Hob's view of the scene was abruptly blocked. Brute had shaken off

Gnasher, and now stood over Hob again. Once more, his meaty fingers reached for Hob's helm. Once more, Hob thought he was doomed.

"*caw! caw!*"

Somewhere out of sight, the crow sounded the alarm.

"Big guy!" said Snivel, tugging at Brute's armor and distracting him. "He's gettin' away!"

Brute turned to see Snivel pointing frantically at the Prince.

Edric was just about to be pulled down off the war-hog, when he sprang from the beast's back. He flew over the outstretched arms of the nearby goblins, and landed on one of the rocks at the base of the gorge's north wall. He teetered there, toes on the edge.

"*caw!*" The crow shot at him out of the mist, trying to knock him back into the arms of the goblins.

Edric twisted to avoid it, and threw himself forward onto the rock. From his knees, he looked up.

Beginning where he lay, a pile of massive boulders ascended the wall of the gorge in steep steps. They towered over him, disappearing into the haze. Edric turned, stood, and swung his sword to drive back the goblins. Then he climbed for higher ground.

Brute growled. It took all the willpower he had, but he let go of Hob in order to chase Edric.

"get him!" Brute roared, running, and launching himself up the boulder pile.

"Yeah, get him!" yipped Snivel, who elected to stay put on the ground and send others up the rocks in his place. "Up there! That way!"

More and more goblins began to climb.

Hob jumped to his feet. Miraculously, he'd been given a chance to escape! He'd done all he could to free Edric. Waiting for Brute to come back and pummel him would do no further good. He turned to run. But a hand quickly clamped down on his arm.

"C'mon! Let's finish the job!" Gnasher growled, hoisting Hob up onto his back. "Let's *kill the human!*"

Buffeted between massive armored bodies, Hob and Gnasher ascended the boulder pile. Hob could just make out Edric high above. The Prince hauled himself up rock after rock, with the crow diving and pecking at his back, and goblins surging after him.

Edric crossed swords with a goblin, beating him back, and sent another crashing down the rocks with a well-placed kick to the head. Then he hurried on.

The goblins pushed and shoved as they climbed, and one elbowed Gnasher right in the side. As Hob fought to keep his grasp on Gnasher's swaying shoulders, he lost sight of Edric. By the time he looked up again, the Prince was gone.

Edric reappeared moments later, rushing out on top of a tall turret of natural stone that crowned the boulder pile. Above this rocky crag, there stood only a shadowy cliff face, sheer and unscalable, where the boulders had fractured from the mountainside. It was a dead end.

A great mound of melting snow twisted up around the crag, having gathered over the winter in a crevice between the back of the crag and the cliff face. Goblins crashed in around the snow mound and fought their way up it, vanishing into the crevice.

"C'mon!" Gnasher cheered. "Now, we've got him!"

He knocked aside everyone in his path as he climbed the last few boulders, sloshed up the snow mound, and tried to force his way into the goblin-filled crevice. However, in the push to get inside, someone shoved Gnasher back, and he lost his footing on the slippery slope.

As Gnasher scrambled to recover, this time Hob *chose* to lose his grasp. He dropped, slid down the snow mound, rolled off a ledge, and landed on a boulder a few feet below. Suddenly, he was on his hands and knees, lost amid the legs of the many goblins now stuck at the base of the crag.

It took Hob a moment to shake off the pain and dizziness that accompanied his fall. By the time he looked up again, Gnasher had gone on without him.

Hob stood, and returned his attention to the crag. It was framed perfectly in the gap between the heads of the goblins towering around him. Its top was fractured into a series of ascending stone steps, and Hob could see Edric retreating toward its peak, the dark crow circling above. Brute emerged next, rushing out of the crevice and onto the rock, followed by many more goblins.

Brute stalked straight toward Edric, sword drawn, while the other goblins encircled them. Soon, Edric was trapped at the peak of the crag. He brandished his sword to keep the goblins at bay, but it was no use.

Brute swung his sword in a great vertical arc, forcing Edric to hurl up his own to meet it. *CRASH!* Their blades rattled and locked. With Edric's weapon suddenly occupied, he was open to capture. The circle of goblins closed in on him like a noose.

Hob felt sick. He wouldn't be able to attempt another rescue; Brute and the others would be watching for him. This had been his one chance, and it had failed.

Then a familiar voice cried out. "EDRIC! LOOK UP!"

It was Stella! Her voice carried on the wind, far too loudly and clearly to be natural. It sounded a little like the Sorcerer's, except it wasn't inside Hob's head. Hob thought maybe she'd placed a spell on it.

Everyone froze and looked toward the cry, including Brute and Edric. It had come from the west—back down the gorge.

As Hob turned, he saw its source at once, high up between the mountain walls, taking shape in the mist as it approached. For a second, he thought it was just another trick of the clouds, the last and greatest of the night's apparitions. Then, there it was, suddenly real, sweeping down over his place in the crowd—a great wooden *airship!*

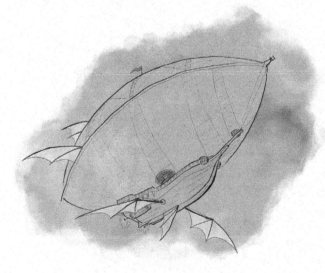

It looked much like a regular sailing ship, with a few key alterations. Extending from its sides were two bat-like wings fashioned of timber and canvas. Mounted at its stern were two massive air-propellers. And instead of sails over its deck, it had a great canvas balloon.

Once it stabilized, the airship threw its propellers into reverse, and began to drift as slowly as possible right over the crag.

Hob had read about airships before, but none had been seen for a hundred years! He wondered where this one had come from.

A dark figure bailed over the railing of the ship's deck. A *gnome!* The little fellow wore a leather harness attached to a long rope that unfurled from the ship. Beard wagging, he tucked himself into a tight dive. Then—*crack!*—his rope went taut, sending him swinging toward the spot where Edric stood cornered atop the crag.

A collective gasp escaped the goblin onlookers, all still frozen in shock and amazement.

Unfortunately, Edric couldn't reach out for the gnome, because his sword remained locked with Brute's.

"*CAW!*" The crow swooped toward the gnome, swiping at him with sharp claws. The gnome managed to swat the crow away, but, in doing so, he sent himself spinning on his rope. *Whoosh!* The gnome spun right past Edric.

Seeing his chance, Brute threw his whole weight on his sword. Edric's blade shook, and his arms began to buckle. He took a small step backward to brace himself, but Brute had claimed the advantage. Edric wouldn't be able to hold him off much longer.

The ship continued its slow drift, now centered over the crag. On the far side, the gnome spiraled through the air, reached the apex of his swing, and fell pendulum-like back toward his target.

"*CAW!*" The crow streaked at him again. But this time the gnome was ready. At the last second, he threw up his boots and struck the crow with both heels. *HOOF!* In a puff of black feathers, the bird was gone, spiraling limply down into the mist. *Whoosh!* The gnome was gone again too, sailing right past Edric.

"Get him, you lugs!" Brute roared at the goblins around him.

But they were still stupefied.

The gnome swung out past the near side of the crag, and then fell back, while the airship drifted out past the far side.

Brute bore down on his blade.

Lacking the strength to drive him off, Edric trembled, about to break.

Hob's breath caught in his throat.

Then, without warning, Edric pulled his own sword away, and lurched to the side. It worked! With nothing left resisting his weight, Brute crashed forward in heap on the crag's top step.

Seeing this, the other goblins finally shook off their stupor, and rushed at Edric. But before they could nab him, Edric sheathed his sword, hopped on Brute's back, and launched himself into the air.

Whoosh! Edric caught the flying gnome mid-swing, wrapping both arms around him and grasping his leather harness with both hands. Suddenly, he and the gnome were soaring away, leaving the goblins behind.

The goblins all gaped, Hob included. He watched in awe as the airship retreated into the mist, Edric and the gnome still swaying beneath it. It kept its eastward course, rising and picking up speed as its propellers came out of reverse, churning the cloud. At once, it seemed unreal again, as if it had never been there at all, a mysterious phantasm, spiriting Edric off to another world.

Then it was gone.

Although Hob was sad at the loss of his friend, he smiled to himself. At least he had helped make things right.

"Let me at him!" roared Gnasher, as he burst out of the crowd at the peak of the crag. He stopped. "Huh? Where is he? Where's the human?"

Instead of finding the Prince there, Gnasher found Brute. Brute got up and socked him right in the nose. Gnasher flopped backward into the goblins behind him, knocking several of them over, and setting off a chain reaction. A terrible brawl erupted atop the crag!

Hob turned to go. Eventually all involved would remember the mysterious little goblin who was *really* to blame for Edric's escape—and he didn't want to be there when they did.

Slipping quietly out of the distracted crowd, Hob dropped onto an unoccupied boulder. He took a deep breath, feeling like he was coming up for air after a long dive.

From there, he descended over rocks and snowdrifts, working his way westward down the steep wall of the gorge. It felt as if he were floating. With nowhere to go and no one to miss him, all he could do was keep moving. He would return to the mountain pass, and then head into the wilds alone.

As Hob reached the floor of the gorge, he took cover behind a boulder, and peeked out. The last lines of the goblin army had already passed. They were mere shadows in the fog a good distance up the gorge. Hob could still hear them muttering, though.

"They're sayin' the boy escaped!"

"They're sayin' he was taken by a *ghost ship!*"

"The humans tricked us!"

"We should go back and flatten their city!"

"That'd teach 'em for trickin' us with their ghost ships!"

"Sure would!"

Hob had to move. If the goblins did try doubling back for revenge on Valley Top, the flooded ravine would stop them. But there was nothing to save *him* from their wrath. He had to get as far away as possible.

Slipping out from behind the boulder, Hob took off. He bounded down the gorge as fast as his short legs and oversized armor would allow. But when he reached the midway point—the fork where the narrow northern channel branched off from the main gorge—a huge, dark shape leapt out of the rocks ahead of him.

SLAM! Hob ran right into it. Massive hands lifted him off the ground, and multiple faces slid down into view.

"We knew we smelled a little goblin …" whispered the heads of Carl the Troll.

CHAPTER EIGHTEEN

Before the Dawn

The cloud was thinning and the sky behind it growing lighter. A rising wind howled at their backs, sweeping waves of mist over them as they picked their way up the rocks—Carl the Troll carrying Hob under one massive arm.

Hob struggled meekly, but only so that in his last moments he could tell himself, *I tried.*

He knew it was futile. Not only was the troll too strong, but Hob had given up his only weapon, and had lost his only means of protection. All he had left were his ordinary clothes and his goggles—still flipped up on his forehead, where he'd worn them under his helmet. Meanwhile, his helmet, breastplate, sword belt, and shield all lay discarded in the main gorge below. The troll had shucked them from him, like a shell from a crab, and had let them drop at the base of the gorge's northern channel.

Now, it was up the northern channel they climbed. Though it was steep and narrow, it was full of fallen stone and easily ascended.

"Where are we going?" asked Hob. He wasn't sure he really wanted to know, but his curiosity always did get better of him.

"Somewhere no one can see us," whispered Carl One, glancing back over its shoulder at the main gorge fading away in the mist below. "You're *mine* this time."

"*Ours,*" Carl Two corrected him.

"*Ours,*" Carl One conceded. "The point is—this is personal."

"Look what you *did!*" added Carl Two.

Hob couldn't help but look. A bizarre injury had befallen the troll. Carls One and Two, its left and middle heads, were the same as ever. But Carl Three, its right head, was conspicuously absent—replaced by a lumpy sack full of turnips on an otherwise empty shoulder. The sack wobbled unsettlingly, poking out from the tattered remnants of the troll's third hood. A smiling face had been smeared onto it with red war paint. Drippy and lopsided, the face was supposed to look happy—but didn't.

"You led us to that terrible woman," Carl One hissed.

"And now Carl Three's a *turnip sack,*" moaned Carl Two.

"There, there," said Carl One. The troll patted itself on the shoulder. "He'll soon be avenged."

Even though Carl Three's demise was ultimately Captain Fist's doing, the troll seemed more than happy to punish Hob for the part he'd played in it.

Carl One peered backward again. The main gorge had now vanished. "This is far enough."

"Look there!" whispered Carl Two, pointing up ahead.

The remains of a single dead tree passed in and out of the waves of mist. It wasn't far off.

"That'll do nicely," Carl One observed. "A fine chopping block!"

They approached the dead tree. It was a squat old mountain pine with a broken-off top, which had grown up through the cracks in a wide rock shelf at the center of the channel. Its roots twisted all over the rock, and its skeletal branches rattled in the wind.

As soon as they reached the tree, the troll forced Hob to the ground. Suddenly, Hob found himself lying on his stomach, with his head facing sideways down the channel, and his neck pressed up against one of the tree's gnarled roots. To keep him in position, the troll pinned him under a crushing foot. Hob couldn't move, couldn't breathe.

A faint scraping noise, barely audible beneath the wind, told Hob the troll was drawing its axe.

Just then, a thick band of cloud moved off, and a bleary light shone down. Hob looked up out of the corner of his eye. Pale pinks and purples bloomed behind the dark mountain peak above. This was the last thing he would see—the beauty of a sunrise never to come. The cloud closed in again, and the light was gone.

"Any last words?" growled the troll.

Hob had none. He simply closed his eyes.

"Suit yourself."

Hob could feel the troll's weight shift as it raised its axe. Soon the blade would fall. Soon it would all be over.

"THERE! THERE HE IS!"

It wasn't the troll's voice. It was Stella's again!

Hob opened his eyes. A dark shape swept up the channel below. It grew and solidified, until suddenly it was overhead. The airship! A long rope ladder dangled below it. Stella held on near the top. Monty and Edric held on near the bottom. When they were right over the troll, Monty and Edric dropped from the ladder.

Edric came down on the troll's back, grabbing the collars of its two remaining hoods to stop his fall. The troll choked, sputtered, and staggered backward. Monty landed on its weapon arm, wrapping himself around it, and biting down hard. His teeth never broke the leathery skin, but, just the same, the troll howled and dropped its axe. Monty recoiled, spitting profusely in an attempt to get the taste of troll out of his mouth. Finally, the troll began spinning and shaking its arm, trying to throw off its assailants.

As the troll spun, Hob was released from underfoot. He rolled away onto his back, wheezing as he filled his flattened lungs.

A moment later, Edric landed lightly beside him, having dropped from the whirling troll. He reached down, helped Hob to his feet, and together they took cover against the trunk of the dead tree.

Hob stared at Edric in silence, struggling to believe he was really there. "How?" he asked. "How did you know it was me?"

"Because of *this!*" said Edric.

He pulled something out of his belt, and held it up for Hob to see. It was Hob's sword—the one Edric had given him at the inn. The falcon-shaped bronze hilt and steel blade shone softly in the burgeoning light.

"Then we spotted your armor at the base of this channel, and we figured you were up here," Edric added.

"And ... you *came for me?*" asked Hob.

"You came for me *first,*" said Edric, smiling warmly. "Besides ... who *else* is going to get us to the Lost City?"

Hob beamed at him. "You can count on me!" he said. "First we head due west from Valley Top, then we find the turtle-shaped mountain, and we—"

"Great, great, I trust you," said Edric, glancing over at Monty, who continued to cling to the spinning troll. "Oh, and let's just keep this between us, okay? I still don't want Stella finding out about the book. It won't do any good."

Hob nodded agreeably.

Then Edric grabbed him, and pulled him to the ground.

CRACK! The tree shuddered above them, as Monty slammed into its trunk.

CRUNCH! In a shower of broken twigs, he landed on his rump beside Edric and Hob, between the tangled roots.

"Enough with the howdy-dos, lads!" Monty said, somehow hopping right back to his feet. "We've got company!"

The troll recovered its axe, and began to charge, while Monty drew a sword, and rushed to intercept. As the troll took a wide horizontal swing at Monty's head, Monty ducked it and batted the troll's shin with his sword. The troll then roared and caught Monty with a fierce sideways kick. Monty rolled across the rock shelf, slid to a stop several paces from the troll, and lay there in a daze. Enraged, the troll stomped over, raising its axe to cleave him in two.

With a quick nod to Hob, saying *stay put*, Edric launched himself into the fray. But he wasn't going to reach Monty in time.

Thinking quickly, Hob grabbed a small stone from between the tree roots, and hurled it at the troll's back. *Thump!* A perfect hit.

Carl the Troll staggered to a stop, forgetting all about Monty, and turning its remaining heads to seek out its new attacker. Hob slipped behind the tree, so the troll saw Edric instead. Still clutching Hob's little sword, Edric looked ready for a fight. The troll gave him one.

Edric waited until the last possible second, rolling away just as the troll's axe smashed down. It chipped at the rock, spraying sparks and shards of stone. Edric circled behind the troll. The troll spun, swinging its axe sideways. Edric dove right under it and through the troll's legs. He popped up behind the troll again, back at the tree.

Having recovered his wits, Monty rushed over to join him. "Those dozy gnomes!" the old dwarf huffed. "What's takin' so long?"

"They'll be back!" Edric assured him. "We just have to hold on a little longer!"

They stood side by side, with their backs to the tree and their swords before them. The troll whirled and lashed out, attempting a heavy vertical chop. SMASH! Edric and Monty sprang apart, and the axe struck the ground between them.

The troll unleashed a wild barrage. Its axe thrashed back and forth, shattering more stone with every missed strike. Edric rolled. Monty leapt. Edric caught the troll's axe handle with his sword, knocking the weapon from the creature's hands. Monty charged the unarmed troll. But it didn't work. WHAM!

With a hammer-like fist, the troll sent him rocketing skyward.

Another shower of twigs rained down on Hob, as Monty landed in the tree above him. Wedged upside down between several upper branches with his coat flipped over his head, the old dwarf struggled to untangle himself.

Taking advantage of the opening, Edric surged to his feet, hacking at the troll with his sword. The troll held out a shield-like palm to stop it. Both heads grimaced. The troll had caught not only Edric's hand but also the bottom part of his blade. Still, the troll's fingers closed tightly around both.

"*Ahhhk!*" Edric screamed, as his hand was crushed.

With its other arm, Carl retrieved its axe from the ground, and brought it up over Edric's head. Edric tried to pull free but was held firmly in place.

Then, before the axe could fall—*thock!*—a small crossbow bolt lodged itself in the back of the troll's weapon hand. The troll howled and dropped its axe again. Instinctively, it clutched its wound, releasing Edric, who staggered away.

Hob looked down the channel in the direction the bolt had come from. Captain Fist appeared there, sweeping out of the mist! She held a compact crossbow in her hands, which she promptly holstered on her belt. It disappeared beneath her billowing cloak.

Hob gasped. The Captain must have sent her men to the Riven Gate without her, and instead tracked the goblin army at a distance, eventually finding Hob's discarded armor at the base of the gorge's northern channel. She'd never planned on letting either Hob or Edric go free.

"It's *her!*" growled Carl Two.

"I *know*," said Carl One. "Get her!"

But as the troll reached down to recover its axe again, Captain Fist pounced. She leapt onto the stone shelf, leveled a sweeping kick at both the troll's heads, and sent it reeling.

Edric ran, quickly reaching Hob's hiding place at the tree.

"Look!" he cried, pointing directly up the channel. "C'mon!"

Hob turned and saw the airship rematerialize there. It was approaching fast.

Edric took him by the arm, and they dashed over to a large boulder behind the tree—right in the path of the airship. Edric gave Hob a boost onto the rock, and climbed up after him.

"LOWER!" cried Stella, from her place atop the airship's rope ladder. She appeared to read something she had written on the back of her hand. "*LAAG!*" she repeated in awkward Gnomish.

The airship descended, and the ladder drew low over the rock. Hob jumped high enough to catch the bottom rung. But before Edric could grab on too, a black-gloved hand closed around his leg and yanked him off the boulder. *Whoosh!*

"*No!*" Hob cried.

The next second, the airship pulled up, and the ladder passed over the tree. Finally untangled, Monty sprang from the upper branches, and caught hold beside Hob.

Only Edric had been left behind. Hob looked back. The Prince now lay on the stone shelf at the base of the boulder behind the tree. Captain Fist stood over him, preparing to shield him from the oncoming troll.

The Captain drew her sword, deflected the troll's axe, and then took a swing at its legs, driving it back a step. Weapon still in hand, Edric jumped up, and rushed at the troll from the side. With the back of its arm, the troll swatted him away. Finally, the combatants receded into the mist. Only the *sounds* of battle remained, ringing out in the distance.

With some difficulty, Hob and Monty climbed up to the middle of the swaying rope ladder—Hob leading the way. They were making room for Edric to come aboard below them on the next pass.

The airship rocked as it ascended, fighting the wind. Once it finally had clearance between the surrounding mountain peaks, it came about and plunged back down into the depths of the channel. Stella, Hob, and Monty trailed on the ladder in a dizzying dive. Hob closed his eyes so he wouldn't faint.

When he opened them again, the ship was leveling off and soaring up the channel. The battle at the tree was coming back into view. The Captain crouched on the troll's shoulders, holding it in a double headlock, while Edric scrambled up the tree. Both had stowed their weapons.

"HOLD COURSE FOR THE TREE!" Stella cried, before reading off the back of her hand again. "*GA DOOR!*"

The ladder came in slightly off target. It brushed the side of the tree, right between Edric and Captain Fist. Edric leapt from his branch, Captain Fist from the back of the troll. Both caught hold of the ladder a few rungs up from the bottom, grabbing on to opposite sides, and finding themselves face to face.

Instantly, they were sailing up the channel, between craggy slopes and through curtains of mist. Edric began to climb the ladder, trying to get away from Captain Fist. She climbed the opposite side, only one rung behind him. Her arm shot through the ropes, seizing him by the tunic.

Hob could only look down in horror.

"KEEP LOW!" Stella cried, fearing Edric might fall. "*LAAG!*"

Dutifully, the airship ascended at an angle just greater than that of the mountain channel, leaving the bottom of the ladder trailing mere feet above the stones.

Taking one hand off the ladder, Edric drew his sword. "Let me go!" he shouted.

Fist obliged, releasing him. But her free hand went straight to her hip. In a flash, her sword was drawn too.

Clank! Edric jabbed his sword down at the hand Fist used to hold the ladder, and she angled her sword to block it. *Clank!* He took a swing at the ropes above her hand, and she blocked this too. *Shwing!* She tried to disarm him with a twist of her blade. His sword flailed out to the side, but he kept his grip.

This sent the ladder swaying back and forth between the walls of the channel, nearly causing Edric to fall off. It was all he could do to hold on one-handed, as he recovered his balance and reset for the next clash. Taking advantage, Captain Fist sprang fearlessly upward, gripping the ladder with two fingers of her sword hand, while reaching up with the other to catch hold above Edric. She hoisted herself past him, leaned out around the side of the ladder, and barred his ascent with her sword. *CRASH!* Their weapons met and locked once more.

"I will *not* let you go!" Captain Fist shouted over the wind.

"You don't have a choice!" Edric screamed.

Then, without warning, the floor of the channel began to rise more sharply than ever. The airship pulled up, but not hard enough. Though the timbers of the ship's mighty wings strained to change its pitch, its ladder's bottom rungs now bounced along the stones.

Whoosh!

The ship broke free of the cloud, punching a swirling hole in the void. The ladder and its crew followed through the gap.

At once, everything was visible up ahead. The rising channel terminated in a rocky cliff—a wedge of stone that projected past the mountain peaks to either side and out over the edge of a vast chasm. They were hurtling toward it, a ship's length from the brink.

Captain Fist took action. She knocked Edric's sword away from hers, and, with a sideways slash, cut the rope ladder. She and Edric dropped onto the cliff. They didn't fall far—only a matter of feet—but they fell hard. The rock caught them, and they were gone. *Whoosh!*

The ship then hurtled out over the open chasm. Hob turned back to see Edric shrinking below, lying on the cliff just above Captain Fist.

"GO BACK!" cried Stella. "*GA TERUG!*"

The ship tilted hard to the right and began to circle. Stella, Hob, and Monty clung to the soaring ladder.

A strange world revolved around them. Thinning clouds filled the bottom of the chasm. And the roar of water rent the air. To the west, framed by mountaintops, Hob was astonished to see the Riven Gate! The great dam stood open, just above the clouds, sending a towering flume cascading down the rocks, crashing and churning into the mist. Hob's route through the mountains—south down the pass and back north up the gorge and channel—had returned him to the ravine.

Rotating at the center of it all was the rocky cliff, and on it Edric and Captain Fist. Hob looked down at them as the ship circled. They had found their feet—and their swords. Edric retreated up toward the precipice, as Captain Fist advanced on him. They shouted at each other over the roar of wind and water.

"Please!" Edric cried. "You saw that army! You know what we're up against! The Sorcerer is back! You *must* let me go!"

"No," replied Captain Fist. She would soon have him cornered. "I swore to return you home by *whatever means necessary*. And that is what I will to do. You will stay here, and become King!"

Edric stopped, his hands wringing the hilt of his sword. "Not while my father's still alive!"

"But he's *not!*" Fist cried, her voice cracking as she struggled to make herself heard. "I know it is hard, my Prince. But you must accept the truth, as I have. He is gone."

"*No!*"

Edric lunged. CRASH! Fist blocked his blade. And suddenly, they were dueling on the cliff.

The rocky peak turned faster and faster as the airship closed in on it. CRASH! CLANK! CLANG! Edric was on the offensive. But Hob could see that Fist was merely toying with him. She calmly brushed aside his every blow, parrying but never attacking, waiting for him to make a mistake.

She didn't have to wait long. Edric hacked wildly at the Captain, overswinging and throwing himself off balance. With a decisive blow, she beat back his sword, opening him up to attack. With a flourish, she caught his blade again, and sent it spinning up into the air. Then she took out his feet with a low kick, and rose to catch his falling sword, hilt in hand. Edric leapt up in defiance. But Captain Fist now held both weapons.

Meanwhile, the airship came about behind her. It flew over the mountain channel again, turning to face out past the cliff, toward the ravine. Then it began to descend.

"MONTY!" came Stella's voice from above. "THE LADDER!"

Both Monty and Hob looked up to see her miming the action of lifting the rope ladder, and pointing at Edric. Hob knew what she meant. Monty, who was lowest on the ladder, would gather up the bottom to keep it away from Captain Fist, and then drop it over Edric when the time was right. Monty gave Stella an exaggerated nod, and began hauling up the rope ladder with a free hand.

"SLOWER!" Stella called up to the ship. "*LANGZAMER!*"

The ship's propellers slammed into reverse to fight the wind rushing up the channel behind it. It teetered dangerously as it drifted toward its target.

Keeping her own sword drawn, Captain Fist slipped Edric's sword into her belt. Then she reached out with her free hand to seize him. "I am sorry, my Prince, but this ends now."

Edric said nothing. His gaze stayed fixed behind the Captain. The next instant, the airship lurched down over her head, causing her to duck instinctively.

"NOW!" cried Stella.

Monty let go of the ladder, and it unfurled just out of Captain Fist's reach. Edric caught the second last rung with both hands and began to lift into the air. He jerked himself up far enough to get one foot planted on the bottom rung, but that was it.

In one motion, the Captain sheathed her sword and lunged, wrapping an arm around Edric's trailing left leg. She dragged behind him up the wedge of stone—toward the cliff's edge. Hob saw only a streak of black as she whipped out a small grappling hook from her belt and jammed it into a fissure in the cliff. A strong, thin rope unspooled behind it.

"STOP THE SHIP!" Stella screamed. "*STOPPEN!*"

The airship's propellers whirled even harder in reverse, shuddering and screeching.

Captain Fist then looped the unspooling rope around her arm, and— *crack!*—it went taut. One of the grapple's steel hooks—barbed and razor sharp—had caught in the fissure and driven itself into the stone.

Thwunk! The whole rope ladder jerked and wobbled as it too went taut. Edric clung to it with all his might, stretched impossibly between the airship and the iron grip of Captain Fist. The Captain leaned out over the brink, feet propped against the cliff's edge, one arm holding Edric, the other roped to the grappling hook.

The airship's propellers continued to battle as hard as they could, but they were no match for the wind. They wouldn't hold the ship in place for long. It began to twist sideways overhead. Together, Stella, Hob, Monty, Edric, and Captain Fist hung out over the chasm, moments from disaster.

Captain Fist stared up at Edric in dismay. "I *will not* fail you!" she shouted. "*Not* like I failed *him!*"

Suddenly, Edric seemed to understand her in a way he hadn't before. "You didn't *fail him!*" he cried, his voice shaking as he fought to hold on to the ladder. "You couldn't have stopped him, even if you'd *known!*"

Fist grimaced. "Then I could have *helped* him!"

"So help *us now!*" Edric replied. "We only *fail him* if we give up!"

"WATCH OUT!" Stella screamed.

Everyone turned to see Carl the Troll burst out of the clouds below. It came charging up the cliff, taking massive, troll-sized strides.

"There they are!" bellowed Carl One.

"Off with their heads!" bellowed Carl Two.

Captain Fist looked back at Edric. "I *will* return you home," she said.

The troll raised its mighty axe. "For Carl Threeee!" it howled.

"… even if it means following you to the ends of the Earth!"

The Captain then released her tether, grabbed on to the rope ladder, and swung with Edric and the others away from the cliff!

Consumed by thoughts of revenge, the troll did not even slow its attack. Instead, it lunged at Edric and Captain Fist as they swung away, dropping its axe, and soaring after them with arms outstretched. Its fingers brushed the hem of Fist's cloak, but couldn't grab hold. And so, Carl the Troll plunged, empty-handed, into the abyss.

CHAPTER NINETEEN

Welcome Aboard

The ladder and its passengers trailed the airship up between the mountain peaks, until they struck open sky awash with orange and mauve.

Below them, the faces of the mountains gleamed with the warm light of daybreak. And to the east, the entire valley opened up, the cloud sea parting over it. Beyond the hazy patchwork fields and the forests yet in shadow, beyond the distant peaks of the Dawning Mountains, the sun was rising on the Kingdom of Yore.

Its light quickly stung Hob's eyes and threatened to make him dizzy— a dangerous prospect while on the ladder. So, with one hand gripping the ropes, he used his other to pull his goggles down over his eyes, finding instant relief.

As the ship flew north, Hob turned for one last look at the Riven Gate. From so far above, he could see the vast lake behind it, its shimmering turquoise waters stretching back endlessly through the mountains. Valley Top came into view next, sitting peacefully at the end of its mountain ridge, looking like but a toy model of itself. Hob had never felt so small, and the world had never felt so *big*.

A chill wind rushed past him, and he shivered. He looked up the ladder, past Stella, to the deck of the airship. The heads of five gnomes peered down over the railing there, beards wagging in the breeze. Stella began to climb toward them, leading the way up the ladder.

The ladder wobbled uncomfortably as everyone ascended, but Hob managed to keep his grip. Before long, he was waiting at the top behind Stella, as the five gnomes helped her over the railing.

Hob didn't recognize any of the numbers on their hats from the meeting at the inn. And when they saw him waiting at the railing, they scurried back a few paces, and huddled together, staring suspiciously. They must have known he was coming, but they didn't trust him.

Stella helped Hob aboard instead. He slid over the railing, and stood for a moment on wobbly legs. Then, struck by the fullness of his exhaustion, he nearly toppled over.

Before he could, Stella knelt down and wrapped him in tight hug. "YOU MADE IT!" she exclaimed.

Hob winced. With their heads side by side, her unnaturally loud voice made his ears ring.

"OH! SORRY!" Stella proceeded to give three booming coughs into her fist, and then continued at a normal volume. "It's a voice amplification spell."

"It works!" Hob confirmed, rubbing his ears.

Stella laughed, releasing him, and straightening back up. "What do you think?" she said, gesturing around the deck of the ship. "In Common Tongue, it's called the *Windfarer*. Isn't it wonderful? No airships like this are thought to exist anymore, not even in the East. That's why the gnomes are so secretive about it. They believe humans would go to war for a thing like this. And they might be right." She paused. "Luckily, they've agreed to help us now. I think Eldwin hired them specifically for this ship. I think he felt it was the only way to finish our quest in time!"

As Stella spoke, Hob gazed around at the Windfarer in awe. It was by far the most fantastic thing he'd ever seen. The deck, where he stood, was long and flat in the middle, but rose up at the prow, where the bowsprit jutted out, and at the stern, where an upper level was built over a block of cabins. It possessed all the standard ship's trappings—hatches, barrels, and coils of rope—but, instead of a mast at its center, it had a steel furnace, which piped blazing hot air up into the great canvas balloon. The balloon stretched overhead, as did the countless creaking ropes that rigged it to the ship. Dozens of tiny gnomes climbed all over the rigging and scuttled about the deck. There was open sky on all sides, and the wind ruffled hat and hair.

"It's amazing!" Hob agreed.

He could have spent ages soaking in every last detail, but he soon got distracted by the arrival of Monty, Edric, and Captain Fist at the top of the ladder. With the gnomes still keeping their distance from Hob, the newcomers got no help climbing the railing either. Monty fared worse than Hob, huffing and puffing and flopping flat onto the deck, while Edric and Captain Fist hopped over with ease.

Upon seeing the Captain standing at the railing, her black cloak billowing in the wind, the five gnomes, already cowering from Hob, squeaked and drew their little swords. They had witnessed the Captain dueling with Edric on the rock below, and didn't seem to understand that anything had changed.

"Run along!" Edric told them. "She's with us now. And so is Hob. *Friends!*"

The gnomes exchanged skeptical glances, but lowered their swords and slunk away.

"So, you're really coming with us then?" Stella asked Captain Fist. "What about your orders to take Edric back to King's Rock?"

"Aye! What *about* them?" growled Monty, his own distrust made plain with every twitching whisker of his mustache.

"My *first* oath will always be to protect the Crown and Kingdom of Yore," said Captain Fist. "And, after tonight, I no longer believe my orders to be in service of that oath. My Prince was right. The goblin army's attack on Valley Top has proven his quest just. It has proven *my King's* quest just. If that was but a fraction of the total force coming, and if the Sorcerer is indeed back in command, then finding the Sunflame is truly our best hope. The Council may disagree, but they have not seen what I have seen."

Stella nodded thoughtfully.

The Captain then knelt before Edric, drew her sword, and presented it to him. "My sword is yours, my Prince," she vowed. "On my life, I will see your quest fulfilled, and you returned home safely. And, if fortune wills it, *my King* returned home safely as well."

Hob could hear the affection, the loyalty, in her voice.

"Your sword is welcome," said Edric, placing a hand on Captain Fist's shoulder, "as are you."

Captain Fist rose, sheathed her sword, and looked to Hob next. She drew his little sword from her belt, and turned its hilt toward him. "I believe this is yours, goblin."

"His name's *Hob*," Monty cut in, as though he'd *never once* called Hob anything less than friendly. "And he saved Edric from that army back there."

"*Hob,*" Captain Fist corrected herself. "And so he did. He kept his promise."

Hob took the sword, admiring it proudly, even if he'd done very little with it. "I doubt my rescue would have worked, if not for this ship," he admitted. He turned to Stella and Monty. "How did you find us?"

"That was all Stella," Monty said.

"It was just good timing, really," Stella explained, trying to sound humble, but beaming nonetheless. "For the sake of secrecy, the gnomes had the Windfarer hidden deep inside the old forest. So, after I'd finished inspecting the ship and crew, and we'd finally signed the contract, the plan was to fly back to Valley Top, drop anchor in the mountains as close as the gnomes would allow, and sneak in on foot to pick you up. We were on our way, flying low, using the pass to orient ourselves in the cloud, when we saw that goblin army marching down from the city. It was terrifying. But lucky. The sight triggered one of my visions. I saw Edric standing on that big rock, surrounded by goblins. And we followed the army until we found him in the gorge." She paused. "I'm so glad we found you too, Hob!"

Edric scoffed. "That sure wasn't the tone you took with me."

Stella glared at him sharply. "That's because you were the one who caused this whole mess. Not Hob. *You.* You promised to stay at the inn. But, by your own admission, you ran off chasing some *girl!*"

"Some *Lady* ..." Edric corrected her, as if it made all the difference.

Stella punched him in the shoulder.

"Okay! Okay! Take it easy!" he chuckled.

"Then promise you won't do anything like that again," said Stella.

"I promise," said Edric, solemnly. "No more Ladies." He smirked. "*Commoners* are much less trouble."

Stella punched him again.

"*Ow!* Now, that one hurt!"

Stella fixed him with her best disapproving stare, but the corner of her lip couldn't help but twist up into a half-smile. Monty laughed.

Then, Hob collapsed.

A sudden wave of terror, shame, and agony crashed over him. He fell to his knees, dropping his sword. He pressed his hands against his temples, trying to stop the pounding. A far-off voice echoed inside his head.

"*YOU IDIOTS! I TOLD YOU THE PRINCE WAS IMPORTANT! BUT YOU LET HIM SLIP AWAY! MARCH FOR SHADOWGUARD AT ONCE! AND DO NOT FAIL ME AGAIN!*"

It took all Hob had left not to lose himself in the fear, the hatred. Then everything went black.

He came-to moments later, in the arms of both Edric and Stella, as they worked together to lift him to his feet.

"Are you okay?" asked Stella.

"What happened?" asked Edric.

"The Sorcerer's angry," Hob croaked. "He knows you escaped, Ed. The crow in the gorge must have regained consciousness and discovered what happened. The Sorcerer uses crows as spies. He can commune with them, even speak through them. I just heard one of his messages." He rubbed his sore head.

Everyone looked worried.

"If this is true," Captain Fist said to Stella, "we should get away from here, before this crow flies up and spots us."

"I agree," said Stella. "Number One!" she hollered across the deck.

Seconds later, Gnome One scurried up beside her, accompanied by Gnome Thirty-Seven. The pair stared at Stella expectantly.

"Give them the first heading," she prompted Edric.

Edric thought for a moment. "West!" he exclaimed, remembering what Hob had told him by the tree. "We set out west from Valley Top!"

Gnome Thirty-Seven translated. Gnome One nodded. And they rushed off again, Gnome One squeaking orders at the ship's helms-gnomes.

The helms-gnomes stood one on either side of the great steering wheel at the front of the raised stern deck. On Gnome One's command, they worked together to spin the wheel, one pushing, one pulling. The rigging creaked and cracked overhead. Hidden mechanisms groaned within the belly of the ship. And the Windfarer swung west.

Valley Top passed by, now off to the south, as the ship and crew sailed out over the Gloaming Mountains. In a matter of minutes, the last glimpses of the valley's distant green fields and woodlands were sinking below the gray-blue peaks behind them.

A long silence settled upon Edric and company. All thoughts lingered on their narrow escape and the many new perils that surely awaited. Hob picked up his sword and held it proudly once more.

When the Kingdom of Yore was completely out of sight, Edric turned his attention ahead. He led the way to the bow of the ship, followed by Hob, Monty, Stella, and Captain Fist.

"And where are we going exactly?" asked the Captain.

Edric stopped at the railing of the bow, and turned to her. The others gathered around him, Hob at his side.

"To a lost city," Edric proclaimed, "to steal the Sunflame from the belly of a dragon, and find my father!"

They all looked ahead again, past the bowsprit, out over the Gloaming Mountains, and toward the wild lands beyond. The distant green expanse was barely more than a suggestion on the horizon and a promise in their hearts—that of their next adventure.

Edric placed a hand on Hob's shoulder and smiled. "Everyone," he said, "welcome aboard."

Rory Madge is an artist and writer. He has trained and worked at Walt Disney Animation Studios, directed cereal commercials, and worked on TV shows for DreamWorks. Now, he's bringing his love for storytelling, both drawn and written, to a series of illustrated novels about a geeky goblin right after his own heart. *The Prince and the Goblin* is his first book.

You can find Rory somewhere up in Canada, ideally near lakes or mountains (yes, a bit like a troll), and online at www.roryandbryan.com or https://twitter.com/RoryMadge

Bryan Huff is an artist, writer, and pizza snob. After going to school to learn how to draw pictures, he spent a decade working for clients like Cartoon Network, Nickelodeon, and Disney. Eventually, he realized it's even more fun to write stories. *The Prince and the Goblin* is his debut novel, the first in a three book series.

Bryan lives in Canada with his wife and two little goblins of his own. Visit him at www.roryandbryan.com or https://twitter.com/Giant_People

CONNECT WITH US

Find more books like this at http://www.Month9Books.com

Facebook: www.Facebook.com/Month9Books
Instagram: https://instagram.com/month9books
Twitter: https://twitter.com/Month9Books
Tumblr: http://month9books.tumblr.com/
YouTube: www.youtube.com/user/Month9Books
Georgia McBride Media Group: www.georgiamcbride.com